ALIZA

my love

Aliza, my love

Published by The Conrad Press in the United Kingdom 2019

Tel: +44(0)1227 472 874
www.theconradpress.com
info@theconradpress.com

ISBN 978-1-911546-70-2

Copyright © James Walker, 2019

The moral right of James Walker to be identified as author of this work has been asserted in accordance with the Copyright, Designs and Patents Act 1988.

All rights reserved.

In part, this novel is loosely based on a true story (see author's note). However, it is essentially a work of fiction and the characterisation as expressed by both the narrative and dialogue is imaginary. In particular, the character *Aliza* is an invention.

Typesetting and Cover Design by:
Charlotte Mouncey, www.bookstyle.co.uk

The Conrad Press logo was designed by Maria Priestley.

Printed and bound in Great Britain by Clays Ltd, Elcograf S.p.A.

ALIZA

my love

James Walker

To Jo for her love and understanding

Author's note: This novel does not set out to show Nazis in a sympathetic light. It is, however, quite deliberately written from a Nazi's point of view, albeit a Nazi who represents the more civilised face of the Party, and who ultimately, and understandably, becomes utterly disillusioned with the Nazi cause.

PROLOGUE

*Sonnenstrasse, Spandau district of Berlin,
Saturday April 15th 1945*

Baron Otto Von Buren's study

Last night, I dreamt Aliza came to me and we kissed.
After we did, she became reproachful, telling me I should be ashamed of myself for the terrible crimes which have been visited on her people. I tried to plead with her, begging her forgiveness, but in my dream she just slipped away, leaving me bereft.

Now, as I glance across my desk at the photograph of my wife, Clara, and my son, Leopold, I'm relieved they should now both be safe and well in the Black Forest. I could so easily have been with them if I hadn't put my duty to my country first.

Yet it's far from as simple as that, for in truth there is another woman in my life, the beautiful Jewish lady, Aliza, whose fate is just as important to me as that of Clara and Leopold. She's surely in far more danger, and I still cling to the hope, however tenuous, of being able to come to her aid, if I can only survive the coming battle, for the Russians are about to begin their assault on Berlin.

So I'm sitting at my desk looking through some of my old diaries, particularly those I wrote in the early 1930s. With the present and the future so hopeless, the past seems my only refuge.

I was born not far from here, in Berlin, in a house, now demolished, on the 10th November 1898, into a devoutly Catholic, aristocratic family. It was impressed upon me from quite an early age by my poetry-loving mother, tragically dead before her time of influenza in 1919, that it was a birthday I was fortunate to share with the polymath Friedrich Schiller, known best for his poetry and plays, none of which, I must confess, have ever much appealed to me.

My family's present fortune is largely based on successful business investments made in property and shares, both at home and abroad, by my grandfather, who died when I was five so I have little memory of him. My father, too, inherited much of his acumen and until his own death, and despite all the upheavals brought about by war and its aftermath, made the family even richer. I was thus able to enjoy a privileged upbringing, and the freedom to seek to pursue a career of my choice, save that when I was still only fifteen war broke out, and once all talk of this being over by Christmas proved a delusion, it became clear to me that by the time I was eighteen I would be in uniform.

After officer training I did not see any action until the spring of 1917, and while I was wounded on two occasions, they were fortunately only flesh wounds. However, eighteen months of warfare on the western front with all its attendant horrors, was still long enough to rob me of any religious faith. This loss was also compounded by the death of my mother, and then, even as I began to pursue a career as a journalist, I had to witness my country reduced to abject poverty with too many former soldiers begging on the streets.

Still a young man, like many others I was drawn towards the National Socialist Party and its charismatic leader for offering the hope of a better future. Anti-semitism played no part whatsoever in my motivation, quite the contrary, and until the terrible acts perpetrates against Jews in November 1938 on *Kristallnacht* I did not believe that the Party would stoop so low.

This terrible event began to seal my growing disillusionment with the cause I had at first so enthusiastically embraced. However, by then I had risen too far and felt that I and above all my family had too much to lose if I were to resign from the Party, let alone actively oppose it, especially once our nation was at war less than a year later and I saw it as my patriotic duty to support our government.

Where, I wonder, did it all go so wrong for our once glorious Reich?

Certainly, it was gross arrogance for Germany, no matter how charismatic its leaders believed themselves to be, to imagine we could ever defeat not only Great Britain and its Empire, but the Russians and Americans, too. But then I now appreciate that arrogance has long been at the heart of the Nazi movement. Further, I now see all too clearly that National Socialism, for all its appeal to notions of unity and patriotism, was in truth a monster, ultimately intent on a policy of evil.

How different it looked to me twelve years ago now, when the Fuhrer first came to power. I thought it was the dawn of an era of glittering achievement for our country and was proud to be a member of the National Socialist Party and the Reiter

SS, but now I may end up being shot by the Russians or being marched off to some godforsaken corner of Siberia.

There were some who predicted, even back in '33, what's happening now. Really, I should have been one of them, but I was too angry with what had gone before and the dreadful condition our country was in. I also believed that only the Fuhrer, supported by the party he had created, had the vision and determination to restore German greatness. If I'd guessed what a terrible disaster we would ultimately face once he committed us to another World War, I believe I would have changed my tune. Now it's far too late, and, as a man of my word, I've pledged myself to take part in our last stand against the forces of communism as the Russian army surrounds our once proud capital city.

Tomorrow morning I will be putting on my uniform and going off to command my Volkssturm company, knowing that our total defeat is now a foregone conclusion. All the same, I believe it's better to go down fighting, even to the last man, than face the ignominy visited on our country back in 1919. The terms of the Peace Treaty of Versailles that year, and all it led to, were monstrously unjust to Germany and its people, and I'll go to my grave believing this to have been the case.

'Herr Baron.' It's the voice of my loyal and thoughtful housekeeper.

'Yes, Frau Solger.'

'Supper is ready for you.'

'Thank you, you're most kind.'

My beloved mother always taught me to be courteous to servants, and now it's second nature to me, but soon, once this war is finally over, my class will be gone with it and all our courtesy, too. The German aristocracy, of which my family, the Von Burens, have been proud members since 1463, has been on the way out since 1918. What's happening now is, I fear, just the final nail in our coffin.

PART 1

BEGINNINGS

1

Saturday November 12 1932

I vividly remember the day I first met Aliza.

It was rather a wet day and I was attending a congress meeting of the Zionist Federation in Berlin, only a thirty-minute drive from my home in the Spandau District of the city.

I had just enjoyed my thirty-fourth birthday, and apart from having become an active member of the National Socialist Party, had been fortunate enough, and had worked hard enough, to achieve success as both a freelance journalist and travel writer.

Some might find it strange that despite being a party member I'd developed a keen interest in Germany's Zionist movement. To me, though, that movement, as a matter of logic, had every potential to offer the perfect solution to those within the party who argued that the Jews ought to be expelled from Germany, much as they had once been expelled from England and Spain.

Besides, I had no personal antipathy towards Jews, and admired what the Zionist movement was seeking to achieve in Palestine, as I had come to believe that the Jewish people would be happier living in their own homeland. This conviction led me to attend several of the movement's congress meetings around the country, where I had interviewed delegates and begun to get to know some of them quite well.

The hall being used for the meeting was crowded with delegates, many of whom had lit up cigarettes even before proceedings got under way, causing a pall of smoke to hang over us all. There was a succession of speakers, all of whom spoke earnestly about what the movement was seeking to achieve in Palestine and some of whom also chose to express their fears about the possibility of the Nazi Party – what the Fuhrer called *'unsere Bewegung'* – 'our movement' - coming to power. Only six days previously the country had voted in a Federal Election, the second that year, which had again failed to give any Party an overall majority in the Bundestag, although ours remained the largest, and I was optimistic that we would soon be able to form a government.

After an hour or so the meeting was adjourned for refreshments, which gave me the opportunity not only to seek some fresh air but also to renew some acquaintances. I soon went back inside as it had started drizzling. I saw a man in front of me whose face was familiar even though I couldn't quite recall his name. He immediately smiled at me and, stretching forth his hand, introduced himself as Bernhard Friedman, reminding me that we had last met at a congress meeting in Hamburg, just a few months previously.

We chatted amicably for a couple of minutes about the speeches we'd heard and then a man and woman came towards us, side by side. I'd never set eyes on either of them before. The man immediately tapped Herr Friedman on the shoulder.

'Hello, Bernhard, it's good to see you again.' he said.

'Why, Max, this is a pleasure. And Aliza, my dear, I trust you're both well?'

Introductions were then made, which revealed that the man

and woman were a Jewish married couple, whose surname was Geisser. I would also have been perfectly content to merely give my name as Otto von Buren, but Friedman was quick to use the prefix *Baron* and add that I was a well known journalist and influential member of the National Socialist Party, and my support for the Zionist movement was greatly valued.

'I think you flatter me,' I said

'But isn't it true that you're acquainted with Joseph Goebbels?' Friedman asked. Goebbels had organised the Party's campaign in three successive Federal Elections.

'Yes, we know each other.'

'I wonder, Baron, have you yet persuaded him to support the Zionist movement?' The question came from Frau Geisser, and was couched in a sceptical, faintly playful, tone of voice.

That was the moment which will remain in my memory for ever.

Alluringly attractive, with perfect skin, regular features and high cheek-bones, she looked to be no more than twenty-five, was as tall as her husband, with a slim, curvaceous figure, and wore her black hair fashionably short. Above all, she had dark, intelligent eyes, whilst her smile as she put her question to me was so delightful that I was quite transfixed by it.

'… I believe that he is open to such persuasion,' I replied, quietly, and in wonderment at the lovely woman who had asked the question. 'Within the Party,' I added, 'there is much debate on the merits of Zionism.'

'Then Baron, I wish you well with your endeavours.'

'Thank you, Frau Geisser, you're most kind.'

You utterly, delightful creature I thought, completely convinced that I had never been introduced to such a gorgeous woman before, whether Jewish or not. I am no womaniser by any means, but marriage had certainly made me no less appreciative of female beauty.

I could not help but wonder at the chances of our paths crossing again at some point in the future. Certainly, there would be more congresses that I might wish to attend.

Before she and her husband moved on she smiled at me once more.

'So pleased to have met you,' she said, fixing me with her eyes.

'And I you,' I replied, nodding my head and returning her smile. Then she was gone.

'A beautiful woman, don't you think?' Friedman said admiringly, once she and her husband had disappeared into the throng.

For a moment I could hardly speak. 'Yes… truly so. Did you say her name's Aliza?

'Yes.'

'And did she and her husband travel far to be here today?'

'Oh no, they live here in Berlin.'

So perhaps mine and Aliza's paths might indeed cross again, I thought, *but then again perhaps not* I also thought to myself. After all, Berlin was a large city and there was no guarantee that I would see her at future congresses. All the same, for all that our encounter had been a brief one, Aliza had made a deep impression on me, and I knew I would certainly not fail to remember her if we were to meet again, unless that was many decades into the future, when her beauty, at least to some extent, might have faded away. Yet somehow I could not imagine her not being beautiful.

2

Wednesday February 1 1933

These, Reader, were Hitler's opening words in his proclamation to the German people upon becoming Chancellor of Germany.

More than fourteen years have passed since the unhappy day when the German people, blinded by promises from foes at home and abroad, lost touch with honour and freedom, thereby losing all. Since that day of treachery, the Almighty has withheld his blessing from our people. Dissension and hatred descended upon us. With profound distress millions of the best German men and women from all walks of life have seen the unity of the nation vanishing away, dissolving in a confusion of political and personal opinions, economic interests, and ideological differences. Since that day, as so often in the past, Germany has presented a picture of heart-breaking disunity. We never received the equality and fraternity we had been promised, and we lost our liberty to boot. For when our nation lost its political place in the world, it soon lost its unity of spirit and will.

*****

February 8 1933

I was standing by the same desk where I'm sitting now, looking out of the window. The lawn was covered in snow. I'd been reading the Fuhrer's proclamation to the people upon his coming to power only a week or so previously and the opening words were very much on my mind. I remember too, what an optimistic and positive mood I was in and how convinced I was that the nation was on the right course, at last, under the Fuhrer's inspiring leadership.

It was almost four months since my meeting with Aliza. I had never forgotten her. About a week earlier, to my pleasure and surprise, I had received a letter from Max Geisser, which naturally brought her even more vividly to mind once more.

The request that it contained had given me an idea. Impulsive of me, perhaps, but the more I thought of the idea, the better it seemed. I'd confided it to my wife, Clara, a few days previously and she had been fine about it.

'Darling, Herr Geisser has arrived,' Clara said, entering the study.

Feeling no doubt at that moment even more aware of the beauty of women than I usually was, I was struck by how attractive my wife appeared that morning. She was most elegantly dressed, which is typical of her, and, as I recall, was wearing a tight fitting, silk dress with 'butterfly' sleeves, which showed off her figure, while her blonde hair was fashionably waved. I loved her, but, in truth, not so much that I could erase the guilty pleasure I felt at the memory of Aliza's beauty and natural charm.

'Thank you, my love, do show him in.'

I smiled at her and she returned this faintly before ushering Max into the study. I gave him a warm smile before shaking hands with him in my usual vigorous manner.

'Max, welcome. It's a pleasure to see you again. This is Clara, my wife.'

Max shook Clara's hand, clicking his heels together in the traditional German fashion when a gentleman meets a lady. 'The pleasure is mine, Otto, and it's a great privilege to meet your lady wife.'

'Would you like some tea or coffee?' Clara asked him, performing a role which would normally have been our maid's, except that she was unwell.

'Some coffee, please – a little milk, no sugar.'

'And you, darling?'

'My usual tea, please.'

Clara dutifully smiled at both of us and quietly withdrew.

Max looked around. I could tell he was impressed by the study. It's changed barely at all in the years since, and is still dominated by its marble fireplace with a large mirror above it, and by its shelves of mostly leather bound books. It was always intended to exude an aura of wealth, learning and good taste, and, unlike today, it was pleasantly warm thanks to the steady heat being given out by a well-banked coal fire.

'I'm most grateful to you for agreeing to see me.'

'Not at all, not at all. Do take a seat.'

'Thank you, Otto.'

I'm quite a tall, slim individual, even now, and in those days, my hair was still dark brown, without even a hint of grey. Max, on the other hand, was somewhat stocky and only of average height for a man. He was clean-shaven, and his black hair had only the faintest touch of grey above the ears. I noticed, too, that the suit he was wearing was of no particular quality whereas I could afford the best. We were also about the same age.

I sat back on the large settee near to the fire, while he sat opposite me. I then took my cigarette case out of the inside pocket of my jacket and offered him a cigarette, but he declined to take it, so I decided I wouldn't smoke either.

'So Max, I have read your letter with great interest, and I'm prepared to help you by writing an article in the party newspaper, *Der Angriff*, on the merits of Zionism…'

Max impulsively clapped his hands in delight. 'Otto, that is most good of you. Such an article would be a huge boon to us.'

'I'm pleased you think so and I'm delighted to help. Now listen, I do have an idea associated with it. It's not exactly a condition, rather something I hope will be of interest to you.'

Max leaned forward in his chair and looked at me intently. 'Please, tell me what you have in mind?'

'Well, if I'm to write this article, and do the best job I can of it, I would really like to have some first-hand experience of what's being achieved in Palestine.'

Max at once nodded vigorously. 'Yes, that makes every sense to me.'

'So I was thinking, I would very much like you to be my guide, at least for part of my visit. I expect you've been there?'

'Why, yes, twice, as part of my work. And it would certainly be a pleasure to assist you, provided I could obtain leave.'

'I'm sure it wouldn't be difficult for you to persuade your superiors within the Zionist Federation that it's in its interests for you to be allowed to accompany me. And should you need a letter from me, or a word in the right ear, I'll be pleased to provide it.'

Max nodded slowly. 'It's an excellent idea, Otto. I do unfortunately need to raise the matter of cost. The Federation might agree to fund my expenses but I can't be certain. I don't wish to plead poverty but my salary isn't sufficient to enable me to afford to pay for such a journey.'

'Please don't worry about that,' I assured him. 'Fortunately I'm a wealthy man and, if necessary, can cover all your expenses.'

'That's most generous of you, I must say. I do hope that you would get sufficient material from the trip to be able to write several articles. I'd hate to think that you'd be out of pocket.'

'Please don't worry. I'm sure the research will hold me in good stead professionally for many years. Given it will soon be spring, I was thinking we could make a party of it. Clara and I love to travel, Palestine is, I'm sure, a fascinating place, and your charming wife - her name's Aliza isn't it?'

I thought it best to give the impression that I wasn't sure.

'Yes, indeed it is.'

'I remember now. Of course, she'd be most welcome to join us at my expense.'

'That's very kind of you and I'm sure she'd very much like to come, I expect, but we have a daughter, Bathsheba, who's only three.'

'Then far too young to be taken on such a journey, of course, but, well… I wonder if some arrangement could still be made?' I was suddenly beginning to worry that my plan wasn't going to work.

'As it happens my parents don't live too far from us and are understandably utterly devoted to Bathsheba. I think they'd be only too happy to look after her. How many weeks do you propose to go for?'

'Well, I can see plenty of potential for writing several travel pieces for other publications, and Clara and I would naturally like to spend some time by ourselves. However, one must be practical. Six or seven weeks should be sufficient plus a week each side for the voyage there and back… however,' I hastened to add, seeing a look of shock on his face, 'I fully appreciate that you couldn't be away from your little one for so long. I'd only need you to act as my guide for a couple of weeks, although you and Aliza would both still be welcome to remain with us for another week if you were able to.'

'You're a very considerate man, Otto. I think that could be arranged.'

'Excellent. I do hope so.'

'Tell me, if I may ask, do you have any children?'

I smiled faintly. The question had touched something of a raw nerve. 'As yet no, but, who knows, my wife is some years younger than I am, and a long holiday might bear many fruits, so to speak.'

Max smiled. 'Yes, I understand.'

The important thing is that when I return I'm sure I'll be able to write a really positive article in the party journal singing the praises of the Zionist movement.'

'I would be exceedingly grateful. Your support for our cause, and your willingness to attend our congresses, has rightly earned you admirers within the Zionist movement, of which I am happy to say I am one.'

'You're too kind, Max,' I replied, with deliberate modesty. Of course, I appreciated praise as much as any man, but I didn't believe I was a conceited fellow, unlike some of my colleagues within the Nazi Party whom I could have mentioned, Goebbels for example. 'I'm pleased to be an advocate of the Zionist cause,' I told Max. 'In my opinion, it alone offers the Jewish people a real future. And I'm prepared to do all I can to promote it within the highest echelons of the Party and the SS.'

*****

It was about then that Clara quietly re-entered the room, carrying a tray with pots of both coffee and tea on it.

'Darling,' I said, 'Max has agreed to the plan that I mentioned to you that we take a trip to Palestine.'

Clara smiled. 'Excellent, I'm pleased to hear that.'

'I'll need to speak to Aliza, of course, and my employers,' Max emphasised.

Clara proceeded to pour the coffee and handed Max a cup. 'Here you are, Max.'

'Thank you…'

She smiled at him. 'I do hope I can have the opportunity of meeting Frau Geisser soon.'

'Yes, Max,' I said, 'you and Aliza must come to us for dinner.'

'That's most kind of you. We'd be delighted.'

'And darling, we must start making arrangements for the trip as soon as possible,' I said, smiling at Clara. 'That's half the fun of holidays.'

'My husband has a passion for travel, Max.'

'I can see that,' Max replied with a smile.

'And you… Max… are you much of a traveller?' Clara asked him.

'I usually enjoy travel once I've arrived, but I find the

disruption it can cause to work can be stressful…'

'Max,' I interjected, 'that's surely a small price to pay for the quality of the experience. It's so life-enhancing.'

'And what are your interests, Max?' Clara asked.

'I love music and playing the piano….although I must confess not all that well.'

'Good, then we've something in common. And your wife… does she share your love of music?'

'Yes, in fact she plays the piano better than I do. And do you play an instrument, Clara?'

'I had lessons as a child but I never took to it. I love to sing, though.'

With that, I positively beamed at her. 'You have a beautiful voice, my love, while mine makes a foghorn sound tuneful. Still, I enjoy listening to music, especially swing.'

'I rather prefer classical musical, especially Mendelssohn. I adore his famous violin concerto,' Max said.

'Oh so do I,' Clara responded, at once.

'I prefer something racier, more modern,' I insisted.

'The Party doesn't approve of swing, darling,' Clara pointed out. 'Nor,' she added, quietly, 'of Mendelssohn.'

'No,' I admitted, 'but I don't have to agree with everything the Party believes in.'

We had had similar debates before and I'd made it clear to her enough times, my adherence to the Party's cause did not come at the expense of being able to use my brain. In some matters the Party's approach was already too fanatical for my tastes, but assuredly I had no realisation at that time of just how much more fanatical it would become.

Max was starting to look fidgety. He gulped down the

remainder of his coffee. 'It's been delightful, but I really have to get back to work. Forgive me.'

'Of course, I quite understand. I'm sure you'll make a positive report to your superiors in order to obtain leave and I do hope you and Aliza will be able to accompany us as well.'

'Indeed, I hope so too. I'll try and let you have confirmation as soon as possible. '

'And then you must come for dinner,' Clara said.

'It will be a good opportunity to discuss travel arrangements,' I added. 'I'm sure we will all have an excellent voyage to Palestine and an enjoyable sojourn there.'

Max and I both stood up and shook hands once more, I was pleased to have been able to win him over to my proposition. There had been nothing disingenuous in my suggesting the need for a Jewish guide during the first stages of our visit to Palestine, whilst the prospect of spending up to a month in the company of Aliza, excited me. Then I thought of my love for Clara and felt a flash of guilt. All the same, there was still a part of me that could scarcely believe my good fortune.

3

I was left in a state of suspense for about a week, wondering if Aliza would be willing to leave her daughter in the care of her parents-in-law so that she could enjoy herself on vacation. But then Max telephoned me to say that he had been able to obtain leave to be able to accompany us, though only for a month, which meant that he and Aliza could only stay in Palestine for a fortnight. He added that his parents had agreed to look after his daughter and that Aliza would be pleased to accompany us. I immediately confirmed the invitation for dinner and this took place about ten days later.

When they arrived, my first thought was that Aliza looked utterly beautiful, dressed in a patterned evening gown, which showed off her figure, her black hair still cropped short, her complexion quite perfect. Above all, I was dazzled by those dark, intelligent eyes, which I had found so compelling when we had first met.

'Aliza, Max, so pleased to see you both again,' I said with a smile, before stepping forward to take hold of Aliza's hand, which I then touched with my lips. As I raised my eyes, she returned my smile and for a brief moment I felt quite transfixed by her, just as I had when we had first met. Recovering myself, I quickly introduced her to Clara, who was certainly more expensively dressed, and had taken care to wear a valuable pearl necklace, which had originally been my grandmother's.

'Delightful to meet you, Aliza,' Clara said with a warm smile before the two of them shook hands. 'And a pleasure to meet you again, Max,' she added, also shaking hands with him. 'Do both come through into the lounge. I expect you'd both like an aperitif before dinner…'

Clara had grown used to her role as hostess at frequent dinner parties, and proceeded to put both Max and Aliza at their ease.

'You have such an attractive house,' Aliza exclaimed as she enjoyed a Manhattan I had prepared for her. 'Have you lived here many years, Otto?'

She looked at me very directly as she asked this question and I almost felt as if we were old friends, for all that this was only our second meeting.

'My grandfather had it built back in the early '60s. I grew up here and inherited the home when my father died. I am, naturally, very fond of it.'

'And do you have any brothers or sisters?'

'A sister, yes. I had two brothers but… well… the war. They were both… killed.'

'Oh, I'm so sorry, I really shouldn't have asked. Please, forgive me?'

I smiled at her gently. 'There's nothing to forgive, I assure you.'

'That dreadful war took too many lives,' Max said. 'I too lost a brother…'

This admission of a shared loss, painful though it was, went some way towards breaking down any feelings of awkwardness at our first social encounter. I didn't particularly want to talk about the war but it loomed over all of us like a malevolent ghost and I felt closer to Max as our conversation revealed that all three brothers had died on the western front within a year of each other. I did my utmost to move the conversation on to light-hearted matters, and also I could not resist showing off my study.

'You have so many wonderful books,' Aliza declared, bringing an immediate smile to my face.

'I'm glad you think so. My favourites are my first editions of Goethe's novels.'

'Really! I do so like the *The Sorrows of Young Werther*.'

'Yes, so do I. And have you also read *Elective Affinities*? I've never quite been able to decide whether it's about fate or free will.'

'Oh,' said Aliza, 'I thought it was just about the natural chemistry that attracts people to one another.'

She looked into my eyes as she said this with a smile playing on her lips and I felt quite stunned. It pleased me, too, that she was clearly well-educated as well as beautiful.

'Yes... perhaps you're right,' I replied slowly.

Clara then declared that dinner was served. As was our practice for such an occasion, we had two maids waiting on us. I had asked them to bring from our cellar certain vintages I specified. In the course of the evening we all enjoyed these and, as had been my intention, they helped to make the atmosphere around the table more relaxed.

As I recall, the conversation was quite inconsequential. In particular, I was careful to avoid talking politics, preferring instead to discuss our forthcoming journey, and who we might meet as well as what we might see once we arrived in Palestine. What also impressed me about Aliza is that she had the ability to ask pertinent questions, be it about my family's history, or my work as a journalist, and also to listen with care as well as interest to the answers I gave her.

While I had naturally been pleased that she found my family home so attractive, Aliza also took care to draw Clara into conversation about first fashion and then music, having no doubt been told by Max that this was something of which she was fond. In short, Aliza was both charming and intelligent without being too ingratiating, which along with her looks left me thinking that Max was a very fortunate man indeed. Even though she might be a respectable married woman I could also imagine her still having many male admirers and that it would be all too easy to be tempted into flirtatious conversation with her. This I was assiduous in seeking to avoid, at least on this occasion, but I still found it hard not to look into Aliza's eyes from time to time and feel bewitched by the sheer force of her personality.

What also delighted me was the discovery that Aliza and I shared an appreciation of popular jazz music. This may still have been a somewhat risqué topic of conversation for Clara given the Party's attitude towards it, but she knew perfectly well that I was not a slave to all of its opinions, and I proceeded to extol the virtues of black American musicians such as Louis Armstrong and Duke Ellington.

'Don't you just love *It Don't Mean a Thing If It Ain't got that Swing,*' Aliza declared enthusiastically in reference to Ellington's latest success, and then began to praise the German composer, Kurt Weill's popular ballad *Mack the Knife*. This might have been somewhat safer territory so far as Clara was concerned, but glancing at her I could tell that she was still not impressed as it was not lost on either of us that Weill had Jewish blood. All the same, helped no doubt by the amount of wine I had drunk by this stage of the evening, I really didn't care and expressed myself to be equally enthusiastic for both pieces of music.

When the time came for Aliza and Max to depart, I simply couldn't resist touching Aliza's hand with my lips once more and once they had left I turned to Clara to say what a success I thought the evening had been.

'Yes, she has charm. Mind you, Max is a little too anxious to please, I think.'

'Perhaps, but I'm sure we'll get on perfectly well.'

She passed her hand across her hair, a gesture with which I had become very familiar. 'Yes, I do hope so, Otto…'

That night, before falling asleep, my mind was full of images of Aliza and enchanting thoughts of what a pleasure it had been to spend a few hours in her delightful company. It made me savour the prospect of what was to come, and I fell asleep remembering not only her smile but her captivating laughter, too, which I thought really special. I would go so far as to say that it was like music to my ears, standing out so strongly in my memory that I cannot think of her without also conjuring it up. Was I already in serious danger of falling in love with her? I think I was.

4

April 6 1933

It was evening when Clara and I met Aliza and Max on the platform of Berlin's central railway station to start our journey, first by train to Trieste and then by ship to Palestine. It was a chilly day, requiring us all to wear thick winter coats and scarves. Clara and I had taken care to pack an ample quantity of summer clothing in the expectation that we would soon be enjoying a much warmer climate.

To mark the occasion I also had a porter take a photograph of the four of us. Ah, the power of photography! Looking at it still serves as a reminder of how comparatively young we looked, especially Aliza, and happy, too, although Clara's smile seems a little more contrived than the smiles of the rest of us.

Following the dinner, once all the booking arrangements were in place, I had invited Max and Aliza for tea and cakes and their visit had gone as well as the dinner. Clara was right to think Max a little too anxious to please, but had our roles been reversed I might well have been the same, and I continued to keep him at his ease. Aliza, too, had been just as delightful, which only served to increase my growing sense of infatuation, for all that I hoped this was not apparent to anyone, including Aliza herself.

To complete what was to be a journey lasting a full twelve hours, we boarded a night train with sleeping quarters, and by travelling first class we were able to ensure that we did so in some comfort. Given that Clara and I also spent much of the journey asleep in our own quarters, we saw little of Max and Aliza. Furthermore, even once we arrived at Trieste and duly boarded our ship, the SS Martha Washington, that was to take us across the Mediterranean to Palestine, there was every opportunity to remain in our own cabins and even to take our meals there if we wished.

However, I was more than happy to eat with Max and Aliza, and to socialise with them, drawn as I was, like a moth to a flame, by Aliza's looks and personality. Although I assured myself that my attraction for her was relatively innocent, and that I had no intention of indulging in more than mild flirtation, I was soon in danger of angering Clara and souring our relationship. Further, whilst Max remained perfectly affable, there was also a risk that I might antagonise him as well, although I surmised he was so used to other men finding his wife attractive that he took it almost for granted, and was perhaps even flattered by it. After all, he had done very well for himself by marrying her, I thought, and could afford to bask, as it were, in her reflected glory.

*****

'Otto, do you think there's anyone on board this ship apart from ourselves and the crew who isn't Jewish?'

'I rather doubt it, my love.'

Clara and I were sitting in the first class lounge of our ship at the time. Up until then, our journey had gone smoothly, the spring weather being perfectly pleasant. All the same, when we had reached Trieste, neither of us had exactly been impressed by the sight of the ship as it was, I thought, at least a quarter of a century old and not in the best state of repair. Conditions on board were also distinctly crowded, although we were at least able to enjoy the relative comfort of travelling first class, whereas most of the seven to eight hundred passengers on board were travelling third class, five or six to a cabin.

'Anyway, our journey will soon be over,' I emphasised. 'We'll be docking in Haifa tomorrow.'

'And not a moment too soon.'

'Our cabin is comfortable, you must admit.'

'It's adequate, I suppose,' she replied grudgingly.

'On the third class deck they're packed in like sardines. Six to a cabin I believe. Mind you, I'm actually encouraged by just how crowded the vessel is. The captain told me yesterday when I met him on a stroll on the first-class deck that it's always the same. Business is booming and with every shipload the Zionist cause is strengthened.'

I then looked at her with concern and, stretching out my right hand, placed it on her left. Her hand felt cold and soft 'Do you still feel sick?' I murmured.

'A little, but I'm better than I was.' Her tone had now softened and she managed a brief smile of affection.

'Good.'

I then glanced around at our fellow passengers and my mind was drawn back to the events of earlier in the day. 'You know, I'm encouraged by a conversation that I had this morning. I was on deck, typing an article for the *Berliner Boersenzeitung* paper, while you were resting, and this young Jew came up to me and started berating me…'

'What on earth for?'

'Oh, in view of my reading material he'd assumed that I must be hostile to the Zionist cause. He went on about the determination of Jewish youth and how Zionism was giving them a sense of purpose with a true belief in their own Fatherland. Also, how they were prepared to work with their bare hands and endure every hardship to make their dream of a Jewish homeland come true.'

Clara looked doubtful. 'Many of the Jews I've seen on board this ship look to be from professional backgrounds. They won't find it easy to cope with manual labour.'

'Perhaps not, but you shouldn't underestimate them. I agree that it won't be easy for the older professional Jews but those who are less well off, and the younger men and women especially, will cope well enough. The young man who spoke to me yesterday was full of zeal and I am sure there are many more like him. By the way, once I told him about my great interest in the Zionist cause he apologised for his earlier manner towards me. You know, he admitted that the Jews have always struggled to be truly assimilated into European society, and therefore needed their own Fatherland if they were to ever achieve real peace and prosperity.'

Just at that moment I glanced up and noticed that Max and Aliza had entered the lounge. I raised a hand in greeting as they walked towards our table.

'Good evening, I'm sorry we're a little late,' Aliza said, with a slight note of embarrassment in her voice.

I remember smiling at her; perhaps, I must confess, a little too warmly. She was as beautiful as ever, and dressed in the same gown, I thought, as she had worn when she and Max had come to dinner before our departure.

'Not at all,' I responded, immediately getting to my feet. 'What can I get you to drink?'

'That delicious cocktail, I had the other night, please?' As she spoke Aliza returned my smile and took her seat next to mine. I sensed, not for the first time, that the attraction I felt towards her was reciprocated. I also found her voice to be as sensual as her eyes.

'Why, a Manhattan, yes of course. And you, Max?'

'A beer will do very well, thanks.'

'And you, my love?'

Clara gave me a rather disapproving stare. 'I'll have the same cocktail, please.'

I tried to catch the eye of one of the waiters and bestowed a friendly smile on both Aliza and Max as I did so. 'It will be a relief to arrive in Haifa tomorrow,' I commented conversationally. 'The storm we ran into last night was most unpleasant.'

'I was rather seasick,' Clara declared, pulling a face as she did so that was indicative of her suffering. I gave her a sympathetic look of concern.

'It should stay calm tonight,' Max said reassuringly. 'And it will be interesting to see Haifa again. There was a lot of building going on when I was last there and it seemed a busy place.'

'And when were you there?' I asked him casually.

'Oh, it must have been two years ago now.'

'I'd prefer us to move on to Tel Aviv as soon as possible,' Clara declared emphatically. 'Didn't you say, darling, there was a half-decent hotel there?'

'It would seem so, my love.'

At that moment the waiter appeared and I ordered the two Manhattan cocktails and two beers.

'I can't wait to see Jerusalem,' Aliza remarked enthusiastically. 'The Holy City, the Wailing Wall, it'll be the experience of a lifetime; I'm sure.'

I smiled at her with an affection that I hoped would not be too obvious, and then turned to Max. 'Have you already been there, too?'

'Yes, on my first visit, five years ago. It was deeply moving.'

'I understand the city is dominated by the great mosque,' Clara commented. I eyed her carefully, suspecting that she was about to become deliberately tendentious.

'Yes, Jerusalem is a Holy City for Muslims as well as for Jews and Christians,' Max replied. He had already struck me as being a rather naïve individual, although perhaps he was simply too anxious to please.

Clara's eyes flashed. 'A sure recipe for conflict, don't you think?'

'With a measure of goodwill on both sides, I hope not.' Max responded, his tone of voice still perfectly relaxed.

'Isn't it the case that the Arabs are opposed to Jewish settlements?' Clara asked. 'I'm sure I read that there were riots about it not so long ago.'

'There were riots about four years ago, I believe,' Max admitted. 'However, I'm sure the situation will have improved since then.'

'I hope so, but my feeling is that the Arabs have lived in Palestine for centuries and are just as entitled to regard it as their Fatherland as you are. In fact, you've been absent for the best part of two thousand years, then suddenly just turn up again, and expect them to accept you. I really don't see it working.'

Max was now looking a little ruffled. 'We only want to share the land with the Arabs and live in peace with them.'

'Fine sentiments, I agree, but what have you in common with them?'

'Common humanity,' Max replied, his tone growing more tense.

'I doubt if that's ever sufficient,' Clara replied. 'But please don't think I don't wish your plans well, Max. It's just that I have genuine doubts that they'll ever succeed.'

Max smiled at her, almost gratefully, I thought. 'I too have doubts,' he confessed, typically anxious, to be conciliatory. 'But I still believe that what we're doing is right and that the Zionist movement will succeed.'

'Well said, Max, well said!' I declared encouragingly.

At that moment the waiter returned with our drinks and put them down on the table in front of us. I promptly picked up my glass and wished everyone good health before I took quite a long gulp of beer in what I suppose was rather a reckless manner.

'I look forward to the day when Max and I can settle in Palestine,' Aliza said in a spirited way.

Max, however, looked uncertain. 'For the time being, my darling, you know that my commitment continues to lie in Germany promoting the Zionist cause.'

'But not indefinitely,' Aliza insisted. 'Sooner or later we must join our brothers and sisters. We Jews have no future in Germany. It doesn't require much perception to see that with Herr Hitler, now our Chancellor, and anti-Jewish legislation already being drawn up, time is running out for all us German Jews! Either we leave Germany for ever, or God knows what will become of us.'

'Herr Hitler will make a great leader,' Clara then declared proudly, throwing back her head. 'He understands the hearts and minds of the German people, he'll take our economy out of recession, and reassert the greatness of our nation!'

Aliza shook her head. 'He's no Bismarck, Clara. I think he'll ruin everything.'

I knew that Aliza was now in danger of making Clara angry so I quickly intervened. 'As I see it our country's been humiliated by the events of the Great War and the Weimar Republic was a total disaster. The nation needs a strong leader and there's no one better than Herr Hitler to provide that leadership and sense of purpose. But please let's not talk any more about politics.'

'No, let's not,' Max agreed. 'I'm afraid that Aliza likes to speak her mind.'

I smiled at her once more. 'That's a quality I greatly admire,' I said with perfect sincerity.

With that, Aliza looked me steadily in the eye. 'I'm glad you do, Otto. The trouble is that in the autocracy Herr Hitler is creating speaking one's mind will soon be a crime if it offends the State. I believe in democracy. It works well enough in England and the United States.'

'But not in Germany,' Clara insisted. 'I agree with Otto; the Weimar was a total failure.'

'It was never given a proper chance,' Aliza said. 'The collapse of world trade has damaged every nation.'

'And who's to blame for that?' Clara asked.

I understood the implications behind this remark only too well as there were many in the Party who blamed the financial collapse on Jewish financiers. However, I wasn't one of them. I believed this a preposterous, even outrageous, argument. Once again I decided to intervene. 'Ladies, let's not bicker. We're on holiday, after all, and it's time we had dinner.'

'Yes, I quite agree,' Max added. 'I'm starving.'

I could tell Clara was still cross whilst Aliza looked serene but defiant. I'm sure she knew exactly what Clara had been trying to suggest, and it was probably just as obvious to Max as well, but he was discreet enough not to appear to notice. It struck me, too, the more animated the conversation had become, the more beautiful Aliza and Clara had seemed. I was left with the image, perhaps unfair, of two magnificent female cats preparing to scratch each other's eyes out.

*****

After dinner the four of us returned to the lounge where we were served coffee. In the background the ship's band was playing dance tunes and three couples had already taken to the floor.

I could see that Aliza was tapping her foot in rhythm with the music and looking as if she would like to dance as well. Max, meanwhile, was recounting his experiences in Palestine to Clara who was clearly becoming bored with the subject. I made an impulsive decision, something of a weakness of mine, I must confess, emptied my cup, and stood up.

'Would you like to dance?' I asked Aliza, holding out my hand.

She looked surprised. 'Why, thank you; that would be very nice.'

I didn't even glance in Clara's direction and instead just led Aliza into a slow foxtrot. I was immediately impressed.

'If I may say so,' I said. 'You dance beautifully.'

'It's for the man to lead and you do so very well,' she responded, returning my compliment with aplomb.

'I don't get much practice, though. Clara isn't that keen.'

'What about Max?'

'Oh, he dances a little.'

'But does he enjoy it?'

'Not very much, I think. He just pretends for my sake.'

'Whereas I can tell that you love it.'

She smiled at me in, I thought, a rather enigmatic fashion. 'And you don't mind dancing with a Jew?'

'Of course not, why should I?'

'But I don't really understand you. You're a Nazi and a member of the SS...'

'The Reiter SS to be exact.'

'What's that?'

'It's really just an aristocrats' club, nothing more.'

'Even so, you must appreciate that your Party despises us?'

'The National Socialist Movement believes in racial purity and that every race belongs on its own soil,' I responded somewhat evasively, perhaps. 'That's why I support Zionism. Aliza, I am absolutely not a Jew-hater, I assure you.'

'Of course you're not, but many in your Party are. You must surely admit that?'

I hesitated before replying. It was true, of course. 'Yes....I can't deny it.'

'And I have the impression that Clara doesn't exactly share your enthusiasm for our cause. Perhaps it might have been better if you and Max had made this trip on your own.'

'No, no,' I spluttered a little, somewhat taken aback by her directness. 'This was largely meant to be a holiday for all of us, and Clara and I both love to travel.'

At that the tune came to an end and I was able to recover my poise.

'Thank you for the dance,' she said to me.

'It was a pleasure. Not only are you a fine dancer but also a very beautiful woman.'

It remains my belief that the right measure of charm and flattery can be an effective way to any woman's heart but all the same, what was I thinking of; being quite so flirtatious with a Jewess in the presence of my wife? Well, as I say, impulsiveness is one of my weaknesses, and knowing how beautiful Aliza was, there remained the constant danger that I would fall in love with her.

'If we weren't both married I'd think that you were making a pass at me,' she replied, in her lovely velvety voice.

'You might think that. I'm an admirer of beauty and you must know how striking you are.'

'Yes, as Jews go, I suppose I'm quite attractive.' I realised she was being ironic.

'That was unnecessary. Can't we be friends?'

'We are friends, Otto, but you know Herr Hitler attributes so many of Germany's ills to Jews when it simply isn't true. We've contributed a great deal to the country, so it's deeply unjust that we should be made scapegoats for the difficulties it has faced since the war.'

I shook my head. 'Whoever said it was a fair world?'

I didn't mean to chide her, however, for I was impressed,

not just by her beauty, but also by her spirited intelligence as well.

We then both returned to our chairs and as I looked at Clara I could tell that she was cross with me. The band started playing another tune and after a few moments Aliza accepted Max's invitation to dance while I leaned back in my chair next to Clara's.

'What were you two talking about in such an animated fashion?' she was cross. 'I'm sure I heard her say something about Jews being scapegoats.'

'She's understandably unhappy about the Party's insistence on racial purity.'

'That's unfortunate. Anyway, you were flirting with her!'

'My love, no!'

'Yes, you were. It was obvious.'

'She's a good dancer.'

'Whereas I'm not, I suppose?'

'You admit yourself that you don't particularly like it.'

'Perhaps it's not my favourite activity, but please stop making eyes at her.'

'I'll try. But look, just because I find her attractive doesn't mean that I'm about to have an affair with her. I find you far more beautiful, I assure you, and anyway,' I added with a smirk, 'I don't think Max would approve.'

'Oh, you're impossible!' Clara was still trying to be cross with me but I sensed that my easy charm was rapidly dissipating this.

'I think Max's rather a weak man,' she added.

'You're too harsh.'

'No, I'm not. I don't know what she sees in him.'

I grinned. 'Intelligence, integrity, reliability, good nature, these are all important qualities I imagine a woman can find attractive in a man.'

'And how would you know? He also talks too much.'

'He's just nervous. Once we reach Palestine he'll be more relaxed, I expect.'

She looked unconvinced. 'Perhaps, but please promise me you won't flirt with Frau Geisser again?'

I held my hands up. 'That's a bargain. I agree.'

She made her familiar gesture of bringing her left hand across her hair. There was obviously still something else on her mind. 'You know, I've never really understood your passion for Zionism. All these attendances at Zionist congresses, both here in Berlin and elsewhere, can't have done your reputation any good at all. It could even ruin you.'

I shook my head and remained relaxed in the face of her criticism. 'I don't agree, my love. The whole point of Zionism is that, in time, it will ensure that tens of thousands of Jews emigrate from this country to Palestine and never return. Max, and many Jewish men and women like him, are dedicated to creating a Jewish State in Palestine, and I believe that if they receive enough support they will succeed.'

She looked unconvinced. 'I don't think so, darling. The Arabs will make their lives hell.'

'Not necessarily, and the alternative is the Jews will become increasingly isolated in our society, deprived of all rights of citizenship, despised and impoverished.'

'Which would perhaps be no bad thing. Isn't our party dedicated to finally freeing this country from the Jewish cancer?'

'Don't use that dreadful phrase, my love!. What I myself think is that we have to seek a peaceful and realistic solution to the Jewish question. Through Zionism the Jews can secure an independent State and our country can say goodbye to them for ever, leaving us as racially pure as we could ever hope to be.'

'But you can't seriously expect all the Jews in our country to emigrate to Palestine?'

'No, of course not, but if a substantial number do so, the position of the remainder will naturally be weakened and they in turn can be encouraged to emigrate to America or elsewhere in Europe.'

She still looked at me dubiously. 'I very much doubt if it will work.'

'You mustn't be such a pessimist,' I responded. 'Have you a better solution?'

She looked askance at me at first, but her expression quickly softened into something gentler and she gestured to me to pass her a cigarette. I did so, gladly, and then lit it for her.

'I simply don't believe that enough Jews will want to give up everything for the sort of hardships they're bound to have to endure in Palestine.'

'Even if they're deprived of their rights of citizenship in this country?'

'Even then. And what about the Arabs? I can't believe they'll ever want to countenance an independent Jewish State in their midst. Nor do I believe the British would allow it to happen.'

I smiled patiently at her apparent ignorance of Middle Eastern affairs. 'But my love, the British have promised the Jews a homeland in Palestine.'

'Darling, I didn't believe you were that naïve,' she riposted with a grin of pleasure, her blue eyes lighting up as she did so. 'Promises can be broken!'

'Yes, I know that only too well.' She had now irritated me a little. 'Anyway, I intend to find out just how successfully the Zionist movement is putting its ideals into practice.'

'And I suppose the price for that is that I must put up with you making eyes at Aliza?'

'I promise you, I won't do that,' I responded gently. Anyhow, once she and Max have gone home we'll have plenty of time to ourselves.'

'Still, you must be careful, Otto. You don't want to be thought of as a Jew lover, and drummed out of the Party.'

'That's not going to happen, my love. I believe I'll become respected for my far sightedness and given the promotion I deserve.'

'I somehow doubt that, Otto.'

I merely grinned at her, but for all my outward self-confidence, I did have serious doubts about ever persuading anyone in the Party who really mattered to support the Zionist cause. Furthermore, though I saw such merit in it, I often found myself reflecting on why that was? My conclusion, however, was that it simply made good sense. After all, its furtherance would, so I believed, help present the national socialist cause in as positive a light as possible, whilst also being consistent with its general principles.

That night a storm blew up and Clara was terribly seasick. Fortunately, I am a good sailor, and was untroubled by the motion of the ship, but still I found it difficult to sleep. Time and again my mind was drawn back to the dance floor and Aliza's alluring image. She clearly - and very understandably under the circumstances - had no time for my Party and what it stood for, of course, and wasn't afraid to say so, but I couldn't blame her for that. Indeed, I just found myself continuing to admire her spirit and wondering if I would have had the same courage to speak out if our roles had been reversed.

Of course, I could just have dismissed her as a Jewess, albeit a very attractive one, who wasn't of my class, and with whom I really had little in common. Perhaps, too, I might have been wise to do so, but as it was, both her looks and personality contrived to hold me in her spell.

5

We finally docked at Haifa on the eleventh of April after a five-day voyage from Trieste. It was now mid-afternoon and the temperature had been rising steadily all day. I was feeling uncomfortable but had no intention of showing it. Both Max and Clara were also clearly suffering in the heat but Aliza appeared to be in her element.

My first priority was to hire a car so we could get to Tel Aviv, which is about ninety kilometres from Haifa. Once we had passed through customs I noticed a tall, moustached British officer standing outside the customs office.

'I'm going to ask him where we might hire a car,' I said to Clara and immediately strode over to the man. My English is reasonably good; it is a sister language of German, after all; and I gave him my name and told him I was a German tourist. Very politely he gave me directions to a garage, for which I thanked him.

'I would like to be able to get to Tel Aviv tonight, if at all possible,' I added.

'I doubt if you'll manage it in daylight, sir, and after that the roads are far from safe. Only the other month someone was murdered travelling after dark between here and Tel Aviv.'

'Were they alone?'

'I believe so, yes.'

'Well, there are four of us in our party and I'd still like to arrive tonight. There's a decent hotel waiting for us, I believe, and we have a reservation. My wife hasn't exactly been happy with the cramped conditions aboard ship.'

'It's your decision, sir, but personally, I wouldn't risk it.'

'Thanks for your advice, but I'm sure we'll be fine.'

The officer was clearly an affable fellow and, keen to obtain as much information as possible, I decided to seize the opportunity to engage him briefly in conversation.

'Tell me, how do you see things turning out here in Palestine with so many Jews now entering the country?' I asked.

'Time will tell, sir. We've imposed restrictions on immigration, but they don't apply to anyone with sufficient skills and assets, so they keep coming. The rules are easily circumvented, too, as anyone entering the country as a tourist doesn't have to register and can then simply disappear into the population at large. The Arabs know this and keep complaining. There'll be more trouble sooner or later, I expect.'

'And what do you think the consequences will be?'

'We'll, increasingly, be put in a very difficult position trying to hold the line between two warring factions,' the officer replied bluntly. 'That will be expensive for us and we'll lose men.'

I looked around me. 'But I've been impressed by the amount of building going on here. It rather gives the impression that the British are here to stay.'

The officer looked doubtful. 'I don't know about that, sir. We only have a mandate from the League of Nations and to my mind what really matters is that the Empire should continue to have safe access through the Suez Canal.'

'So the Arabs and the Jews may be left to their fate?'

'You could put it that way, sir.'

'And do you think the Jews can create their own homeland here?'

'Quite possibly; in many ways they're already doing it. I admire their industry and dedication but the Arabs understandably resent the progress they're making. They see the Jews as no better than any other infidels intent on stealing their land in the same way as the crusaders did. It's a recipe for bloodshed, in my view.'

'What about some division of the land between Jews and Arabs, isn't that possible?'

The officer looked even more doubtful. 'It is, I suppose, but this is a small country and the Jews are very much in the minority.'

'Still, their numbers are growing. What if they were to be counted in millions?'

'There's always strength in numbers, I agree, but so much of the land is desert…'

'…But with sufficient irrigation and cultivation?'

The officer's expression became defensive. 'Look, don't get me wrong, I wish the Jews well, and I hope they succeed in what they are trying to achieve here. All the same you still have to question whether it will work in the long run.'

'And what about oil? Isn't it in the British interest to remain here as long as possible in order to safeguard the oil supply from the Mosul oil fields in Iraq?'

'You're clearly well informed, sir.'

I nodded and smiled a little before looking up at the bare slopes of Mount Carmel that dominated the town. I then glanced at Clara and the Geissers, who were not unreasonably becoming impatient with me for talking so long in the heat.

'Well, thank you, officer; you've been most helpful.'

He stood to attention and saluted me.

Half an hour later, after bartering with the Arab owner in a mixture of sign language, English and French, a car was hired.

'Right everyone, as soon as we've filled up with petrol we can be on our way,' I declared, happily.

'Isn't it too late for that, darling?' Clara suggested.

'No, not if we get going within the next ten minutes.'

'But I know the road to Tel Aviv isn't good,' Max interjected. 'And we certainly aren't going to get there now in daylight. Don't you think we should stay here for the night?'

I looked at him impatiently. 'No, we'll be fine. Don't worry.'

'Well, if you're sure, darling?' Clara asked me intently.

'Yes, I'm completely sure.'

In the event, the drive to Tel Aviv passed off without incident, though the calibre of driving among the people of Palestine was, it must be said, not that of Germany. It didn't take long to locate our hotel, which struck me as being reasonably civilised. Having been shown to our rooms, we then changed for dinner.

Clara and I were the first to reach the hotel's dining room. Having been shown to a table, we sat waiting for the others to join us. I was still in a good humour.

'I'm pleased the journey here from Haifa was such an easy one,' I said, conversationally.

Clara frowned at me. She'd already told me that she had developed a headache and was less approving of our surroundings.

'We could have been murdered.'

I grinned at her. 'Well, we weren't. Now we can enjoy a good meal, I hope. I'm feeling hungry.'

'And you can continue to flirt with Frau Geisser and make eyes at each other,' she retorted.

'Darling, that simply isn't true.'

'I'm not blind. Don't lie to me. And you promised me you wouldn't.'

I sighed, trying to maintain my patience. 'I'm simply being a gentleman; that is all. They'll be going home soon enough and then it'll just be the two of us. Please don't get so upset over nothing.'

'Oh very well, I'll continue to grit my teeth, I suppose, but it won't be easy.'

I glanced in the direction of the dining room entrance. 'Here they come. Please be nice!'

As Aliza approached, I stood up and couldn't stop myself smiling warmly at her. I thought she looked ravishing in the long turquoise evening-dress she was wearing and I was half-inclined to tell her so but then checked myself.

'I trust you're feeling refreshed?'

She returned my smile. 'Yes, thank you.'

'You made the right decision, getting us here tonight,' Max told me as he and Aliza took their seats. 'I must confess I was a bit worried at first.'

'I assure you there was no need to have been. I always carry my revolver with me.'

Aliza looked shocked. 'What, loaded and ready to fire?'

I grinned at her. 'Yes, I saw enough action in the war to know how to use it.'

Aliza looked me steadily in the eye and calmly asked, 'Have you ever killed a man, Otto?'

Her directness took me somewhat by surprise, but I decided

that her question still merited a straight answer.

'Yes, but it is not something that I remember with any pleasure. I was simply doing my duty, as were those whom I killed.'

'So you killed more than one?'

'I'm afraid so, yes, but I will never know the exact number. The battlefield is a confusing place.'

We continued to hold each other's gaze. I glanced at Clara and sensed that she was becoming angry.

'My husband is a brave man,' she said, almost with a note of defiance in her voice. 'You were decorated for it, weren't you, darling?'

I nodded. 'Yes, I had that honour.'

'We have a photograph of him being decorated by the Kaiser himself,' Clara declared proudly, pointedly directing her remark at Aliza.

I began to feel decidedly uncomfortable. 'Let's not dwell on the war. It's all in the past and for the most part best forgotten.'

'You see, my husband is not only brave but modest, too,' Clara declared.

'Please, my love, you're embarrassing me. I'm really no braver than countless other men who served their country. I just give thanks I survived when so many of my comrades did not. Some of them were twice the man I could ever hope to be.'

A waiter then arrived to hand out menus and take our drinks order. It was a relief to talk about more mundane matters and I was careful too not to make any direct eye contact with Aliza, but I could still sense that she was studying me in a pensive fashion.

'You know, I think you exaggerate the qualities of your fallen comrades because you feel guilty that you lived and they did not,' she suddenly remarked. This time her directness took me completely off my guard.

'That may be so, although I didn't know that you were a psychologist, Aliza,' I responded without any hint of sarcasm. 'One man at least, a good friend, lost his own life saving me, and if our roles had been reversed I don't know if I would have acted as he did. Call it guilt if you like but I know that I'll never forget him or his courage.'

'I'm intrigued. Tell me, what happened exactly?' Again, we were making direct eye contact across the table, and once more, I began to feel uncomfortable, sensing Clara's mounting hostility.

'I'd prefer not to. The memory is a painful one.'

'Of course, I can understand that.'

'Can you really?'

'Yes, I believe so.'

'And you, Max, were too young to play any part in the war, I expect?' Clara asked, while at the same time flashing her eyes angrily at me.

'No, no, I was an ambulance driver in the last few months of the war. I didn't see action, it's true, but I did witness a good deal of death and suffering. Enough certainly to convince me that war is a terrible thing.'

'Yes, I entirely agree with that sentiment,' I added. "So let's not dwell on the war; what matters is the future, a bright new future, I trust, with a resurgent Fatherland and a Jewish State in Palestine.'

A few moments later the waiter returned with our drinks and, as soon as he had departed, I raised my glass.

'To a bright future for us all,' I declared.

6

The following morning, after a restless night, I got up early and decided to go for a short walk on my own. In truth the Great War had understandably left me rather a poor sleeper and I am invariably an early riser. All was still quiet, it was already becoming pleasantly warm, and I enjoyed being able to take in the atmosphere of the place without anyone disturbing me.

Feeling refreshed, I returned to the hotel for breakfast and noticed that Aliza was sitting by herself at a table in the restaurant. She seemed even more beautiful than ever. I often used to wonder, when thinking of Aliza, how such a lovely woman could exist at all.

'Good morning, I've just been for a walk. May I join you?' I asked her.

'Why of course.'

'And you slept well, I trust?'

'Yes, very well, thank you.'

'I expect that Clara will join us shortly.'

'And Max as well, no doubt.'

I sat down opposite her and leant back in my chair. 'I'm looking forward to some proper sightseeing. This country is so steeped in history.'

'Yes, it's very special. But, you know, you really continue to intrigue me.'

'Do I? In what way, I wonder?'

'What do you think, Otto? You're a Nazi who likes Jews. It's a contradiction in terms!'

Once again, here she was, probing away at me; I could have been offended but I wasn't. I gave a shrug. 'Yes, I suppose it is a contradiction.'

Aliza smiled at me with a warmth and beauty that almost took my breath away. 'You are certainly happy enough to flirt with me.'

It was true, of course, but I feigned surprise. 'Do I really? I think you're a beautiful woman and I merely wish to behave in a gentlemanly way towards you.'

'Thank you again for the compliment, but I suspect your wife sees it rather differently. She looked very cross last night.'

I sighed. 'Well, she's wrong to be so. I've never been unfaithful to her.'

'Would you like to be?' Aliza asked me softly.

This time I really was almost lost for words. 'Are you seriously propositioning me?'

'No, I'm just curious, that's all. Anyway, imagine the scandal if it was discovered that a member of the SS… sorry Reiter SS… was having an affair with a Jewess.'

'You're teasing me, I think. Of course, I enjoy the company of beautiful women, whatever their race, but I don't believe that I am a flirt and I love my wife.'

'That is to your credit.'

'And you?'

'What?'

'Is your marriage a happy one?'

She looked straight into my eyes before responding. 'Why,

yes, I suppose so, and we have our child, of course.'

'Then we are both blessed.'

'And perhaps one day Max and I will settle here in Palestine.'

'You should certainly do so, and sooner rather than later. As you've said yourself, there is no future for Jews in Germany.'

'Yes, I understand that only too well. You know Herr Hitler is a messenger of hate and that's the worst of all cancers.'

'He stands for racial purity and strong government; that's all.'

Suddenly, she looked incensed. 'How can you say that? I think he's just a demagogue. He and his supporters, men like you, I'm afraid, will drag Germany into the gutter.'

This could well have been the moment when our burgeoning friendship came to a juddering halt, but instead I simply smiled at her indulgently. Once again what really struck me was not what she said but how particularly beautiful she was when animated.

'On the contrary, we are hoping to give the Fatherland a new sense of pride and purpose.'

'But Otto, that purpose is to destroy the influence of all, so called, foreigners, even though we may have lived in Germany for generations, as well as to remilitarise with the intention of seizing back the Rhineland and much else besides. Sooner or later that will very likely lead to another war and, if it does, Germany will lose just like it did the last time.'

I shrugged again. 'Just because we suffered a defeat in the Great War doesn't mean we would be bound to do so again.'

'So you admit war is Hitler's major objective?'

'No, I didn't say that. Certainly, I believe we should do everything possible to avoid it, but if the German people cannot be reunited by peaceful means, regrettably there may be no alternative.'

'Mark my words, it will come to that,' she declared emphatically. 'I can't believe that France, Great Britain and America would stand by and let Hitler trample over Europe any more than they were prepared to let the Kaiser do so.'

I couldn't help but be impressed by the passion behind her argument. I was not, however, prepared to concede anything.

'I think you will find that attitudes have changed. Nations have lost the appetite for conflict and the carnage of war.'

'Has Germany, though?' she fired back me.

'A good question; time will tell.'

With that, she shook her finger at me. 'You know you are really such a hypocrite.'

This time her attack did make me wince slightly but I remained in a good humour, still rather enjoying our verbal jousting match.

'How is that?' I asked her calmly.

'You exude gentlemanly charm and are happy enough to flirt with me and yet you espouse a cause that is completely undemocratic and despises my race.'

At that, I laughed at her, refusing to be stung by her words. 'And yet you don't dislike me, do you?'

'Perhaps I am too easily flattered,' she conceded. 'I want to dislike you, though, because you are no more than the civilised face of…of…an evil ideology.'

'Now I'm hardly likely to agree with that, am I? Even so I admire your spirit. That and your good looks is what I find most attractive about you.'

She threw up her hands in frustration. 'Oh, you're impossible.'

With that, I began to laugh. 'That's exactly what Clara accused me of only the other night. You two are really quite alike, you know.'

Aliza looked cross at the very suggestion. 'I think it's just as well that you and I will not be enjoying each other's company for too much longer. You can be very irritating, Otto, yet also attractive, and as we're both married, that's dangerous. Perhaps it's fortunate I'm expecting Max here at any moment.

I said nothing. I had not been expecting such frankness from her. She gave a little cough, then, very consciously changing the subject, said:

'At least Max and I won't go home without first seeing Jerusalem. God willing, it will, one day, once more, be the capital of an independent Israel.'

I glanced towards the door of the restaurant and saw Clara walking through it. She appeared to be scowling at me.

'Well, I hope you're right,' I said in response to Aliza's words.

'I know I am. It is part of our nation's destiny.'

I stood up and dutifully went to kiss Clara on the cheek. 'Good morning, my love, I hope you slept well?'

'No, not really.'

Clara swept passed me, ignoring my gesture of affection, and sat down opposite Aliza, whose presence she did not even bother to acknowledge. 'And where have you been?' Clara asked me.

'I went for a walk. When I returned Aliza had already come down for breakfast, and we've been chatting about the merits of National Socialism, haven't we, Aliza? I think it fair to say you don't have a very high opinion of our esteemed Chancellor.'

'No, I don't,' Aliza replied flatly, though looking a little anxious, I thought. She was obviously acutely conscious of not wishing to annoy Clara and looked relieved when Max came walking through the restaurant door. He appeared to be especially cheerful.

'Good morning, everyone, I hope you all slept well? Another fine day, I see, and the Purim Carnival to look forward to this evening.'

'And what's that?' Clara asked him.

'It's an annual event. We're lucky to be here at the right time of year. The streets will be decked with garlands; there'll be dancing, and then a parade, apparently. It's a joyous celebration. We must all be sure to watch it.'

I gave him one of my more ingratiating smiles. 'We'll be delighted to do so, won't we Clara?'

'Yes, it sounds fun.'

She was back to being her usual gracious self, which pleased me. I was reminded of my dear late mother who had accused me of marrying beneath me. 'Clara is not of our class, I'm afraid,' I recall her telling me in a regretful tone of voice.' Whereupon I had said, 'It does not stop me loving her, mother.' At which my mother had replied, 'no, I realise that only too well, but even so it may cause you some social embarrassment in the future.'

I had dismissed my mother's comment as pure snobbishness, because Clara was merely the daughter of a doctor of medicine rather than of a member of the aristocracy, and nothing that she had done since had ever given me any reason to regret our marriage.

It made me think, too, of what either of my late parents would have made of the rise of Herr Hitler to power in

Germany. My father, I believe, would have been supportive as he had been crushed by Germany's defeat in the Great War and the chaos that followed, but as for my mother… well I somewhat doubt it. She would have been much too inclined to look down on the man because of his humble origins.

I almost smiled as well, at the thought of what she would have made of Aliza. Of course, she would have been totally polite towards her, even charming, but behind her back she would probably have been just as critical as she had been of Clara. However, that reflection didn't stop me from seeing Aliza as the very embodiment of all that was finest in her race and above all to begin to open my eyes to the dangers inherent in notions of racial superiority. Surely it was, in truth, pure nonsense for the Nazis to claim that pure-blooded Germans were superior to Jewish people. Weren't we all *people*, after all? I did not, though, yet share her insight that Fuhrer was a messenger of hate, unleashing the worst of all cancers. That understanding still awaited me… or perhaps I should say that it still eluded me

7

The evening air was still and warm and the streets of the Tel Aviv were alive with the sound of people enjoying themselves and of bands playing.

Aliza was clearly enthralled by it and I thought she seemed happier than at any time since we had first met. I was still mulling over what she had said to me in the restaurant over breakfast.

'Isn't it wonderful?' she remarked. 'So much colour and jollity everywhere!'

'Yes, I'm impressed,' I responded, completely truthfully. I was also, you may correctly surmise, deeply impressed by Aliza.

'It's as well that we've managed to find ourselves such a good view and without too much of a crush,' Max commented. He was right, for, from where we were standing, we could see the carnival wending its way towards us, even from quite a distance. 'And what do you think of the theme of the parade, Otto?'

I smiled at him indulgently. 'Very appropriate, I must say.'

'I think so, too. Deliverance and return to the Promised Land. It's what the Jewish nation has been seeking for nearly two thousand years.'

'And now at last becoming a reality,' I added.

'It has to be worth celebrating, that's for certain,' Aliza declared emphatically.

We continued to watch the parade coming nearer to us and

then Clara cried out. 'Look, what's that float coming towards us with swastikas. It has the head of a dragon.'

'People are wearing masks as well, shaped like books. They must represent the ones that were so stupidly burnt in Germany.' Aliza responded.

'What was stupid about it?' Clara asked her.

'I would have thought that was obvious. It was hardly the behaviour you'd expect of a civilised nation.'

Clara bristled a little. 'Germany is one of the most civilised nations on earth!'

'Not if its government supports the burning of literature it disapproves of,' Aliza said.

'Let's not argue, please,' I urged them. 'This is a night for celebration after all…'

'Hey, there's Daniel,' Max called out. Then he started to wave. 'Daniel, it's me, Max.'

A short, chubby faced man with curly hair waved back and then walked quickly towards us.

'Hello Max, it's good to see you again. What brings you to Tel Aviv?' he asked as the two men embraced.

'We are here on holiday.'

'I see.' Daniel was smiling at Aliza as he spoke and they also embraced fondly.

'And may I introduce our friends?' Max said. 'This is Otto and his wife Clara, who have come from Germany with us to see for themselves what the Zionist cause is achieving.'

'Hello, it's nice to meet you.'

Daniel politely held out his hand and I was pleased to shake it with all my usual firmness.

'We were good friends with Daniel and his wife in Germany

before they emigrated here a couple of years ago,' Max explained

'A fortunate coincidence you should happen to meet up in such a crowded place,' I remarked.

'Yes, very,' Daniel responded. 'You're not Jewish, I take it?'

'No, but I am a supporter of the Zionist movement. Max has been acting as our guide and I must say I'm impressed by what I've seen.'

'I'm pleased. Certainly we believe we are really achieving something worthwhile here.'

'Daniel,' Max interjected. 'I should explain that Otto is a prominent member of the National Socialist Party. He believes the German government should be actively supporting the Zionist cause.'

A look of total astonishment immediately crossed Daniel's face. 'A Fascist who believes in Zionism, eh! My God, whatever next? I thought your kind hated all Jews?'

Daniel's disparaging tone made me feel annoyed. 'I assure you, I do not, sir.'

'Perhaps you don't, but there are many like you who do. You appreciate, I hope, that many German Jews are emigrating here to escape from anti-Semitism?'

'Their motives for coming here are of no concern to me,' I replied stiffly. 'What matters is that I am prepared to advocate support for such emigration in the highest echelons of government.'

'If that's your genuine intention then I wish you well.'

At that moment our conversation began to be drowned out by the sound of music as a carnival float approached with a jazz band on board. I smiled in recognition of the tune they were playing, having made a mental note to question Daniel further, regardless of his hostile manner towards me. Once the float passed by and the sound of the music died away, I seized my opportunity.

'Tell me, do you believe the Arabs will ever accept you in their midst?' I asked.

'They're already doing so,' he responded emphatically.

'There are tensions, though, you must admit.'

'Some, but we will overcome these in time,' Daniel replied.

'And if the British leave?' I asked.

Daniel turned to face me and allowed a slight smile to pass across his face. 'I pray for that day so we can create an independent Jewish State.'

'But might that not be a recipe for bloodshed with the Arabs?' I couldn't help asking.

'Possibly, I don't have any illusions about the struggles that might lie ahead. I simply know that this is our God given homeland and that we must fight for it if we have to.'

I found myself admiring the man's spirit but I was in a tendentious frame of mind. 'Even to the exclusion of native Arabs whose race has lived here for more than a thousand years?'

This question clearly irritated Daniel. 'Look, we don't want to deprive them of anything. We are cultivating the desert, creating new villages and towns, and with God's grace can come to live side by side with the Arabs in peace and harmony.'

'That may take a long time to achieve, though, don't you think?' I said.

'Perhaps, who can say, but even if it takes another two thousand years it will have been worth the struggle,' Daniel said. 'What can be worse than being dispossessed of one's homeland

and despised by the likes of Herr Hitler and all the other Jew-haters?'

'I admire your determination,' I said, 'but you would hardly expect me to agree with your remarks about the German Chancellor.'

'Of course not.'

'Surely all this questioning can wait for another time,' Clara insisted, tugging at my arm as she spoke. 'I thought we came out to have a good time and watch the parade, not debate the future of Palestine.'

'I'm sorry, my love, you're right, of course.'

'Anyway, I must be moving on,' Daniel insisted. 'But it's been good to see you again, Max.' He then reached into the inside pocket of his jacket and brought out his wallet. 'Here's my card. Do telephone me. Erica and I would love to have you both over for a meal before you leave. Your friends would be welcome as well, of course.'

'That's kind of you; I'll be in touch soon.'

With more embraces and short farewells Daniel disappeared into the crowd as quickly as he had emerged from it.'

'An interesting man,' I remarked to Max. 'What does he do by the way?'

'He's a chemical engineer,' Aliza answered on Max's behalf.

'Really,' I said.

'Yet again, I found myself bewitched by her figure and attractive laugh. Then, out of the corner of my eye I thought I saw Clara scowling at me. I checked myself and decided to concentrate on the carnival as well as the pleasant evening air, for all that this was far easier said than done.

8

The sun hadn't long risen, when I went out for an early morning stroll. We had reached Jerusalem late the previous afternoon and as in Tel Aviv I was anxious to capture the atmosphere of the city while it was still peaceful. I hadn't, however, gone more than a few metres from the King David Hotel, which we had booked into, when I heard a familiar voice call out to me.

'Otto.'

I turned and saw Aliza coming towards me, looking simply wondrously pretty, and smiling.

'May I join you?' she asked me.

'Why, of course.'

'I've been so excited, I just couldn't sleep,' she explained. 'Arriving here is the fulfilment of a dream. It's such a special place.'

'Yes, indeed it is.'

'You don't sound very enthusiastic,' she said admonishingly.

'Oh no, I am, I assure you. It's just…well, I have no faith. The war did for that.'

'I have none either. We are not practising Jews, after all, as you must have realised.'

'So what excites you so much about this place?'

We were walking in the direction of the old city and even as I asked this question we both caught a glimpse of the golden dome of the Al-aqsa mosque glinting in the early morning sun. Aliza pointed towards it.

'That wonderful building for a start, but more than that, just the whole history of the place and what it represents to my people as well as Christians and Muslims.'

'And yet it has been a backwater since the end of the crusades.'

'Not in the minds of Jews and Christians. That still makes it one of the most important cities on earth.'

'Historically, I agree.'

We grinned at each other, and I sensed that we felt equally at ease in each other's company. I thought of Clara, though, probably still asleep in bed, and remembered my promise to her not to flirt with Aliza. It was, however, much harder said than done, when I found the woman walking next to me sublimely beautiful and intelligent; for all that she had no time for either my Party or our leader. I glanced at her. Her response seemed to be an echo of my own thoughts.

'I left Max in bed. You weren't intending to go too far, were you?'

'No, no, just a little way into the old city and then back again. No more than fifteen minutes.'

I couldn't help thinking how unimaginably fortunate her husband was in that he shared the bed of this utterly magical woman. Aliza looked at me pensively. 'It's at this time of day that I most miss our daughter. I seem to hear her calling out for me. I don't regret coming here for a moment but the thought of her still makes me feel guilty.'

'She's being well looked after by her grandparents, I'm sure.'

'Oh yes, I've no doubt of that, but even so it's the first time I've been without her for more than a day since she was born.

With every hour that passes I miss her more and more.'

'Well, you'll be going home quite soon.'

'Yes, that's true.'

We walked on in silence, getting closer to the old city wall. There was still hardly anyone about, but soon we saw a small flock of sheep coming towards us. They were being guided by a shepherd; an old man wearing a turban.

'This is still a very poor country,' Aliza remarked. 'Our hotel is very modern, of course, but a scene like this hasn't changed since biblical times.'

'Some things never change.'

Again our eyes met and I was acutely conscious of a deep sense of mutual attraction. Suddenly, I even felt an overwhelming desire to kiss her, but, thinking of Clara, looked the other way instead.

'Perhaps we should go back,' I suggested, though hesitantly. 'If Clara knew we were out walking together alone she would be furious with me. I've promised her faithfully that I wouldn't flirt with you,' I said, as a kind of confession.

She smiled enigmatically at me. 'But you're not; I asked if I could join *you*, after all.'

'I don't think she would see that as any excuse.'

'Well, let's just go a little bit further, please. We practically have the city to ourselves, after all, and it's too good an opportunity to miss.'

I allowed myself to be persuaded. I wanted to appreciate the atmosphere of the old city while it was still so quiet and I decided to enjoy the pleasure of Aliza's company while I still could. In that moment I felt certain, too, that this short period of time that we had spent together would remain with me, as a gloriously happy memory, for the rest of my life.

We were soon strolling through the narrow streets of the old city; the history of the place bearing down on both of us.

'You know, I'm reading a book about the crusades,' I explained. 'Jerusalem was captured at the climax of the first crusade in the year ten ninety-nine and remained under the control of the crusaders for nearly ninety years. That's four generations. Do you think it might take the Zionist movement that long to put down really deep roots here?'

'I've no idea how long it will take, but as you must be aware many Jews believe that Israel was given to our race by God and has therefore never ceased to be our true homeland.'

'And do you believe that?'

'I just know that the Jewish race has been in the wilderness for too long and needs a home somewhere. Here will do as well as anywhere just so long as we can achieve our purpose by peaceful means.'

We walked a little further in pensive silence before Aliza blurted out a question to me that had clearly been on her mind for some while.

'I still don't really understand what made you become an active member of the Nazi party? I mean, I know I've accused you of being a hypocrite, and I honestly believe that your Party is evil but....'

'...I am not such a bad fellow after all.'

'No, no you're not,' she conceded wistfully. 'But don't you see what a tyranny Hitler will create?'

'No, I don't. I'm no democrat, don't forget. And, to answer your question, I genuinely believe that it's only my Party that can deliver the strong government our country needs to restore prosperity and a true sense of national pride. That's why I joined it, that and my disgust at our humiliation in the last war, as well as my belief that my party represents the country's future, of which I want to be part. You see I'll admit I am not without ambition and want to make a difference for the better, if I can.'

'Yes, I can understand that a little. But as a matter of principle…'

'But haven't I made it clear, I am a Party member as a matter of principle.'

My answer made her sigh with obvious regret, while I glanced at my watch. 'I really think we should go back now,' I said gently. 'This walk has given me an appetite.'

She reluctantly agreed. 'Very well, I suppose so.'

'Don't worry, we can come back later with the others.' Except that I sensed it would not be the same.

As we walked back towards the King David Hotel, I couldn't help thinking how much its impressive edifice and very modernity represented a stark contrast to the old city we had just left behind.

'You must tell me what your friend did to save your life during the war?' Aliza suddenly asked.

I was slightly taken aback, wondering what had prompted such a question.

'It's been on my mind to ask you again ever since you first mentioned it,' she explained as if reading my thoughts

'I thought I said I didn't want to talk about it…'

'Well, if you'd rather not? I'm just curious, that's all.'

I smiled at her. I had never really discussed what had happened with anyone before, not even Clara except in the most cursory terms. It had really been too painful. Also, we would be back at the hotel in no time. Even so, and despite the old fear that it would stir too many bad memories, she had again succeeded in breaking down my defences and I felt a sudden compulsion to speak about it.

'The story is quickly enough told. During the spring offensive in the last year of the war we were in No Man's Land under machine gun fire. There were many casualties, as you can imagine. I gave the order that we should fall back. Then I was hit in the leg; the pain was.... excruciating. I thought, is this the end, am I going to die?'

I paused, feeling again the agony of the experience.

'You don't have to say anything more, Otto,' Aliza said. 'I apologise for raising it again, I really do.

'No, no, it's quite all right. You see even though I had gone down I was still under fire. I could have been hit again at any moment, Gunther was my Company Unteroffizier. We had fought alongside each other for the best part of a year and had become good friends. He didn't hesitate to come to my aid; carried me in fact. He was a big man, strong as an ox, but when we were almost back to our trench he was hit in the head by a bullet. He was killed outright, while I was able to crawl the last few metres to safety.'

'You would have done exactly the same for him?'

'Would I?'

'Yes, of course.'

'I'm glad you have such confidence in me, Aliza.' Then I laughed ruefully. 'I could never have carried him, though. He was much too heavy.'

She grinned and our eyes met in what was, I now saw beyond

doubt, a conspiratorial fashion. We were now at the front steps of the hotel.

As we entered the reception area I was confronted by the sight of Clara coming out of the lift. She glared at me.

'Good morning, my...'

She instantly cut me short. 'Where have you been?' She spoke in an accusing tone of voice, her eyes fixed upon Aliza. I determined to remain relaxed.

'For one of my usual early morning walks. Aliza asked if she could join me. We've been into the old...'

Again Clara cut me short. 'Oh, did she indeed.' Her tone was scornful.

'It was pure coincidence...,' Aliza tried to assure her, but Clara affected not to listen. She had already turned on her heel, walking in the direction of the dining room.

I just shook my head, glancing at Aliza with an apologetic expression on my face, and then followed Clara, fearing that this time I'd find it far harder to assuage her anger. Nonetheless, I decided that I really didn't care that much and I was simply astonished by how relaxed I'd felt in Aliza's company. She had the power, through her very direct nature and sexual allure, to bring me out of myself so that I could talk to her about even the most painful of subjects with barely any flashbacks of remorse.

9

'You *promised me* you wouldn't flirt with that woman again!' Clara shouted at me, her face flushed. We had returned to our room after breakfast and were preparing to go out. The meal had been a rather strained affair with Clara saying hardly a word, but her face speaking volumes as she scowled across the table at me.

'And I've kept my word,' I protested lamely.

'How can you have the nerve to say that? How I kept my temper over breakfast, I will never know.'

'Please keep your voice down, my love.'

'No, I will not! Either she and her husband go home now, or I will!'

'Please be reasonable, my love. They're due to leave anyway in a few days. And I swear to you that I'm *not* flirting with her. When she told you it was a coincidence that we were together, she was only speaking the truth.'

Clara glared at me and continued to walk up and down in an animated fashion. I tried to take her in my arms but she pushed me away.

'Don't touch me!'

'Please,' I appealed to her plaintively. 'Do you seriously expect me to tell them to leave?'

'Oh, I suppose not, but if I catch you together alone again, I'll leave and return to Germany. I mean it!'

'It won't happen again, I swear it. Now come on, they'll be waiting for us, I expect. The old city is really fascinating. You'll love it, I know you will.'

The remainder of the day was taken up with sightseeing and passed without any apparent incident. Clara, however, was sullen and uncommunicative, and frequently strode off on her own, leaving me to scurry after her with Max and Aliza following on behind. Eventually I felt obliged to apologise to them for her ill humour.

'I'm sorry; Clara is not in the best of moods today.' As I said this, I looked sheepishly at Aliza who creased up her eyes in sympathy.

'I expect it's the heat,' Max remarked, obliviously. 'It's getting too much for me as well.'

Regardless of Clara's opinion of him, I appreciated his ability to look for the best in everything, and tried to enjoy our sightseeing, although Clara's sulkiness and Aliza's beauty were constant distractions to me. In the end I was relieved to return to the hotel for dinner.

'I've got a terrible headache,' Clara declared irritably when I reached the privacy of our own room. 'And I'm not hungry either. In fact I'm going to bed.'

'Are you sure, my love?'

'Quite sure; you can continue to flirt with that woman as much as you please in my absence.'

'That remark is unworthy of you. I'm really not flirting with her.'

'Deny it as you wish, I'm going to bed. You can make my excuses for me.'

'Oh, very well.'

Since before our marriage, our courtship having lasted about a year, I'd realised that Clara could be bad-tempered. However, I'd never previously had cause to appreciate how jealous she could be as well. I felt irritated and was slow to change for dinner while she quickly undressed and curled up in bed with her back to me.

'I'm going for dinner, then,' I told her but she barely grunted in acknowledgement.

As I made my way to the dining-room I made a point of trying to relax and determined to appear my usual urbane self. I noticed that Aliza and Max had already sat down at one of the tables. Aliza smiled warmly at me as I approached them, its effect was to immediately brighten my mood.

In Clara's absence, the tension that would otherwise, I suspect, have been all pervading, was removed. I increasingly enjoyed myself, chatted amicably about the day's sightseeing, drank too much wine, and, when the resident pianist began to play, couldn't resist inviting Aliza onto the dance floor. As we waltzed I was struck by the thought that we would probably never get another opportunity as she and Max would soon be going home.

'You're leaving the day after tomorrow, aren't you?'
'Yes.'

We looked into each others' eyes. 'I'll miss your delightful company, Aliza.'

'It's for the best, I think. I'm really beginning to miss Bathsheba. She's too young to be without me for longer than is absolutely necessary.'

Suddenly, I lost my way a little and stumbled slightly.

'Are you all right?' she asked me.

'Yes, I'm sorry, I just wish Clara wasn't so... so possessive.'
'She's your wife, she's entitled to be.'
'But it's not only that,' I said. 'I'm afraid, well... she doesn't like Jewish people very much.'
'I know she doesn't,' Aliza assured me. 'And we both know that there are many others in Germany who feel like her. That's why the Zionist cause is so important and needs to succeed.'

The dance drew to a close and we returned to our seats. Following her news, I found it hard not to feel dejected and gulped back the last of my wine. Then I felt an urge to smoke and offered Aliza a cigarette. She had smoked with me in the past but this time she declined. I knew already that Max was a non-smoker. I decided not to smoke after all.'

'I'm feeling tired,' she told me. 'I think I'll go to bed now, but thank you anyway.'

I looked at Max and smiled. 'Aliza tells me she's homesick and misses Bathsheba.'

'I miss her too.'

'I'm sure you do, but I wanted to assure you what a great help you've been to me.'

'I've been only too pleased to be of service.'

I couldn't help wondering, though, how much he really meant that, given my amorous behaviour towards Aliza and the growing tension between her and Clara. Surely he must have noticed some of that? In the circumstances he had appeared to remain remarkably relaxed and that was surely to his credit.

Aliza rose to her feet. 'Well, goodnight, then.'

I stood up too and bowed to them both. 'Goodnight to you.'

Aliza smiled at me in what definitely seemed to me a fond way, and as she and Max made their way out of the room I sat back in my chair, watching them depart. I had to admit to myself that Clara had reason to be jealous.

******

Less than two days later the four of us were together in the lobby of the hotel. Aliza and Max had packed their suitcases and were awaiting their taxi. Their ship was sailing from Haifa to Trieste that very evening, so they were in good time to catch it before its departure. Meanwhile, Clara seemed in the best humour I had seen her in since our arrival in Palestine.

'I hope you enjoy the remainder of your stay here,' Max said, addressing both myself and Clara.

'I'm sure we will,' I assured him.

'And would you say your impression of what the Zionist cause has been able to achieve here has been a favourable one so far?' Max asked.

'Very much so. I will be writing an article to that effect when we return to Germany, I can promise you. There is Arab resentment to take into account, of course, but I will not make too much of that.'

'Thank you, I would appreciate that very much. As my friend Daniel said when we were in Tel Aviv, this is our God given homeland. We have nowhere else.'

'Quite so.'

'I hope we've remembered to pack everything?' Aliza asked anxiously.

'Don't worry,' Max told her. 'I checked our room very carefully. I'm sure we haven't forgotten anything.'

That Aliza was something of a worrier was a trait in her personality that I had noticed before. On this occasion she was clearly on edge and the expression of concern on her face was spoiling her natural beauty. I wondered if I would ever see her again.

'And you're sure you have our passports?' Aliza asked her husband.

Max gave her an indulgent look. 'Yes, they're here in my pocket, completely safe.'

She looked around and smiled directly at me. 'Well, Otto…. we have enjoyed our time with you very much. Perhaps we'll see you and Clara again when you return to Germany?'

'I do hope so. The last few weeks in your charming company have been a pleasure.'

I couldn't resist taking her right hand and planting a kiss on it. I sensed all the while that Clara was starting to seethe again. However, for those brief moments I decided to ignore her. It was as if Aliza and I were quite alone.

I shook hands with Max. Without saying a word, Clara did the same, before also shaking hands limply with Aliza.

'A safe journey to you both,' I said to them.

'Thank you so much, Otto,' Max replied.

'Think nothing of it. Goodbye.'

After they had left Clara found her voice. 'I hope you don't have have any serious intentions of seeing that woman again?'

'Of course not, my love, I was merely being polite.'

'Huh! You looked to me as if what you really wanted to do was take her in your arms and kiss her on the lips.'

'Nonsense! Anyway, they've gone now and we can enjoy ourselves.'

'I certainly hope so.'

I couldn't help thinking, though, that I would never forget

the time I had spent in Aliza's alluring company. For all too brief a period of time we had been like soulmates brought together by a strange combination of circumstances. Although, from a purely rational perspective, I don't believe in such a phenomenon as fate, my emotions told me that beyond doubt it existed.

******

In the course of the next few weeks Clara and I continued to explore Palestine. At first Clara remained sulky but I went out of my way to be unfailingly attentive, which gradually broke down her hostility towards me. Memories of Aliza, too, became less intense so that by the time Clara and I reached the city of Safad, north of Lake Tiberias, I had good reason to believe that the normal harmony of our marriage had been restored.

We were having breakfast together in the dining room of our hotel. It was far from being the most comfortable that we'd stayed in, but Clara nevertheless appeared more relaxed than at any time since we had arrived in the country. The previous night we had made love, leaving me to think that it was this that had put her in such a good humour. I was particularly pleased to have been able to resume our usual sexual life after a painful period of rejection. Also, I couldn't help remembering my conversation with Max, all those months before in Berlin. Certainly, I'd done nothing to guard against pregnancy and had no reason to believe that Clara had either.

Before breakfast, I had picked up an English language newspaper from the lobby of the hotel without bothering to give its contents even a cursory glance, but now decided to do so.

'Bad news,' I exclaimed.

'What is it, darling?' It was only the previous night that she had begun to use that term of endearment once more.

'The Arabs are in revolt against British rule. There's been trouble in Haifa. Apparently, the Arabs aren't happy about the new harbour facilities that we saw under construction when we arrived. As I told you, they're due to be opened shortly.'

'You wanted to be there for the opening ceremony, didn't you?'

'Yes, and I still do.'

'Will it be safe, though?'

'I don't see why not. Anyway, our ship leaves from there the day after the opening, so we'll have to risk it.'

'I'll go and pack then.'

As Clara made her way upstairs to our room, I watched her go and couldn't help thinking how attractive she looked. Then I walked to the hotel desk to pay. There was a short, rather fat, middle-aged Palestinian man standing behind it. I had spoken to him before in English.

'You are leaving us today, sir?' he asked me.

'Yes, we're making our way to Haifa.'

'I would not advise that, sir. There's been rioting in Haifa. The road there isn't safe, either.'

'What, even in daylight?'

'There was a robbery only last week. At gunpoint, so I have heard. They were an English couple. Now with this latest trouble…'

I cut him short. 'We'll be fine. I'll make sure I fly a National Socialist pennant from our car.'

He shrugged his shoulders and I proceeded to pay the hotel bill. I also decided to make light of the man's warning.

'Why the flag?' Clara asked me casually, as we prepared to depart.

'It makes it clear that we aren't English. If there is any trouble on the way, it should help to protect us.'

'Are you sure it's a good idea to be travelling at all?'

'Yes, of course. As I said, we have a ship to catch. We've been away long enough and need to get home.'

At first our journey was uneventful. I began to feel increasingly relaxed and even a little wistful.

'I've really enjoyed our time here. In some ways I will be sorry to leave,' I confessed to Clara. 'I hope it's given you pleasure as well, my love?'

'Only since Aliza left us. You really were drooling over her most of the time she was with us. God, how it made me cross.'

'Really, my love, you exaggerate.'

'No, I don't. You couldn't see your face whenever she walked into the room.'

'Well, that's behind us now.'

'I hope it is.'

'Of course, I swear it.'

'Look out!'

Instantly, I realised that several Arabs had suddenly run into the middle of the road, not all that far ahead of us. They were frantically waving their hands in the air, clearly intent on getting me to pull up, and then I noticed one of them was holding a rifle. The road we were on was a poor one and I'd been maintaining no more than a steady fifty kilometres an hour. Now I made a split second decision to put my foot on the accelerator.

'I think they intend us harm; one of them has a gun. Keep your head down!'

Clara screamed at me 'No!' but it was too late. I was now within only a few metres of the Arabs, leaving them with no choice but to scatter in all directions, or face being run down.

My one fear, as I drove past them, was that the gun that one of them was carrying was loaded, and a shot would still be aimed at us before we were out of range.

'For Christ's sake, don't raise your head,' I shouted at Clara, fearing that she might be about to do so too soon. 'He could still aim a shot at us!'

I was going so fast along the bumpy road that it was becoming a struggle to maintain control of the wheel but I didn't dare slow down. At any moment I expected to hear a gun being fired and all of my worst experiences in the war seemed to flash before my eyes.

I glanced in my rear mirror, and with an enormous sense of relief, noticed the Arabs were now barely in sight. We were approaching a bend in the road as well and I knew that once I had negotiated it we would be safe. I was already driving into the bend, however, and, fighting to control the wheel, managed to negotiate it successfully without ever feeling the sickening pain of being shot.

'We're safe now!' I cried out to Clara.

'We could have been killed!' she screamed back at me.

'If I had pulled up they would have robbed us and then perhaps shot us, too.'

Now I had the wheel of the car under control and felt able to slow down. I realised, though, that I was shaking and I breathed slowly through my mouth. Clara was clinging to me and sobbed in my ear, as much, I suspect, out of shock as fear. I briefly took my right hand off the wheel to give her a reassuring hug and, fortunately, the remainder of our journey to Haifa was uneventful.

The official ceremony to open the new dock facilities was a subdued affair as a consequence of the uprising. Armed police and soldiers were in evidence on many streets and a strict curfew in place, forcing us to spend more time in our drab hotel than I would have wished. It was a disappointing end to our long sojourn in Palestine.

Clara, too, was frustrated as well as increasingly critical of the whole Zionist enterprise.

'With this level of hostility towards the British mandate,' she remarked, 'can you imagine what it will be like if the Jews were ever permitted to establish their own State here. I tell you, the streets would run with blood.'

I resisted being drawn into any argument with her. Nonetheless, on our last full day in the country, I made a point of engaging the Arab owner of the hotel, who spoke broken English, in conversation.

'Do you think the uprising will be easily brought under control?' I asked the man casually.

'I expect so.'

'And what has caused it, do you think; this… this resentment of British rule?'

The man gave me a fixed, but not unfriendly, stare before responding. 'It's because we don't like the Jews. The British have allowed too many into our country and they keep coming.'

'They could still help make Palestine a more prosperous place, couldn't they?'

The man pulled a face. 'Perhaps, but if they think we will

just lie on our backs, should they want to take over, then they're mistaken.'

The following morning we boarded our ship to return home, and as I stood on the deck watching the coastline of Palestine recede into the distance, the man's words kept coming back to me. It made me fearful that the Zionist enterprise, for all its enthusiasm, was doomed to end in bloodshed. I wondered, too, if I would ever see Palestine again.

At the same time Aliza's image kept returning to the forefront of my mind and I couldn't help but ponder how likely I was to see much, if anything, of her in the future.

10

Mid April 1934

'I'm home, my love.'

I was in an excellent mood. It had been a particularly successful day and I was eager to share my news with Clara.

'I'm in here,' she replied, her voice coming from the lounge.

I strode into the room where I found her relaxing on a settee. I was intent on planting a kiss on her lips, but as I approached her she only scowled at me.

'I'm feeling ill,' she moaned.

'Have you been sick again?' I asked her gently.

'Yes, a little; I'm beginning to wish I had never become pregnant.'

I felt a flash of anger at such a suggestion. 'Please don't say that.'

Tactfully, she sought to change the subject. 'You seemed happy when you came in?'

My face brightened again. 'Yes, indeed, what I have written about our visit to Palestine is to be published shortly in *Der Angriff*.'

'That was only what you were expecting, surely?'

It was not the response I wished for.

'Yes… but, they could have turned me down, and I have even better news as well.'

'Oh, really.'

'I have arranged a meeting at SS headquarters next week. It's the opportunity I've been seeking to gain approval for my proposal that the solution to the Jewish question lies in encouraging mass emigration to Palestine.'

Clara merely yawned. She was clearly bored by the whole topic. 'Well, you know my views on that.'

'Yes, I do.'

I looked towards the drinks' cabinet in the corner of the room. Whatever Clara might think I still believed it had been a successful day and I was determined to celebrate.

'I'm going to have a drink. Would you like one?'

'Yes, why not. I'll have a martini, please.'

I proceeded to pour us both drinks, deciding that I would have my usual scotch and water.

'I must tell Max the good news,' I remarked casually as I handed Clara her glass.

Clara gave me a piercing sidelong glance. 'You won't be seeing his wife as well, will you?'

'No, of course not. I'll telephone him, that's all. I haven't seen Aliza since the day she and Max left Palestine.'

'I should hope not. Make any attempt to have an affair with that woman and I'll divorce you like a shot.'

I felt exasperated. 'You really never had any cause to be so jealous, you know.'

'Oh, didn't I?'

'No, you did not. You insult me in fact to suggest that I would have an affair with any other woman when you're the woman I love. Haven't I proved that to you often enough?'

She looked affronted. 'There's no need to be so angry with

me.' Then she smiled coyly. 'Kiss me.'

I put down my glass and came and sat next to her. I was happy to do as she asked and took her in my arms, even as I did so smelling the rich perfume that she was wearing. Our lips met…

'Excuse me Sir, Madam…'

Both of us jumped apart. It was Hilda, our rather stout, elderly cook. She was standing nervously by the door.

'Shall I serve supper…?'

'Yes, of course, Hilda. Thank you.'

Hilda had already scurried back to the kitchen, and with a grin, I took Clara in my arms again and drew her lips towards mine.

After supper I went into the study in order to telephone Max while Clara returned to the lounge to rest. She had eaten little and still complained of feeling unwell.

Since our return from Palestine I suppose I had spoken to Max a couple of times on the telephone. We had also met once for lunch when I had related our experiences in Palestine after he and Aliza had returned to Germany.

I telephoned at about half past eight that evening.

'Hello?'

I instantly recognised Aliza's attractive voice. Previously, it had been Max who had answered when I had rung.

'It's Otto von Buren here. I hope you're well?'

'Why, yes, it's good to hear from you. Max has told me that you enjoyed yourselves after we left.'

'Yes, we did. There was one incident just before we were due to return, but nothing too serious. Is Max at home?'

'No, I'm afraid he's out for the evening. I will ask him to

telephone you back. He has your number, I take it?'

'Yes, tell him to ring me tomorrow evening if that's convenient for him. I have some good news.'

'Oh, what's that?' Her tone of voice was friendly but her willingness to talk made me feel slightly nervous as Clara was within earshot. It even made me wish I had shut the door before picking up the telephone.

'What I have written about our excursion to Palestine is to be published in *Der Angriff*,' I replied quietly.

'Oh good, I'm pleased.'

'Well, good to talk to you. Goodbye, Aliza.'

'Goodbye, Otto.'

The instant I put the telephone down, I sensed that it had been a mistake to address Aliza by her name. Nervously, I made my way into the lounge where Clara was once again lying back on the settee. She immediately turned her head towards me and glared.

'You've been speaking to her, haven't you?'

'She answered the telephone, that's all,' I replied with a note of irritation in my voice. 'Max is out so I left a message for him to telephone me.'

'I wish you would drop this obsession with Zionism once and for all!' she snapped.

'No, Clara, I will not! And anyway it's not an obsession. All I'm doing is promoting an idea that's beginning to find favour in the highest echelons of the party.'

'Oh, I'm too tired and feeling too ill to talk about this any longer. I'm going to bed.' With that, she stood up and walked straight past me with a scowl still on her face.

'Goodnight, my love. I'll come to bed soon.'

'Do as you wish.'

I sighed and, going to the drinks' cabinet, poured myself another Scotch. I was prepared to make allowances for Clara's pregnant state, but at times like this, I couldn't help finding her moodiness and bad temper hard to tolerate. I allowed myself to daydream about what life would be like with Aliza.

A sexual life with her might be good, perhaps even very good, but then again she had already demonstrated what a strong willed and opinionated person she was, so the reality, I rather suspected, was that she was capable of being every bit as difficult as Clara. It was one thing, I realised, to be attracted to spirited women, quite another to live with them for any length of time.

All the same, I still fantasised about Aliza. I have inherited something of my mother's love of poetry and over the years have composed my share of poems including ones on the theme of love. When I felt driven to compose one entitled *Beyond Compare* I certainly only had Aliza in mind. It was then put away amongst my other poems in a draw, where even if Clara was ever to come across it she could never know with certainty who it was really dedicated to.

The loveliest woman I ever saw,
Was to me, beautiful beyond compare;
With flesh fine as any marble,
And endowed with the lushest of flowing hair;
A gentle voice,
Like a sweet musical air;
A chuckle of a laugh,
To bring to the darkest mood a complete repair;

Eyes like the finest jewels,
So deep in colour as to be especially rare;
Lips that were crimson,
With a smile to bring me to heaven's stair;
And a spirit powerful enough to convince me,
Such a place is really there.

From time to time over the years since it was written, especially when feeling out of sorts, I've derived pleasure from reading the poem, its words always conjuring up in my mind how beautiful Aliza was the first day I set eyes on her.

11

About three weeks later, I was sitting in a large, well-lit room in SS Headquarters, Berlin. It was sparsely furnished with just a long, simply carved wooden table and eight matching chairs, four of which were unoccupied. There was a miserable coal fire in the grate and the walls were bare apart from a picture over the mantelpiece of Adolf Hitler in an intentionally dominating pose. Everyone present was wearing their black SS uniforms with the exception of me, and the man who sat at the head of the table.

Reich Minister of Public Enlightenment, Joseph Goebbels, was dressed in a smart grey suit and was smiling thinly at me. In front of him was a draft of the first of the articles to be published in *Der Angriff*.

'I do not recognise the Jews you describe here, Otto. Did you really find them so industrious?'

'Mainly, yes I did. It was a surprise, I assure you.' At these words, there were grins around the table. 'It's not the behaviour we expect of Jews in this country, of course, but in Palestine they are like men….and women reborn.' In saying this I felt hypocritical and disloyal to Aliza and even to myself, but this nest of SS vipers was hardly the place to make a stand against Nazi ideology concerning Jewry.

I glanced across the table at the blond haired Brigadefuhrer, Reinhardt Heydrich, who was eyeing me closely. He was attending the meeting on behalf of the head of the SS, Reichsfuhrer Heinrich Himmler. We had never met before but I could sense that he was a cold, calculating individual.

'So tell us what exactly you're proposing, Baron?' Goebbels asked me intently.

'Well, Reich Minister, that the party gives its official support to the Zionist movement and accords it special status.'

My words were met with an instant guffaw from the fourth person present at the table, SS Chief of Staff Max Wolff. 'What, support a load of Jews? The Fuhrer will think it a ridiculous idea!'

Goebbels looked at him in annoyance. 'I think I'm in a better position to be a judge of that than you are, Max.' Wolff gave a shrug of the shoulders and looked down at the table.

Feeling duly encouraged I went on, 'Gentlemen, I believe that with the right measure of support the Zionist movement can succeed in Palestine and, in so doing, establish a homeland for the Jewish people.'

'Ah, but just how many Jews would that rid us of, do you think?' Goebbels asked me, his eyes seeming to bore into me.

'That's difficult to answer with any certainty, Minister, but the population of the country is small at present…'

'Can you be more exact?'

'Why, yes, Minister. The most up-to-date figures available put it at around one million one hundred thousand. But, with due expansion of cities like Jerusalem and Haifa combined with careful irrigation and cultivation of the land, I see no reason why in time it couldn't support another million at least.'

'Are we talking centuries here?' Heydrich asked. His tone of voice was sarcastic, but I was more struck by how high pitched, almost feminine, it sounded.

'No, not at all,' I responded calmly. 'A generation, no more.'

Goebbels' eyes lit up. 'So the entire Jewish population of Germany could be settled there!'

'In theory, Minister, yes, it could quite easily. Of course, one has to take account of Jewish emigration to Palestine from elsewhere in Europe.'

'And we all know that the Jewish population of Europe is nine million at least,' Heydrich was quick to add. Once again his tone was sarcastic and I began to feel slightly irritated.

'But there is no government anywhere, of which I am aware, that is actively encouraging emigration to Palestine,' I shot back.

'And what about the British?' Wolff asked. 'Aren't they supposed to have curtailed the numbers allowed into the country?'

'Yes,' I nodded, 'but those restrictions don't apply to the wealthier Jewish immigrants, and those controls they do have are easily circumvented. I was told quite specifically by a British officer that many enter the country as visitors and simply don't go home.'

'And nothing is done to deport them?' Wolff enquired.

'No, not so far as I'm aware. The British simply don't have the resources. Anyway, while the Balfour declaration holds good, I think they are quite happy to turn a blind eye. The restrictions are merely a sop to the Arabs.'

'Ah yes, the Arabs,' Goebbels mused. 'Will their understandable resentment of Jewish immigration prove the real stumbling block?'

I caught his eye and did not look away.

'It would be naïve of me to pretend that it might not present a serious difficulty in the longer term, Minister, but that would not be our problem. Let the Jews and Arabs fight it out between themselves…'

'With the British caught in the middle,' Heydrich added with a smirk.

'Quite probably,' put in Goebbels. All that matters from our perspective, though, is that the maximum number of Jews should emigrate from this country to Palestine.'

'Just string a few of them up and the rest will start leaving in droves,' Wolff suggested, in a calm, rather sinister tone of voice.

'It may yet come to that, Max, but I am prepared to follow more civilised methods to begin with,' Goebbels responded icily.

Despite the image of the noose before my own eyes I allowed myself a brief smile. I could sense that I was about to win the argument.

'Are you proposing that we give *money* to the Zionist movement?' Heydrich cut in. There was no mistaking the sneering tone in his voice.

Again, I felt irritated but did my best to suppress any outward show of annoyance. 'Not necessarily,' I responded, 'although I think there is a case to be put for financial support where appropriate. Don't forget as well that we are already allowing any Jew who emigrates to Palestine to retain some of their assets.'

'And isn't that generous enough?' Heydrich suggested.

'Perhaps,' I said, 'but for the present simply favouring Zionists over all other Jews is the main thrust of what I am proposing and that, by itself, need cost nothing.'

'I agree,' Goebbels added. 'Gentlemen, you will be aware

that policies are in hand that are intended to isolate the Jewish vermin within our midst, but I can see the merit, at least at this time, of being seen to be the friend of Jewish nationalism. After all it can be argued that it has a kinship with the ideals of our own movement. What is your view, Reinhardt?'

I tensed. I expected nothing but a torrent of scorn from the man sitting opposite him.

'I am sceptical, Minister,' Heydrich said, 'but indeed I suppose such a policy would do us no harm if it works and really costs us very little.'

Now I felt a rush of pleasure. I still suspected that Heydrich had no heart but at least he wasn't stupid as well. What Wolff thought didn't really now matter. Even so, Goebbels afforded him the courtesy of asking for his opinion as well.

'It sticks in my throat that we should actively encourage any Jewish movement. I wouldn't have anything to do with any of them,' Wolff said bluntly.

Goebbels, however, was unmoved. 'None of us around this table is a Jew-lover, but we must be practical. Otto has seen Zionism at work, and to afford support to an organisation dedicated to the creation of a Jewish homeland seems to me to be substantially in Germany's interests. I shall speak to the Fuhrer, and Reinhardt, will you speak to Heinrich?'

'Yes, of course, Minister.'

'So, it is agreed then,' Goebbels declared with a wave of the hand. 'In principle, we see no reason why the SS should not support the Zionist movement. Congratulations, Baron, on a job well done.'

'Thank you, Minister, you are most kind.'

'The detail of the policy will have to be worked on, of course, but that need not concern us today.'

Goebbels got to his feet, glancing at his watch as he did so. 'Now, if you will excuse me, gentlemen, I have another meeting to get to. *Heil Hitler!*'

'*Heil Hitler!*' came the chorus of responses from around the room, including, I regret to say, from me.

Goebbels walked rapidly out of the room, and Wolff, after merely a nod in the direction of myself and Heydrich, immediately followed him. Heydrich, meanwhile, lingered slightly and grinned superciliously at me.

'I too would like to offer my congratulations,' he declared. There was still a sarcastic edge to his voice, however.

'Thank you, but I thought you weren't at all enthusiastic about my proposal.'

'I am not. Like Max, I don't welcome the idea of offering succour to any Jewish organisation, but that doesn't mean I cannot see the potential value of the exercise. Well, I must be going, too. Good day, Baron.'

'And to you, Brigadefuhrer.'

For all Wolff's hostility and Heydrich's faint praise, I felt a surge of elation and left the room a happy man. With Goebbels' endorsement I was now more confident than ever that the Party would make support for the Zionist movement part of its official policy.

12

Late June 1935

'This is what I've been expecting!' I was sitting at the breakfast table with Clara. I had just opened the morning's post and read the contents of the letter signed personally by Reichsfuhrer Heinrich Himmler. There was a note of triumph in my voice and with a flourish I turned to Clara and handed the letter to her.

'See, I have been appointed to head the Jewish desk. Now, I can really achieve something!'

Clara glanced at the letter and looked unimpressed. 'That will mean you will be answerable to Heydrich. I thought you said you didn't like the man?'

'I don't, not really, he's too full of himself, but he's no fool, either. We will get on well enough, I'm sure. Aren't you pleased for me; it is promotion, after all?'

'Why, of course,' she said half-heartedly. I thought she looked tired and then she began to yawn. She had, after all, been up half the night with our baby son Leopold, who was now thankfully sleeping soundly.

'Would you like some more coffee?' I asked her solicitously.

She smiled at me limply. 'Yes, if you would, I need something to keep me awake.'

I proceeded to pour her a cup.

'You know I'm out tonight,' I reminded her. 'It's that meeting to which Max has invited me.'

She curled her lips down slightly. 'Must you spend so much time with your Jewish friends?'

'They are not friends, merely acquaintances. Anyway, if I am to do my job properly, attending such events is unavoidable.'

'I suppose so,' she conceded grudgingly. 'But if you attend every meeting and function you're invited to, what time will you have left for me and Leo?'

'I will not accept every invitation, I assure you, and anyway you could accompany me to some of them.'

'Not while Leo is still a baby and not if it means I have to make small talk to Jews. I had quite enough of that in Palestine. And you'll work longer hours in the office as well, I expect.'

'I'll try not to.'

'But you will, I know you, Otto.'

I smiled at her sheepishly.

'Will that woman be there tonight?' She asked the question abruptly with that toss of the head I had come to know so well.

'What woman?' I asked her in turn, disingenuously.

She tutted at me. 'Frau Geisser, of course.'

'I've no idea.'

'Well, if she is, do try not to flirt with her.'

I felt irritated. Was I never to be allowed to forget that I was fond of Aliza? I decided to ignore Clara's remark completely and, glancing at my watch, rose immediately to my feet.

'My word, is that the time, I must be going.'

'I suppose you'll you be travelling straight from the office to this meeting of yours?' Clara asked me.

'Yes, I'm afraid so, but I should still be home by ten at the latest.'

The remainder of my day passed quickly. I enjoyed a pleasant, and extended, lunch at one of my favourite restaurants with some Reiter SS colleagues, who were full of congratulations when I informed them of my appointment. I also drank a little more wine than I would usually have permitted myself.

Several times, too, I reflected on our travels around Palestine and my mind kept bringing me back to an alluring, if by now frustratingly cloudy image of Aliza. Would she in fact be there this evening, I wondered? It was a tantalising question but one which I nevertheless did my best to suppress as I was uncertain whether I really wanted to see her again anyway.

Max had invited me to address the meeting, which was being held in a hall, and as the afternoon wore on I tried to concentrate on what I intended to say and to make a few notes. Later, as I made my way to the hall by car, I couldn't help my sense of anticipation mounting at the prospect of possibly seeing Aliza once more.

As soon as I entered the lobby of the building, Max came hurrying to greet me.

'Welcome, Otto, it's so good of you to join us.'

'Not at all, Max, it is a pleasure to be here, I assure you. I have some good news for you as well. I have just been made head of the Bureau of Jewish affairs.'

Max looked delighted. 'Why, that's excellent news, indeed. Many congratulations.'

'Thank you. It's an opportunity to achieve something really positive.'

'And will you be informing the meeting of your appointment?'

'Why, certainly, it's all official, and I'm to take up the position at the end of the month.'

'Well, please come through. There aren't all that many people here, I'm afraid, but you'll recognise some that are from previous events, I'm sure. Aliza is here, too, by the way.'

'Oh, is she really?'

Max led the way into the hall itself. I was immediately struck by its poor lighting and quickly judged that no more than twenty people were already seated. Even from behind I thought I could recognise Aliza sitting in the front row, and as soon as we reached the high table from where I was to speak, and I turned round to look at the audience, I could see her smiling at me.

I naturally returned her smile and would have gone forward to greet her had Max not immediately introduced me to everyone present. Within a few moments I was on my feet beginning to make my speech. It was on much the same lines as ones I had made before to similar audiences except that this time I was able to proudly announce my appointment. I ended, as usual, with a warm endorsement of the Zionist movement as well as an assurance that it could look forward to the full support of the government, before sitting down to a little polite applause.

As I was speaking I was conscious of Aliza's eyes upon me. I felt that there was warmth behind them, which pleased me not a little, and added to my sense of confidence, not that I didn't believe myself to be an assured public speaker anyway. Max then thanked me for what I had had to say and called for questions. There was a pregnant pause. Aliza then raised a hand.

'Can the Baron please tell us whether he believes the government is likely to give financial support to the Zionist movement, and in particular to allow emigrants to Palestine to exchange their Reichsmarks at full value?'

She looked me straight in the eye as she asked this question and I thought I detected a mischievous glint. It made me feel slightly uncomfortable and I was conscious that she was testing my easy rhetoric.

'That is a very good question, I would like to be able to give such an assurance but I am afraid that I am unable to do so at the present time. However, it is a matter that will, I can assure you, receive my close attention as soon as I take up office.'

'We are all grateful for that I'm sure,' Aliza responded, 'but without sufficient financial support, would you not agree, everything else you have referred to in your speech this evening amounts to very little?'

It was as if we were together in Palestine again, and not being too surprised by the directness of her riposte, I stood my ground. 'No, I would most certainly not say that, although, of course, I accept that the cost of emigration is an important issue. We are, as you will all be aware, though, living through a period of considerable global financial difficulty and the government's first priority must be the German economy. Nevertheless, I am confident that with time it will be possible to provide a measure of financial support for the Zionist cause.'

'Ah, but how much time, Baron?'

'That, I really cannot say, I'm afraid. I can only repeat that it is an issue which I am prepared to address.'

'Thank you, Aliza,' Max added, sounding as if he had found her line of questioning unnecessarily hostile. 'Any more questions, anyone?'

A man put up his hand, but his question was inconsequential

and I answered it with ease. Finally, a middle-aged man stood up at the back.

'Why should we trust a word you tell us when the government you represent hates all Jews and is preparing to deprive of us of our rights of citizenship?'

The man's voice rose to a crescendo of anger as he completed the question and there were murmurs of support from around the hall. I was now beginning to feel rather uncomfortable.

'I am a man of my word and my appointment is an official one. The policy of the Party is to promote the Zionist cause and I assure you it has only respect for those of your race who wish to establish a Jewish homeland in Palestine.'

'You and your kind hate us,' the man shouted back.

'I assure you that is not the case. The destiny of your people simply lies in your own homeland; that we can surely all agree upon.'

'Shall we move on,' Max added hurriedly. 'I do not see anyone else wishing to ask questions so I will take the next speaker.'

I had to sit through two more speeches in all, together with the questions that followed them, an experience I found increasingly difficult. The tone of the meeting became ever more hostile towards the Nazi Party with much condemnation of the proposed new laws. Although I did my best to remain outwardly relaxed, I soon began to wish that I was elsewhere.

All the while, I sensed, too, that Aliza's eyes were on me. I allowed myself a glance at her occasionally and each time believed that she was actually smiling at me with her eyes. I felt as if she had been teasing me with her line of questioning, but had to admit to myself that she had been acute enough in appreciating that without financial support fine words would never be enough. I envisaged battles ahead to persuade the Party to back my ideas with hard cash, but tried to remain confident that I would be equal to the task.

'Well, thank you for coming, everyone,' I heard Max saying at last. 'There is coffee and cakes being served for anyone who would like them.'

I was pleased to stand up. Aliza, after promptly doing the same, immediately walked towards me.

'It's a pleasure to meet you again, Aliza.'

She held out her right hand and I put my lips to it.

'And you, Otto; you spoke well.'

'Did I really? I thought from the way you questioned me that you might have felt otherwise?'

'No, no, not at all, I am sceptical of the government's good faith but not of yours.'

'That is kind of you.'

'Otto, will you stay and have coffee with us?' Max asked me.

I hesitated. 'I really ought to be going, I'm afraid, I promised Clara…'

'How is she, by the way?' Max asked.

I looked Aliza in the eye, less pleasant and singularly unwelcome memories of Palestine suddenly intruding into my mind. 'She's well, thank you.'

'And your son?'

'Thriving, I am pleased to say.'

'Oh yes, many congratulations,' Aliza added. 'You're a proud father, I'm sure.'

It was at that moment I first noticed a change in Aliza's

appearance. She smiled gently at me and looked down at her tummy.

'Yes, I am pregnant again. Max is delighted. The baby is due in about three months. We both hope it will be a boy.'

Aliza's radiance suddenly seized me as if by the throat. I began to feel self-conscious and more anxious than ever to escape from the hall. Her beauty, I decided, was simply too alluring, too dangerous.

'Well, I really must be going,' I insisted, beginning, even as I uttered these words, to make my way towards the door.

'Goodbye Max, Aliza.'

'Goodbye, Otto,' she responded with another smile and a wave of the hand.

As I drove home, I couldn't get Aliza out of my mind. Her deliberately tendentious line of questioning could easily have made me angry, but instead it had merely stirred happy memories of our time together in Palestine. I remembered, too, how well we had danced together and, although I tried to forget her, her image refused to go away. She also remained on my mind long after Clara and I had gone to bed and I had switched out the light.

13

Mid April 1936

I was sitting at my office desk at SS headquarters in Berlin. Opposite me sat an ambitious young man whom I had appointed to the Bureau, Hauptscharfuhrer Adolf Eichmann. I had been impressed by his intelligence and attention to detail but now I was beginning to wonder if I had misjudged him.

'I have read this pamphlet of yours with interest,' I remarked. I was conscious that I was frowning and I was thumbing through the document even as I spoke. 'When I appointed you I believed that you were in favour of a pro-Zionist policy but after studying this I can see that I was wrong.'

'I regret to say, Baron,' Eichmann gave a slow nod, 'that after careful consideration I have come to the conclusion that a strong Jewish state in the Middle East would be against Germany's interests and also against the interests of native Palestinians. It's obvious, too, that the policy isn't working. According to the latest figures, emigration to Palestine is still falling rather than rising.'

'Yes, I have seen those figures,' I replied irritably. 'The numbers are not down by much, though.'

'No, but the trend has been consistently downwards for some months.'

'Yes, I suppose so. But you know my view as to that. Jews must be given a greater financial incentive to leave.'

'No! The Fuhrer would surely never countenance such an idea. Our first priority must be the welfare of the German people, not Jews.'

I felt tired. 'Look, you know that I am only trying to find a just and peaceful solution to this question.'

'Yes, I accept that, of course. Nonetheless, you should be careful, Baron.'

'Careful, why I should be careful?'

'If I may say so there is talk that you count too many Jews amongst your friends.'

'No I do not. They are acquaintances, no more than that. If I am to do my job properly I must maintain contact with leaders of the Zionist movement. I would have thought that much is obvious.'

'Speaking for myself, I agree, but others see it differently.'

'And who are these individuals? Can you name them?'

'Forgive me, but I would prefer not to.'

Now I was becoming angry. 'Do I have no support, even amongst my own staff?'

'I am not suggesting that, Baron.'

'Clearly I no longer have yours. But you are wrong. Allowing Jews who emigrate to exchange their marks at near parity would be fair and perfectly affordable. Palestine may be a small country and Jewish and Arab conflict inevitable, but with time and the cultivation of the desert a viable Jewish State could be created.'

'And that is precisely my concern, Baron. A strong Jewish state will simply bolster the Jewish financial conspiracy around the globe.'

'I simply do not accept that such a conspiracy exists.'

He looked at me aghast. 'Of course it does. It is the stranglehold that the Jews have on the world's finances for their own selfish ends that is to blame for the global economic depression.'

I shook my head wearily. 'Well, you are entitled to your opinion, but I must remind you that I am here because of the widespread acclaim that my article in *Der Angriff* received. I still believe that the highest echelons of the party agree that Zionism offers a real solution to the Jewish question.'

'Frankly, Baron, I doubt that.'

'Well, I still have a job to do in this Department and I intend to carry it out to the best of my ability. I continue to believe that encouraging as many Jews as possible to support the Zionist movement is in this country's best interests.'

'I am sorry, Baron, but in my view any emigration that furthers the prospects of an independent Jewish State would be against our national interests.'

Now I felt exasperated. 'So what would you do?'

'What is most important is that the Jewish stranglehold on our society is broken for ever. We are already beginning to achieve that…'

Suddenly the telephone on my desk began to ring and I picked it up. When I was told who was on the line I was shocked, a reaction that must have been all too obvious to Eichmann.

'Thank you,' I said to the operator. 'Just ask her to hold a moment, please?'

I then glanced at Eichmann. 'It's a personal call I must take. We will talk again, of course.' He merely nodded and quickly left the room.

'Put her through, will you.'

'Otto, is that you?'

'Yes, Aliza. This is an unexpected pleasure, but what on earth are you doing telephoning me when I am at work?'

'I thought it the lesser of two evils. I do not believe your wife would have been amused if I'd tried to contact you at your home. Can I see you, please?'

'Why?' I asked her bluntly.

'I need to ask a personal favour of you. I wondered if I might even be able to meet you for lunch today…, if you are not too busy?'

I felt intrigued and glanced at my diary, which was sitting open in front of me on my desk.

'Yes, I don't see why not. There's an excellent restaurant called Heising in the Wilhelmstrasse not far from here…Do you know it?'

'No, but I'm sure that I can find it easily enough. Could we meet at a quarter past one?'

'Yes, of course.'

'I will see you then.'

She rang off, leaving me to stare out of the window and wonder what it was she wanted to see me about so urgently. I felt tense, remembering what Eichmann had just said to me. Since September 1935, with the passage of the Nuremberg race laws, any kind of sexual relationship with a Jew had become illegal and especially for a man in my position, I knew that I was in dangerous territory.

My marriage to Clara, despite, or perhaps because of the arrival of a child, still had its stormy periods. However, our relationship was not an unhappy one, and I certainly wasn't about to risk anything for Aliza, however strong her sex appeal.

Anyway, I decided that she probably just wanted to talk to me about some issue or other relating to the Zionist movement and that, as such, our meeting for lunch would be a perfectly innocent affair.

Two hours later as she walked into the Heising restaurant I was already seated and waiting for her. She was wearing a small hat with a feather, perched on the back of her head, and a dark, tight fitting dress that showed off her figure. She had now given birth, I assumed, to two children without it having any obvious effect on her waistline and I sensed that many other male eyes were drawn to her entrance.

I quickly got to my feet and, taking her outstretched hand in mine, placed a kiss on it.

'It is a pleasure to see you again, Aliza. Do please sit down.'

'Thank you, Otto. I'm grateful to you for agreeing to see me at such short notice. It's very kind of you.'

'Not at all.' I then gestured towards the menu sitting on the table in front of us. 'The food here is excellent and naturally I will be pleased to pay for both of us.'

'Really, that's unnecessary.'

'Nonsense, I insist. Tell me, can I take it that you are now a mother again? I have had no contact with Max since last year.'

A warm smile spread across her face. 'Yes, indeed.'

'Is it a boy or a girl?'

'Another girl but healthy, which is what matters most of all. We have called her Zara after Max's grandmother.'

Suddenly a look of profound sadness crossed her face. 'It is not all good news, I'm afraid, which is why I wanted to see you.' Her voice had dropped to barely more than a whisper and she leant towards me so that I could smell the perfume she was wearing. 'You see, Max and I are thinking of separating. He is determined to leave for Palestine as soon as possible whereas…'

At that moment, a waiter caught my eye and with Aliza's approval, I ordered a bottle of wine. I then looked at her intently.

'I cannot believe what I just heard you say. Surely, you are not serious?'

'We have been arguing about it for more than a year; well before Zara was born in fact.'

'But I thought you were as happy to settle in Palestine as Max?'

'No, not any more. Not in fact since we were there with you. It made me realise that it was not a place where I wanted to live. This country is my home and has been my family's home for generations.'

I sighed and glanced around anxiously. Her voice had become louder and more vehement, attracting the attention of other customers.

'I'm sorry you feel like that,' I responded quietly. 'But you must realise that… well, Jewish people, I greatly regret to say, have no future in this country. I am very sorry.

'I know that only too well. Which is precisely why I'm here.'

I was nonplussed. 'I don't understand….'

'I want to be exempted.' She leant close to me again and whispered the words. 'I want to legally cease to be a Jew. Can you help me to make that possible?'

I shook my head. 'But I believe that only the Fuhrer has that power.'

She lowered her eyes and then looked at me eagerly. 'There is something I have never told you before. My mother was not a Jew.'

I looked intently at her. 'So if it were not for your marriage you would only be a Mischling – a half-Jew?'

'Yes, and I am thinking that my chances of being granted exemption would increase if Max and I were to divorce.'

'Quite possibly, and you are not a practising Jew, are you?'

'No, I told you that, and did either Max or I show any inclination to attend a synagogue while we were with you in Palestine?'

'No, of course not.'

'And my mother was a Roman Catholic. I am quite prepared to adopt that faith if I have to.'

'Then why not be satisfied with that; after all you do not look particularly Jewish.'

'Yes, but what about my children? If I could gain complete exemption perhaps their status could be improved as well.'

'I think you need the advice of a good lawyer. I could perhaps recommend one and if you need money…'

She shook her head vigorously at which moment the waiter returned with the wine and proceeded to uncork it before giving me the opportunity to taste it.

'Yes, that's excellent, thank you.'

'And would you be ready to order now?' the waiter asked.

We both did so whereupon she fixed her eyes on me again. They were as beautiful as ever though profoundly sad.

'So you cannot help me?'

'Beyond what I have just suggested, you are asking the impossible of me, Aliza. The kind of exemption you are seeking is only going to be granted by the Fuhrer to persons who have demonstrated their commitment to the Party and to the Fatherland.'

'But look, if I were to divorce Max, and be seen to have adopted the Catholic faith, are you saying to me that you could do still do nothing to help me?'

I was silent for a few moments. 'I do not know whether I will still even be head of the Jewish Bureau in a few months' time, and I assure you that I do not have the ear of the Fuhrer or any of his ministers. I'm very sorry.'

'You must have met the Fuhrer?'

'I have been introduced to him briefly, on two occasions, but that is all.'

'And ministers…, you must work with some?'

'Yes, of course, but I'm not on that close terms with any of them. Do you also seriously expect me to say to Reich Minister Goebbels that I am acquainted with an attractive Jewish lady who needs a favour from the Fuhrer? And, oh yes, she would like that extended to her children as well.'

My tone was gently chiding rather than fiercely sarcastic but even so, Aliza looked devastated and close to tears.

'Otto, I am desperate. I just want to be able to live in peace in the land of my birth. Forgive my intrusion, I should leave.' She began to stand up.

'No, nonsense, lunch has been ordered and you know I am pleased to see you.'

She sat down again. 'I thought you might be. I haven't forgotten the way you used to look at me when we were in Palestine. God in heaven, how it annoyed your wife!'

This brought a faint but definite smile to my face. 'You know, you should stay with Max, if only for the sake of your children.'

'Not if he remains determined to emigrate to Palestine.'

The waiter now arrived with our meals, which we proceeded

to eat, for the most part in companionable silence. I don't even remember what we ate. I couldn't help reflecting on how furious Clara would be if she ever learnt of this meeting and I was determined to make no mention of it.

'Are you all right?' Aliza asked me curiously.

'Yes, it just isn't very warm in here,' I lied.

'Personally, I feel quite hot. Tell me, though, why do you say that you might not be head of the Jewish Bureau in a few months?'

I shrugged. 'A number of reasons,' I confessed. 'Emigration figures to Palestine are down a little, you were right to be sceptical about the level of financial support from the government, and now one of my own officers has produced a pamphlet attacking the whole notion of an independent Jewish State. He claims that such a development would simply help to strengthen what he called the 'Jewish conspiracy'. I am afraid, Aliza, that if men like him get their way, the entire Jewish population of Germany will end up being herded into ghettos and allowed to starve. You really would be better off staying with Max and emigrating. Couldn't you persuade Max to live somewhere else in Europe…, Britain perhaps?'

'I would still prefer to remain in the land of my birth, and anyway he believes in the cause. You must realise that?'

'Yes, of course I do.'

She then put her knife and fork together and smiled coyly at me. Not for the first time, I felt overpowered by her sheer beauty and sexual attractiveness.

'I really must be going.'

'But you haven't finished. Have coffee with me.'

'No, I really must be going. Forgive me for troubling you.

And look after yourself.'

'And you.' I stood up as she did and once more kissed her hand. I wanted to ask her to keep in touch but the words wouldn't come and with a final regretful smile she turned and walked away.

Feeling tense, I took out a cigarette and proceeded to smoke. I had only told her the truth but that didn't make my strong sense of regret any easier. It offended my natural sense of chivalry towards women in general, and Aliza in particular, not to have been able to help her beyond suggesting that she see a good lawyer. I was left hoping that she would find some way of reconciling her differences with Max and that they would leave Germany as soon as possible.

14

'*Yes, he was with a Jewess, Gustave told me. He saw them together in Heisings and overheard part of their conversation. I tell you he's nothing but a Jew lover.*'

It was Eichmann's voice and I wasn't sure if he was with someone or talking on the telephone. His words - or at least what I could make out of them through the closed door - made my stomach turn over but did not deter me from what I was about to do. After only a moment's hesitation I tapped on the door of his office.

'I'll ring you back…,' I heard him say. 'Yes, please come in.'

I was already feeling quite out of sorts and what I had just heard him say did nothing for my mood. As I walked in I didn't feel too inclined to make any eye contact with the man. It was obvious that he was embarrassed.

'I thought you should know that I have decided to resign,'

'I'm very sorry to hear that. Is it really necessary?' The tone of his question was sympathetic but I did not take it to be genuine.

'I thought you'd be pleased, given how opposed you've become to everything that I've been trying to achieve? Numbers emigrating to Palestine are down again.'

'Yes, I know.'

'Anyway, it's now, regrettably, clear to me that everything I have advocated and worked for is simply doomed to failure.' I could not disguise the bitterness in my voice.

'Even so, I'm surprised by your decision. When we spoke a few weeks ago you still seemed to believe that your support for Zionism was accepted by the highest echelons of the party.'

'I hoped that was the case, yes, but I had a meeting yesterday with Heydrich and he made it very plain to me that this was no longer the case. That pamphlet you wrote has been very well received, apparently. It will probably lead to promotion, especially once I'm gone.'

I could see a look of triumph in his eyes, but in fairness to him, he was prepared to be magnanimous in victory.

'Don't imagine I've ever doubted your sincerity.'

'Thank you, but we both know sincerity alone is never enough. That is why I have decided it's best I resign.'

'Permit me to give you some advice?'

'Very well, if you must.'

'You have been seen in the company of an attractive Jewess…, one of your Zionist acquaintances, no doubt.' He cleared his throat. 'I would be very careful if I were you…'

Now I began to feel angry. 'Yes, I could hear dimly through the door what you were saying on the telephone just now but I can assure you that I was only with the woman in question on one occasion and at her request. She was born a Mischling and was seeking exemption. I told her there was nothing I could do to assist her. She accepted that and I have no expectation of seeing her again.'

'Very wise…'

'Well, there's nothing more to be said then. I'll go and prepare my letter of resignation. I want it to take effect immediately so I should be gone by the end of the week.'

'What will you do?'

'I don't know. Travel perhaps.'

Later the same day, as I returned home, the future was naturally very much on my mind. Certainly, I would have liked to travel again, but the birth of Leopold had changed things. Also, I did not welcome having to discuss my decision to resign with Clara, but I realised I could not put if off any longer. I knew I really ought to have spoken to her sooner but somehow the very idea had stuck in my throat.

'There is something I need to tell you, darling,' I said to Clara after supper. She looked suddenly stunned, as if I was about to confess to some indiscretion of a sexual nature. 'I have decided to resign from my position with the Bureau, I've prepared my letter of resignation in fact...'

I'd hardly expected her to be upset by my revelation and as it was she positively beamed at me with pleasure. 'Congratulations, darling, you've come to your senses at last then?' Her words stung.

'It's not a question of that, my love.' I was now feeling irritated. 'It's simply that I've been, reluctantly, forced to the conclusion that I'm never going to be able to achieve what I had hoped for...'

'You were naïve to have imagined that you could.'

'That may be so,' I conceded. 'What, however, finally forced me to make this decision was a conversation I had with Heydrich the other day and also a pamphlet produced by Eichmann attacking the very notion of an independent Jewish homeland. It's gone down very well, apparently. It's clear to me that the Party will never agree to reduce the cost of emigration to Palestine, so I see no point in continuing in office'

I felt, and no doubt looked, dejected and would have

welcomed some expression of sympathy from Clara, but instead she was simply triumphant at having been proved right, at least in her own eyes.

'I'm just delighted that you won't be associating with Jews any longer. It's tainted our lives and you've simply become known as "a Jew-lover".'

'How can you say that?'

'I see the way we're regarded at functions and how limited our social life has become.'

'That has been because of the pressures of my work and the fact that we have a baby.'

She looked at me, sceptically, shaking her head.

'I think we should have a holiday,' I suggested. 'We can't really travel as we did but we can still have a few weeks away. I thought, perhaps, the Black Forest; what do you think?'

'That would be very nice,' Clara said.

We discussed holiday arrangements for a while, then Clara asked me whether I'd given any thought to the future.

'Not much, to be honest. I'll think about it while we're away.'

I spent the rest of the evening finishing my letter of resignation. I intended to take it, in person, to the office of Reichsfuhrer Heinrich Himmler. A telephone call the following morning quickly established that the Reichsfuhrer was elsewhere, but I took the letter to his office anyway, and gave it to his personal secretary.

I felt a certain sense of relief. In my heart I had recognised for some time that the policy I advocated was becoming a fruitless one, and I welcomed the fact that I'd now be spared the burden of advocating it in the face of increasing opposition from the likes of Eichmann.

When I returned to my desk to clear it, I also decided that a few courtesy calls were in order. Eichmann's comments about my having been seen with Aliza were still particularly rankling me and I reflected, too, on whether she had really meant what she said about leaving Max. I hesitated slightly, then had a call put through to him. A few minutes later I heard his familiar voice and proceeded to explain my decision to him.

'This is a sad day for the Zionist cause in Germany,' he told me, his voice charged with emotion.

'I'm sorry, Max. I'm sure you'll appreciate that I have done all I can…'

'Of course, Otto. I know you have.'

'I've met with too much opposition, I'm afraid. The antipathy the party has towards your race has clouded judgements.'

'You'll forgive me for saying it's hardly a surprise to me.'

'Quite so, I was too optimistic, I see that now. So, will you be emigrating soon?' There was a prolonged silence at the other end of the telephone. 'Hello, are you still there?'

'No, I'm afraid emigration is now out of the question. Aliza has refused to go.'

'Really?' I feigned surprise. 'I thought that she was full of enthusiasm for the idea…'

'At one time, yes, but not any more. It's caused some friction between us.'

'Nothing too serious, I trust?' I was trying to keep the tone of my voice as casual as possible.

'We're still together.' he replied with a defensive edge to his voice. It was obvious to me that he didn't want to discuss Aliza with me.

'Well, give her my regards.'

'I'll do that.'

'And the children are both well?'

'Oh yes.'

'Goodbye then.'

'Goodbye…and thank you.'

For a while after replacing the receiver, I sat looking out of the window. I was relieved Aliza hadn't, apparently, carried out her threat to leave Max, or at least not yet. After all, I believed in the strength of the family and didn't approve of divorce or separation. Yet, above all, I still couldn't help thinking that they would be much safer emigrating to Palestine, as it was obvious to me that neither of them had any future in Germany.

Aside from this, I felt that the pull of loyalty towards Clara and Leopold conflicted with my feelings for Aliza. It was a reality that made it hard for me to take any initiative in keeping in contact with her although my concern for her welfare remained a compelling reason for doing so. In the back of my mind, too, I did not want to be seen to be taking too obvious an interest in her in case Max came to realise the true extent of my feelings for her.

In the face of these dilemmas, I'm afraid I allowed time to drift by more than I would have liked until finally, by sheer good fortune, I happened to meet Aliza in the street in Berlin. It particularly stands out in my mind as the meeting happened on the thirtieth of September 1938, the very day the Czechoslovak government capitulated, enabling our armed forces to peacefully occupy the Sudeten territory following the Munich agreement, which the Reich had reached with Great Britain, France and Italy.

When we had that accidental but fortuitous meeting, Aliza

smiled at me as delightfully as ever, which came as a relief to me as I was concerned she might not have forgiven me for declining to take any steps to try and have her exempted. It was a busy day for me at work but I was so pleased to see her again that I decided to invite her to have a cup of coffee with me at a nearby cafe, to which she happily agreed.

'So how are you and Max?' I asked her once we had taken our seats and been served. 'You're still together, I trust?'

'Oh yes, we've resolved our differences… as much as anything for the sake of the children.'

I looked at her keenly, wondering how happy she really was but she gave me no further clue that she might not be, preferring instead to immediately ask me what I thought of the Munich agreement.

I gave my honest response. 'I'm very impressed. After all, it's yet another great success for the Fuhrer and all achieved without a single bullet being fired. It's really quite astonishing how much he's accomplished in the last five years.' In saying this I had in mind not only our remilitarisation of the Rhineland and peaceful annexation of Austria but also the transformation of the nation's economy.

'But will this satisfy his ambitions, do you think?'

'I really don't know. At least the agreement has preserved the peace for now. But, be that as it may, I'm pleased for you and Max… And if I can be of any service to you in any way at all in the future, please do not hesitate to get in touch.'

'That's very kind of you, Otto.'

I was conscious of course that my tone was too formal, but I didn't really know what other tone it was rational for me to adopt with Aliza. Again, she smiled at me so that I felt the bond between us, which I had been so conscious of during our days in Palestine together, had not gone away. She then proceeded to ask me about Clara and Leopold, which encouraged me to reach for my wallet and pull out a recently taken photograph of him.

'He looks like you, I think,' she told me.

'Really, I see so much of Clara in him. And how are your daughters… Bathsheba and…'

'Zara. They're both well.' And with that she also reached into her handbag and produced a family photograph, which I duly admired, before she suddenly looked at her watch. 'I'm sorry, Otto, I can't stay any longer, I'm afraid.' She then gulped down the remainder of her coffee while I insisted on paying the bill. I wasn't sure why she was in such haste, and I chose not to ask her.

'It's been so nice to see you again, Otto,' she told me as we both stood up.

'The pleasure's been all mine, I assure you.'

With that she leaned forward and kissed me on the cheek before quickly walking away. She was wearing just a touch of rose scent to enhance her femininity, which was appealing. Indeed, even the thought of it is enough to instantly transport me back to that special moment in time. I found myself willing her to turn round but she never did so. I knew I also needed to be elsewhere, but felt compelled to sit back for a little while, finish the remains of my coffee, and savour the pleasure a few minutes of her company had given me.

Only a few weeks later came *Kristallnacht*, which with the ransacking of so many Jewish businesses, schools, synagogues and hospitals, as well as nearly a hundred murders of Jewish people and thousands of arrests, undermined my faith in the National Socialist cause. The excuse was the assassination of one of our diplomats in Paris by a Polish Jew, but I saw absolutely no justification in such an outrageously disproportionate response and said as much to Clara.

Her response that it was merely 'unfortunate' thoroughly irritated me but when I threatened to tear up my Party card she pleaded with me not to be so foolish.

'You cannot afford to take that risk, Otto. You will be blacklisted and God knows what will become of us. Please think of my interests and those of Leopold before you do anything so foolish.'

I was concerned that she was right and merely brooded on the matter. Then, within a year came our invasion of Poland, plunging us into war. The nation was informed that it was only in response to Polish aggression on the border, but my work kept me close enough to the higher echelons of power to know that this was no more than a baseless excuse, made possible by the Non-aggression Pact, signed with the Soviet Union only days beforehand. Nonetheless, as the conflict widened I decided that my first duty was to remain loyal to both the Party and to my country, whilst, of course, Poland was quickly overrun and carved up between the Reich and the Soviet Union.

And then in the spring of 1940 came more astonishing victories, which left the Fuhrer in command of so much of Europe, including the golden prize of Paris, bringing to mind the great victory achieved over France in the Franco-Prussian war seventy years previously. It seemed that the Fuhrer was positively invincible, so even when the Luftwaffe failed to achieve dominance over the skies of England and any thought of an invasion of that country had to be postponed, it did little to tarnish the prevailing sense of euphoria.

I had singularly mixed emotions over such success given my fierce memories of our humiliation in 1918. Of course it was impressive, I might even say astonishingly so, as the scale and speed of the conquests left even those of Charlemagne or Napoleon Bonaparte in their shadow. All the same, what deeply concerned me was that it would encourage the Fuhrer and his regime to ever greater acts of repression and brutality against the Jewish race across the length and breath of the conquered nations of Europe.

15

Berlin Spring 1941

I was sitting at my desk here in this study. It was a Saturday and I was examining my morning post. It looked uninteresting, bills, official communications of one sort or another, but then also an envelope addressed to me in a hand which I didn't recognise. My curiosity aroused, I used my knife to open the envelope and I pulled out the letter. I caught a whiff of scent, which instantly triggered my memory. It was as if I was in Jerusalem in the summer of 1933. I caught my breath.
Otto,

Please forgive me for writing to you but I am desperate and I don't know who else to turn to for help. Max has been taken away. I fear that it is only a matter of time before they come for me and the children as well. I wish I hadn't been so stupid and had agreed to leave Germany when we had the opportunity. I am afraid I had too much pride...

'Have you seen my purse, Otto?' Clara had suddenly appeared at my study door. I instantly put down the letter and slipped it underneath one of the other, nondescript, communications.

'My love... I'm afraid I've no idea where it is...'

'I need it. I'm going shopping.'

'If it's money you want, let me give you some.'

I felt inside my jacket pocket and took out my wallet from which I produced some Reichsmarks.

'Thank you. Is it bad news?'

'What?'

'…Whatever you were reading?'

I tensed. 'No, no it's nothing,' I replied.

Clara looked at me sharply. I could tell she didn't believe me.

'Well, I must be going. I'll be back in a couple of hours, I expect.'

'Where is Leopold?'

'Freda's looking after him,' Clara was referring to the child's nanny. 'They're in the nursery together.'

I kissed my wife fondly on the cheek and waited for the sound of the front door being closed before looking at Aliza's letter again.

Please can I see you again? My telephone number is…
For the sake of our old friendship and common humanity please help me. I understand that it is a very hard thing to ask of you but I still beg you to contact me.
Yours affectionately,
   Aliza

I picked up the telephone. I hesitated, then I rang the operator and asked to be put through to the number Aliza had given me.

The telephone rang and rang, I was on the point of replacing the receiver when I heard her familiar voice.

'Hello.'

'Aliza.'

'Yes…Otto?'

'I received your letter.'

'It's good of you to telephone me…'

'Aliza… I wish I could help you but I just don't see how I can.'

'Otto, I don't have anyone else to turn to. I am so frightened.'

'Aliza, why didn't you follow my advice? You and Max could have been in Palestine years ago, safe and well. And your children too.'

'I'm sorry…' I could hear her voice breaking with emotion. 'I never thought it would come to this…'

'I'm afraid it has. Once the Party began to reject my policy, I realise now it was always likely to come to this sooner or later. Aliza, I'm really, really sorry but I'm afraid I can't help you.'

'You selfish bastard!'

'Aliza!'

She'd slammed the phone down on me. For some moments I remained where I was standing, holding the receiver. Then I took a deep breath, replaced it, and composed myself as best I could.

I reached for my cigarette case, took out a cigarette, and lit it. Looking out of the window, I found my mind returning to that morning in 1933 when I'd welcomed Max into this very room and proposed our joint trip to Palestine. That he was now an inmate in a concentration camp, and Aliza might soon share a similar fate, was something that I really didn't wish to dwell upon, but I still found myself compelled to do so. I picked up the telephone again.

'Hello.'

'Aliza, it's Otto.'

'Leave me alone!'

'Aliza, I apologise, please forgive me. I was so disturbed by your letter; I wasn't myself. It's just very difficult to know what I can do to help you. This wicked regime we live under has made even good Germans impotent to help without risking the destruction of themselves and their own families, and how would that destruction help Jewish people in Germany? Please listen. There is one person who I could appeal to on your behalf. You see, since we were last in touch with one another I've become better acquainted with Reich Minister Goebbels. I'm now head of the press office in the Department of Film. It's part of his Ministry so he's effectively my boss and we see each other quite regularly. In fact, I'm due to have a meeting with him later this week…'

'Oh Otto, thank you! Thank you so much.'

'But Aliza, you must not be too hopeful. Of course, I will seek to speak to him in confidence and I hope he will respect that but revealing any friendship with a Jew has become dangerous. He may well dismiss my appeal completely.'

'I understand Otto. I'm just so grateful that you're willing to approach him at all on my behalf.'

'I see your address from your letter. If you will allow me, I'll call on you once I've spoken to Goebbels…' Suddenly, I heard the front door slam.

'Clara's just come back, I expect, I must go. Take care.'

'Thank you,' Aliza responded softly

'I'm home,' Clara called out. I immediately put the receiver down and composed myself as best I could.

'Do you like this cocktail dress, I've bought myself?' Clara asked me, holding it out in front of her for my inspection, as she entered the study.

'Yes, it looks very nice,' I said despondently.

'What's wrong with you; not in one of your bad moods, I hope?'

'No, of course not, my love, it looks beautiful, really it does.' I forced a smile and going to Clara took her in my arms and put my lips to hers. She was clearly surprised by such a sudden and ardent display of affection but still yielded to my embrace quite willingly.

'Are you sure you're feeling all right?'

'Of course.' Except that even as I kissed Clara I had the image of Aliza in my mind and couldn't help feeling an unshakeable sense of regret.

****

I entered the overly-large office of Reich Minister Goebbels in the Ministry of Public Enlightenment and Propaganda with a gnawing sense of apprehension, which made it hard for me to concentrate on the matters which I had supposedly come to discuss. Fortunately, Goebbels was in a good humour, and did not appear to notice, talking rapidly and fluently as was his wont so that within as little as twenty minutes the moment of truth was upon me. After he had given some instructions to one of his secretaries, he then asked her to leave his office and then we were alone together.

'You look troubled, Otto, is anything bothering you?' he asked.

I coughed. 'A little, Minister, you see there is a matter of some delicacy that I would like to raise with you, if you are able to give me a few minutes of your time?'

He smiled at me. 'Of course, Otto, what is it?'

I cleared my throat. 'It concerns a certain Mischling Jew...'

He already looked shocked, which was hardly surprising. Still I had begun and there was now no turning back so I embarked on a brief explanation of who Aliza was and how I had come to know her. 'Frankly, Minister, she became something of a friend and has approached me with a request that she might... might be exempted from any classification as a Jew, both for her sake and that of her children.'

He looked at me sternly and at first said nothing. which made me feel distinctly uncomfortable, as if I was a boy again and had been summoned to the headmaster's office to explain some particularly awful misdemeanour.

'But on what possible grounds?' he finally asked.

It was exactly the question I had been expecting and had come armed with only one rather lame answer. 'She and her husband were extremely helpful to me on my visit to Palestine. As I've already said neither she or her husband are practising Jews and her mother was Roman Catholic.'

'But her husband is a full-Jew?'

'...Yes, he is.'

I thought he might then ask me some probing questions about Max but instead he snorted. 'And you seriously expect me to raise this woman's plea with the Fuhrer?'

'...Only if you saw any prospect of success.'

'Well, I'm sorry, Otto, but I certainly don't...'

Again I coughed. I had to make one last throw of the dice. 'And there is no way in which she could be, how shall I say, removed from the record?'

He wagged a finger at me. 'Absolutely not, Otto, absolutely not!'

'I quite understand, Minister, forgive me for troubling you on this matter.'

At this he smiled faintly and became more relaxed. 'She's attractive, I assume?'

'Oh yes, very.'

'Then I will forgive your foolishness in making such a request. You know, in the early twenties I had an affair with a woman who I then discovered was a Mischling. I quickly broke it off, but I must confess I went on loving her and continued to see her occasionally for a few years. Now, look, I'm happy to forget that we've ever had this conversation.'

I muttered my thanks and couldn't wait to withdraw, still feeling like a boy who has been let off lightly for breaking the rules, but also relieved to be able to breathe fresh air again. Most of all, for all that my request had ended in almost inevitable failure, at least I could now look Aliza in the eye and tell her I'd tried.

*****

Two days passed before I could bring myself to visit Aliza, knowing how painful it would be for both of us for me to have to tell her to her face that I could bring her no comfort. However, it wasn't fair on her either to put this off any longer especially when it would only require a five-minute detour from my usual route to and from work to reach her front door.

I made a point of finishing work a little early on what was a pleasantly warm and sunny evening and drove to the street I was looking for within twenty minutes. Her address was an apartment block, which I was able to park outside. It appeared smart and modern with a lift, although I preferred to climb the stairs to its third floor where I arrived in a carpeted hallway. Here I halted and composed myself. Whatever happened, I knew I couldn't stay long, and in the event of my knock going unanswered, was prepared to write her a note giving her my work telephone number.

As it happened, within moments Aliza appeared. For all that I was the bearer of bad news, she instantly brought an affectionate smile to my face as I doffed my trilby hat to her and felt a palpable sense of happiness at being in her company once more. She was still very much the beautiful woman I remembered, wearing a primrose-coloured dress, and with her hair fetchingly waved.

'I'm glad to find you at home, Aliza. If I might say so, you're also looking as lovely as ever.'

'And you were ever the flatterer, as I recall, Otto. Come in…, I'm sorry if the apartment's something of a mess.'

'That really doesn't matter…'

As I stepped inside a child's face appeared around the corner of a door, looking at me curiously.

'This is my younger daughter, Zara,' Aliza explained. 'Bathsheba is with a friend who lives nearby. I expect her home quite soon.'

I offered the child a smile in greeting but couldn't help a slight sense of irritation that her presence would preclude any serious conversation with her mother. However, Aliza, was quick to tell her to stay in her room and play.

'I have something important to discuss with this gentleman, so please be good and try not to disturb us.'

She then led me into the sitting room, which was indeed rather cluttered by various books, magazines, and toys, scattered around, as well as a clothes rack in one corner, but was, nonetheless, clean and elegantly furnished. She offered to make me either tea or coffee and I accepted tea..

'Come into the kitchen with me while I make it,' she said and I was content to follow her, enjoying the sense of intimacy this created between us. In happier circumstances I would have liked nothing better than to reminisce about the past and renew our acquaintance in a relaxed and friendly fashion but now was not the time.

'So what news have you for me?' she asked, fixing me with her eyes.

'I'm sorry Aliza, it isn't good, I'm afraid…'

Her face fell a little but she remained composed. 'Well, you did tell me not to be too hopeful.'

'Yes, I did, but I tried, Aliza, I really did. Goebbels was surprisingly understanding and wasn't really offended that I should make such a request…'

'That's something at least.'

'… But he still made it clear that it was impossible for him to intervene in any way. I'm so sorry.'

She was clearly upset but still managed a little smile and placed a hand on my wrist. 'You did your best, Otto, I know you did. I couldn't ask for more and will always be grateful, I promise you.'

'Thank you, Aliza, I appreciate that.'

I then decided to offer her my further sympathies over Max's fate. 'What happened to him exactly?' I asked. 'And have you any idea where he might have been taken?'

Aliza gave a heavy shrug, as if she were so worn out with despair, worry and gloom that there were limits even to how much she could feel about the disaster she was about to impart to me. 'Otto, the Gestapo came for him one evening nearly three weeks ago. He's continued to be active in the Zionist movement, you see, and apart from being a Jew I imagine he's now considered to be politically undesirable as well. As to where he is now, I don't know, but I imagine a camp, somewhere or other.'

'Oh no, what disastrous news! Poor Max! But why are you so certain that you and your daughters are at risk; after all, I take it the Gestapo didn't interrogate you?'

'No, they were only interested in Max, but I just feel that it can only be a question of time before they come for us as well.'

'But you haven't been personally active in any political way, I assume?'

'No, or certainly not since the war started.'

'Then I think you may not be at too great a risk. I'm also really sorry about Max and I wonder how you are now placed financially? If I can help you in any way in that regard then I would be more than pleased to do so.'

'Thank you, Otto, I'm grateful for such an offer. At least I have some savings. My landlord, a kind man, has also agreed to waive my rent for three months and I'll look for part-time work. You see, I was a secretary before I met Max.'

'But you'll find that a struggle, given your status.'

'Yes, of course, but there are still a few Jewish employers around who might be able to offer me a job.'

'Well, if you find you can't manage, you must not fail to tell me. I'd prefer it, though, if you didn't contact me. Rather, permit me to continue to visit you, say once a month. It won't take me far out of my way when I'm travelling home from work.'

'All right, I would appreciate that. What worries me more than anything is that I might be taken away, leaving Bathsheba and Zara to fend for themselves.'

I tried to reassure her that this was most unlikely to happen and emphasised that I'd not heard of any plans to round up Berlin's Jewish population and force them into any sort of ghetto as had happened in Warsaw, or into camps. How utterly naïve I was about the vile intentions of the Nazis!

Aliza and I sat down together at her kitchen table and drank tea in a spirit of companionship that we had not enjoyed in eight years. For just a few minutes I was even able to imagine us once again side by side in Palestine with the world still at peace until I heard the sound of her front door being opened and moments later her elder daughter, Bathsheba, appeared.

My first thought was how much like her mother she looked. I guessed she must be twelve or thirteen and could envisage her blossoming into just as beautiful a woman. Meanwhile, she eyed me rather suspiciously, I thought, while Aliza introduced me to her as an old friend. Drinking the remains of my tea, I decided the time had come to depart and quickly did so, whilst reaffirming my promise to call again in a month's time.

Before walking away I couldn't resist taking hold of Aliza's right hand and placing a kiss upon it. Such a gesture brought a radiant smile to her face and I felt the pull of that sexual attraction between us, which I'd been conscious of since the first day we'd met. All the same, I was convinced that our relationship was bound to remain a platonic one. After all, I still loved Clara and did not wish to be unfaithful to her, whilst the Nuremberg racial laws were also a disincentive to any thought of a sexual relationship with Aliza.

16

For the next eighteen months I lived, if not a double life, then certainly one punctuated by regular visits to Aliza's apartment; on average about once a fortnight, I would say, that felt increasingly to me as if we were engaged in a clandestine affair, even if the truth of the matter was rather different. Had one or both of her daughters not always been present then I doubt if my powers of self-control would have been sufficient to prevent me from falling into temptation, even at the risk of a fierce rebuttal. As it was, I had to be content with just a few minutes in her company, sometimes a little longer if I allowed myself to linger over the tea she always offered me. I always kissed her hand when we parted and came to savour the entrancing smile that she invariably bestowed on me in return as something particularly special to be kept in my heart until our next meeting.

Conversation between us was usually limited to little more than essential practicalities as, unable to find work, she became increasingly dependent on the financial support I insisted on providing. This was, inevitably, a drain on my reserves, but not to the point that it prevented me from keeping Clara in the manner to which she had become accustomed since we had married. Clara herself certainly never had any reason to suspect anything. Furthermore, as my visits to Aliza were always comparatively short – though extremely important to me and,

I think, to Aliza too - my excuse of occasionally having to work late was never one that Clara had cause to question.

Gradually Aliza and I took to embracing fervently whenever I said goodbye to her, and I would accompany those embraces by giving her a kiss on her lovely soft cheeks, though I resisted what was admittedly often an almost overwhelming temptation to kiss her on the lips. I don't know how she would have reacted had I done so... or what the consequences might have been, but somehow I always restrained myself, a nagging sense of guilt forever playing its part.

The German invasion of Russia in the summer of 1941, followed some five months later by Japan's attack on Pearl Harbour, bringing the United States into the war, proved to be catalysts for more than just passing conversation between myself and Aliza concerning the war's progress. At first the invasion went so well that no propaganda was required to manipulate the truth, and it seemed to be only a matter of time before both Moscow and Leningrad were in German hands. There was even talk of a German Reich that would stretch to the Pacific Ocean in a grand alliance with Japan, creating a completely new world order. But remembering history, I was sceptical of this, and confided my scepticism to Aliza:

'Russia is a vast country and its winters are terrible. The Emperor Napoleon advanced all the way to Moscow only to see his Grand Army destroyed. Ours could go the same way as I doubt if it's much better equipped to cope once the weather turns colder. I fear that the Fuhrer has overreached himself.'

'He covets Russia's oil and other natural resources, I expect,' Aliza responded perceptively.

'No doubt, in which case it would have made more sense to

me to send all the divisions now fighting in Russia to North Africa. The oil fields of the Middle East are well within striking distance of Egypt.'

'Perhaps the Fuhrer now thinks himself invincible?'

'In which case, like Napoleon before him, he may well be in for a nasty surprise.'

As so often, that particular conversation was then cut short by my realising that I'd already stayed too long, but we were to return to it again, especially when winter inevitably brought a halt to our progress in Russia and we found ourselves at war with the United States.

'It's not good news,' I declared gloomily. 'Soon enough the Americans will doubtless come to the aid of the British in North Africa and set about planning an invasion of Europe.'

'But aren't they likely to be preoccupied with fighting the Japanese?' Aliza asked.

'Only to a degree. The Americans are rich and powerful enough to commit resources to a war against Germany as well. Mark my words, the Fuhrer will come to regret ever invading Russia, let alone declaring war on the United States. I think historians in the future may find it laughable that a comparatively small nation such as Germany had the audacity to declare war on an almost infinitely wealthy and powerful country that is more than 4,000 kilometres from East to West, and more than 2,500 kilometres from North to South.'

'And Russia is even bigger.'

'Indeed. And Russia is even bigger.'

'Otto, you think Germany will lose the war, then?'

'It's too early to say, but the fact is that we're now at war with the three most powerful nations on the planet. Japan will help us to an extent, but I think it's been foolish to imagine that we can ultimately win a war against not only the United States and the British Empire but also nationalist China as well. I know, too, that I joined the Nazi Party in the hope it would restore our pride in ourselves as a nation. I never did so in the expectation it would involve us in another world war that could leave Germany in an even worse position than the first one, and could indeed end in our total destruction.'

This was an admission I would have been unlikely to make to Clara. Her enthusiasm for the 'great struggle' (as she liked to put it) on which the nation had embarked was at this time still quite untarnished and she would have seen my remarks as not only defeatist but also treasonable. With Aliza, however, for the short while we were together each month, I could afford to be more honest, and the frank rapport between us which had worked so well when we first came to know each other in Palestine was easily re-established. So much so in fact that I decided to admit to her how disillusioned I had become with the Party and everything it stood for regardless of its successes.

'You were right all along, I see that now,' I confessed. 'I was blind to the warning signs, thinking that the Party would never go so far. It was *Kristallnachnt* that brought home to me what senseless cruelty we were inflicting on such a tiny minority of our population. I wish I'd had the courage to resign from the Party but when I said I might do so to Clara she was horrified. She said we'd be ruined and I had to think of her and Leopold. I'm a coward, I'm afraid; at any rate a moral one at least.'

'I think you were just trying to protect yourself and those you love,' Aliza said, charitably. 'Isn't it what most of us do?'

'Yes, I suppose it is.'

Meanwhile, Aliza's fear of being taken away sooner or later increased when in September of 1941 all German Jews were required to wear a Star of David whenever they went out, thus exposing them to ever greater abuse. She declared, bravely, that she was prepared to wear it like a badge of honour and hold her head high, but I was deeply unhappy about such stigmatisation and said so.

Even so, as time passed and we moved deeper into 1942, I began to take it for granted that my regular visits to Aliza would continue indefinitely, and certainly until the war was either won or lost. Such confidence, though, was shaken when in the July I became aware that there had been a rounding up of many Jews in Berlin, presumably with the intention of transporting them to various camps.

These developments made me greatly anxious on Aliza's behalf and, although it was only about a week since my previous visit, I decided to go again just to ensure that all was still well. My relief, when she came to the door to answer my knock, was palpable.

'Why Otto, this is a pleasant surprise, what brings you here so soon?' she asked me.

'Forgive me, Aliza, may I come in for a few minutes?'

'Why, of course.' At which point she stood to one side so I could enter what by now had become familiar surroundings.

'I don't want to alarm you but I've heard that there's been a round-up of many Jews in the city. I believe they've been transported away. I was worried about you.'

'Well, as you can see, I'm still here. Naturally, I appreciate your concern. I'll happily make you tea, if you would like a cup?'

'Yes, that would be good.'

Invariably, whenever I arrived, one or both of her daughters would make a brief appearance but on this occasion they failed to do so.

'Are you alone?'

'Yes, for a short while. Both the girls are with friends. I must say, it's very rare that I get any time to myself.'

'And then I arrive to spoil it.'

'But only with the best of intentions, Otto.' She gave me such a knowing smile, it almost took my breath away.

'Whilst you look as beautiful as ever.'

'Ah, what a flatterer you are, Otto.'

'No, I merely speak the truth.' I felt such a frisson of sexual tension between us that I could easily have taken her in my arms and kissed her, but I hesitated, and the opportunity passed. She moved into the kitchen to make tea. Within five minutes Bathsheba returned and I was left to contemplate what might have been. Ten minutes later I said goodbye in my usual fashion, and whilst returning to my car, I concluded that it was probably for the best that I hadn't kissed her passionately as I wished to do. As our relationship remained platonic my conscience was relatively untroubled, and I was able to look Clara in the eye without feeling that I had actually betrayed her.

I also recognised that I had no right to imagine that Aliza was not still in love with Max. I knew that from the summer of 1941 onwards letters written by him had begun to arrive at regular intervals from Sachsenhausen concentration camp. Indeed, she had shown me some of them, often heavily censored, and never expressing any criticism of his living conditions. Nonetheless, they were an undoubted comfort to her and she'd been able to write back. From the late summer of 1942 onwards they stopped coming, causing her to become understandably more anxious about his well-being.

'Do you think you could make some enquiries for me in order to find out what's happened to him?' she asked me when I visited her in the November.

'I might be able to,' I responded, not wanting to disappoint her. 'There's a former colleague in my old department who I could speak to.'

Once I'd left her, however, I had second thoughts. Asking for a favour of this nature might raise eyebrows; equally, I might end up being the bearer of bad news. In the end I decided to put it off and make my excuses to Aliza.

By the end of 1942 it was apparent to me that the tide of war was turning against us with our army in full retreat in North Africa and bogged down in an ever more terrible conflict in Russia. After the events of July, Aliza was also understandably more apprehensive. I tried to play down her fears, but in truth, every time I paid her one of my monthly visits, I had to prepare myself for the worst. By early February there was also no disguising the fact that we'd suffered a dreadful reversal in the battle for Stalingrad and I was now convinced that the war would eventually be lost. I didn't admit as much to Clara, but when I paid Aliza a visit I didn't hesitate to share my pessimism with her.

'So how much longer do you think the war will last?' she asked me as we sat in her kitchen drinking tea together.

'That may well depend on when the British and Americans are ready to mount an invasion of Europe. I can envisage them invading Italy before the year is out, and the Italian army will then collapse like a pack of cards. It's only efficient against a foe that doesn't fight back. All the same, Italy is a mountainous country and easily defended. What matters far more is when the British and Americans will consider themselves strong enough to invade France as well, and that I can't say. Assuming, though, that they successfully mount an invasion by, say the spring of next year, then I can see us being defeated within another nine months. Of course, the greatest threat must be from Russia. If we're forced into headlong retreat then their armies could be in striking distance of Berlin within a year. I expect that would result in the mother of all battles. It could last weeks, even months.'

'So, whatever happens, the war will go on for more than another year?'

'I think so, but that's just my opinion, of course.'

'Still plenty of time for me and the girls to be taken away,' she said gloomily. 'You know my nerves are more and more on edge. I worry so much about Max; I don't suppose you've had any success in finding out what's happened to him?'

I shook my head. 'I'm sorry, no…'

'And whenever there's a knock on the door, or I hear shouting, or someone running up the stairs, I'm frightened that we're about to be taken away. It's got to the point that I'm not sleeping well, thinking every time I go to bed that they'll come for us at dawn.'

Realising how real the risk was, I decided that the best comfort I could offer was to simply stretch out a hand and place it on hers. 'And you know, I pray every night that you and your girls will be spared.'

'Thank you, Otto, I appreciate that. She then leant towards me and kissed me on the cheek. Such an intimate exchange of gestures seemed to set every nerve in my body on edge and I wanted to take her in my arms. Yet again, however, fate seemed to be against me as we were interrupted by Zara and I was soon looking at my watch, realising that I'd already stayed longer than intended.

'God go with you, Otto,' she said softly.

'And with you, Aliza, until we meet again.'

*****

By the end of February 1943, it was common knowledge that there had been another round-up of Jews in Berlin and this time on a scale that far outweighed the numbers taken the previous year. Again I decided to visit Aliza's apartment without further delay, utterly dreading what I might find, and this time there was to be no reprieve.

Aliza's front door had been daubed with paint and this was enough to tell me the worst, although I still went through the motions of knocking loudly. Of course, there was no response. At first I just felt numb and slowly walked away, but I'd barely reached the street when I realised I was in tears.

*****

Over the course of the next few days I was in something of a daze, finding it hard to concentrate either on my work or more mundane matters at home.

I had been uncomfortably aware of the existence of concentration camps since the 1930s as a means of incarcerating political opponents of the Reich and certain other so called undesirables. That Max had ended up in Sachsenhausen had not therefore come as much of a surprise me once his political activism as a Zionist fell so much out of favour. When it came to the Jewish population at large, however, I clung to the hope that they were merely being resettled in the East following the conquest of Poland and large swathes of Russia. Certainly, this was the message which was being sold to the German people by Goebbels very own Reich Ministry, for which, of course, I worked. All the same, I remained fearful that this portrayal was but a euphemism for herding them into ghettos where they could all too easily be allowed to starve.

Once again I decided to resort to the same tactic I had employed two years previously. I would be brave and go straight to the top, asking for a reassurance from none other than Reich Minister Goebbels. Admittedly, my personal meetings with him had become less frequent than they had once been, but fortunately I knew that I was due to see him again before the end of the month and found myself counting the days.

When I entered his office he was very much his usual confident and assured self despite the fact that the war was no longer going in our favour and as an intelligent man he must have had considerable fears for the future of the Reich, whatever was said to the contrary in public. If anything, our personal relationship had also continued to strengthen with the passage of time so I felt more relaxed than on the previous occasion about raising the matter with him that was of such concern to me once we had concluded the purpose of our meeting.

'Forgive me, Minister,' I began, 'but you'll recall, I hope, that rather delicate matter I raised with you a couple of years ago. Of course, we agreed to forget about our conversation, and I hesitate to raise it again, but you see the woman I spoke of has now been taken from Berlin, and I must confess I'm most concerned for her welfare.'

'Ah yes, Otto, I remember,' he responded without any hint of displeasure. 'She's that pretty Jewess you like so much, isn't she?'

I could tell he was practically smirking at me, which made me feel slightly uncomfortable. '… We were friends, Minister.'

'I'm sure you were,' he said with a grin, leaning back in his chair. 'So, how can I help you?'

'I would be grateful for some reassurance, Minister. Our policy of resettlement of Jews in the East, is it progressing well, are they being provided for?'

'Of course, Otto, let me assure you their needs are being taken care of.' 'They're on farms then, Minister?'

'You need not doubt it. Naturally, they've been put to work, both for their own benefit and for the greater good…'

At this point he stood up and went and looked out of the window before becoming more expansive. 'Look Otto, I understand your concern but let me make it plain that what we are accomplishing is a revolution. The Fuhrer has been in power for a mere ten years and think what he has achieved! Honest pure blood German were starving in the streets in January '33, our nation was the victim of the Versailles Treaty and the International Jewish conspiracy. Now we have rid ourselves of that pernicious influence for ever and are masters of Europe.'

I could not disagree whilst it would have been impolitic of me to have made any mention of our terrible defeats both in Russia and North Africa. I therefore thanked the Minister for both his time and the reassurance he had been able to give and left feeling that, although life was hardly going to be easy for Aliza and her children on some farm in the middle of nowhere, at least they should not be starving.

In the months to come I continued to seek comfort in Goebbels' reassuring words. Meanwhile, however, the war continued to go against us with the invasion of Sicily by British and American troops in July and then the mainland of Italy in September. Furthermore, the bitter fighting on the Russian front went on unabated with little to show for it on either side, leaving me with a nagging concern for Aliza in case she were to become the innocent victim of some savage Russian advance.

Worse was to come in the autumn when the bombing of Berlin by the British intensified. Gone now were the days when Berliners could take a relaxed stroll in the Tiergarten or down the Unter Den Linden, imagining that on a day-to-day basis life could for the most part continue much as it had before the war. We were now very much a nation under siege and it seemed quite preposterous to me that we could ever have imagined we could prevail once so many powerful nations united against us.

17

Berlin, early February 1944

'Clara, you really must leave. The city's become too dangerous. If not for my sake then at least for Leopold's.'

I was trying to be as insistent as possible but Clara could, as you may have noticed, be extraordinarily stubborn at times.

'I don't want to leave you, Otto, don't you understand that? And surely we are still safe enough here. No bombs have fallen within what...half a kilometre at least.'

'Not yet, but they will sooner or later, and do you think it's fair on Leopold that we should have to spend night after night in the cellar?'

'He enjoys it, you know he does?'

'Do I? I'm not so sure. And anyway if this house received a direct hit I doubt if the cellar would afford us enough protection. At the very least we would probably have to be dug out. Do you really want to put Leopold through that?'

'No, I suppose not.'

'Take him to the country, please. After all, we have our house in the Black Forest and you'll both be completely safe there.'

'Oh very well.'

I sighed with relief. Clara threw her arms around me. I looked down into her eyes and could see how tearful they'd become. Her face was ageing but she was still attractive to me and it pained me to see her in such obvious distress.

'I don't want to be shut away in the country,' she complained. 'I'm a city person, you know that.'

'Of course, but it has to be for the best.'

She nodded lamely.

'And who's going to tell Leopold?' she asked me.

'I will.'

'He'll miss you.'

Now it was my turn to feel upset. Leopold – who was now ten years old - and I were close and I didn't welcome the prospect of being separated from him. I looked away for a moment, my eyes concentrating on the snow-covered lawn outside.

'And will it ever be safe to return to Berlin again, I wonder?' Clara asked.

'Not while the war lasts, I'm afraid.'

'… which could still be years, couldn't it?'

'… Possibly.'

Even Clara, fiercely patriotic though she was, had recently begun to recognise that Germany now faced the possibility of defeat. I, for my part, knew that it was inevitable and continued to blame this, above all, on the increasingly disastrous war against Russia.

'So you think it could be over even sooner?'

'That depends on when the British and Americans invade France. They will, probably do so in the spring.'

'But they will be thrown back into the sea, surely?'

'I'd like to think so, but if they are not then….'

'It could be over in less than a year?'

'Perhaps, after all this war has already lasted longer than the last one.'

'We must never surrender to the communists, never!' Clara asserted vehemently.

'Nor will we, but invasion on two fronts would crush us anyway.'

'It's all just too depressing.'

'I agree, but I'm sure you and Leopold will be safe in the Black Forest, whatever happens.'

'I'd better go and pack then.'

'You can take the Mercedes. It has a tank full of petrol and I can give you some canisters full to the brim as well. It'll give you as much as you should need for the journey.'

'Will you speak to Leopold now?'

'Yes.'

'I'll call him then.'

I nodded, although, even as I did so, I felt my courage desert me. In the last war I had faced machine guns but having to tell my only child that I was sending him and his mother away suddenly seemed an equally daunting task.

As Leopold entered the study I was reminded of how much like his mother he was in appearance, blonde, good looking, in every way seemingly the type of Aryan youth that the Party eulogised. He was, though, also shy, serious, and over-protected by his mother, causing me to regret that Clara and I had not had more children.

'Leopold, my boy, do come in. I've got something important to tell you.'

'What is that father?'

I cleared my throat. 'For safety's sake, your mother and I

have decided it would be best if the two of you left Berlin for a while.'

'But not you as well, father?'

'No, Leopold, I'm afraid it isn't possible. I must remain at my post.'

Leopold was totally crestfallen and lowered his eyes. 'Then I won't go, father,' he insisted stubbornly, pouting his lip as he spoke and clearly on the verge of tears.

I placed a hand on his shoulder. 'Look at me, Leopold.'

'Yes, father.'

'I only said for a while. When the bombing stops you'll be able to return. Until then you must promise me to be brave and support your mother.'

'And when will the bombing end, father?'

'Not too long. The Luftwaffe will soon gain the upper hand, I'm sure. Now I want you to help your mother pack.'

'Are we going immediately then, father?'

'Not today, it's already too late, but tomorrow morning straight after breakfast.'

At these words, Leopold began to cry and threw his arms around me.

'I'll come and see you as soon as I can,' I told him reassuringly before offering a handkerchief. 'Now come, wipe away those tears for me, and be a brave boy.'

'Yes, father,' he mumbled.

The three of us spent one more night together in the cellar. It was inevitably a cold, dark, cramped environment, but I couldn't help reflecting on how lonely it would also seem once Clara and Leopold had departed. I struggled to get to sleep but eventually must have done so because the bang that went off certainly woke me. I immediately sat up, startled by the sheer ferocity of the explosion, which had also instantly woken both Clara and Leopold.

'That sounded terribly close,' Clara said in alarm.

She had barely spoken the words before I heard another even louder bang.

'And that one even closer,' I commented. The noise reminded me of my time in the trenches and of having to take cover during periods of heavy bombardment. Comradeship had helped to see me through that experience and I was pleased on this occasion to be able to offer comfort to Leopold as he snuggled up next to me. There then came a noise that seemed to be almost on top of us.

'That's blown out the windows, for certain,' I remarked, trying to sound as relaxed as possible although in truth I felt increasingly apprehensive.

'I'm frightened, father,'

'It's all right Leopold, we are safe here.'

'*Unless we get a direct hit, of course*,' I thought, but did not say. If I had had any doubts about insisting that Clara and Leopold leave Berlin what was now happening above us had dispelled these completely. My one regret was not having persuaded her to leave even sooner.

We heard yet more bangs but, fortunately, none as close and after a while nothing at all. The raid had ended so at last I was able to fall again into a troubled sleep. By dawn I was awake, curious but at the same time afraid to see what damage had been inflicted, both on the house above us and those close by.

We found that all but one window had been blown out, as I feared would be the case, and then Clara gasped in sheer horror.

'The house next door; look, it's nothing but a pile of rubble!'

'We've certainly had a lucky escape, I agree.'

'I'm not leaving you!' Clara exclaimed.

'Nonsense, you've got to go for Leopold's sake; now more than ever in fact.'

'But I can't bear the thought of leaving you here on your own. Next time….'

'You won't be here and I'll be safe enough. It's no worse than being in the trenches.'

It was Clara's turn to throw her arms around me and I held her tight before our lips met in a lingering kiss.

'I hate this war,' she whispered in my ear causing me to draw in my breath with surprise at the expression of any such sentiment.

'You know, this is the first time in more than four years of conflict that you've made such an admission. In fact I thought you were still an enthusiastic supporter of the war.'

'No, not any more, it's becoming too awful. I never imagined that it would come to this. You thought it would though, didn't you?'

'I've had that fear for quite a long time, yes. As soon as America entered the war I knew we couldn't expect to fight and win on two fronts.'

'I see that now.'

'I've also had plenty of experience of the devastating effect of high explosives,' I added, pointing with my right hand towards the ruins of our neighbour's house. 'So now you and Leopold must go, you really must. I'll be all right, I promise.'

Clara merely nodded and within the hour, she and Leopold were ready to leave. Inevitably, the parting was a painful one, for all that I considered it a necessity. After Clara and Leopold had finally driven away from the house, and I'd waved a last farewell to them, I felt an overwhelming sense of loneliness, bordering on despair.

18

With Clara and Leopold's departure I found myself thinking even more intensely about dear Aliza's fate. I still clung to the belief that she ought to be safe but the image that Goebbels had given me the previous spring no longer seemed so comforting in the dead of winter. I imagined dear Aliza, along with her daughters, huddled together without warmth and with dwindling supplies of the bare necessities of life and hoped that in fact they were able to enjoy the comfort of a warm fire together with ample amounts of nourishing food. I also still had that nagging fear that they might be at risk from the Russians but tried to find comfort in the thought that in all probability they were a hundred miles or more behind the Eastern front and therefore far safer from the threat of bombs than I was.

Berlin, in the midst of this cruel war and aerial bombardment, had become a deeply depressing - and also of course extremely dangerous - place in which to live. Increasingly, I recognised fear in the eyes of its remaining population, much as I remembered seeing fear in the eyes of my fellow soldiers on the western front. There were shortages, too, of everything and even one decent meal a day had become a luxury to be savoured. More and more restaurants had inevitably either shut down or been bombed out, although for the time being at least the Heising restaurant was still able to open its doors.

The place felt like some haven of civilisation and peace to me, and I regularly ate lunch there. I was still troubled sometimes by the memory of the meeting I'd had with Aliza there, but that alone was never enough to keep me away. I had my favourite table after all, the food served was still tolerable, and having eaten, I invariably smoked a cigarette and sought to relax for a little while before making my way back to my office.

Of course, the restaurant was often crowded, usually with quite prominent members of the party and of government, and one lunch time, not long after Clara and Leopold's departure, as I sat eating my lunch there, I looked up and saw a familiar face coming towards me. There was a look of mutual recognition in the man's eyes as well.

'Baron, it's good to see you again. I trust you are well?'

'Yes, quite well, thank you,' I responded guardedly as we shook hands. 'It's been a long time. I see you're an Oberstarmbannfuhrer now,' I added, glancing at his uniform.

'Yes, I have that honour. May I join you?'

I allowed a hint of a smile to cross my face. 'By all means.'

I had never warmed to Eichmann, and didn't regard his sudden appearance as the most welcome of surprises, but it wasn't in my nature to be either rude or offhand.

'So, what are you doing these days?' Eichmann asked me in a friendly fashion, so I proceeded to explain.

'Oh, I'm still in charge of the press office of the department of film. I must say that in comparison with so many, I've had a quiet war. What about yourself? Your rank must go with particular responsibilities.'

'I'm still involved in Jewish affairs.'

'Really; in what capacity exactly?'

'I'm in charge of transportation administration.'

'You mean transportation for our political opponents to work camps?'

Eichmann gave a nod. 'Yes, indeed.'

Seeing a waiter approaching I requested some coffee while Eichmann ordered himself a meal.

As I recall, Eichmann did not say much else; he seemed more interested in his Wiener Schnitzel than in talking to me, as indeed I have no doubt he was. I do, however, remember one remark of his which he voiced over his strawberry cake and whipped cream and his coffee. 'Otto, I know that deep down you see Jews as fellow Germans, but they are not. They are vermin, and I am sure you are aware that vermin can only have one fate.'

'What do you mean?' I asked.

But he merely sipped at his coffee and said nothing.

As I made my way home, first by tram and then on foot, I kept thinking with utter horror of Aliza's fate, and that of the many prominent Jews in the Zionist movement, whom I had come to know. Some had settled in Israel or fled to other corners of Europe where they remained safe, but by no means all; and many including Max, could well now be dead.

After I had cooked myself a light meal and eaten it, I sat at my desk with a cigarette in one hand and a glass of whisky in the other, asking myself, over and over, *how has it come to this?* What Eichmann had said to me had been enough to shatter my illusion that Aliza and her daughters were relatively safe somewhere. The truth of the matter, I was now convinced, was that Goebbels had lied to me and that it was far more likely that they had been sent to a concentration camp just as Max had been.

I'd once foolishly believed in the National Socialist cause, in racial purity, at least in theory, although increasingly less so in practice, and I had been as swept away as any man by the Fuhrer's charisma, but nothing I decided could justify the herding of tens of thousands of human beings into camps. It was, I felt, completely unacceptable, and Eichmann's use of the word *vermin* had naturally given me a deep fear that something even more terrible was being committed and that the inmates were being allowed to starve or worse.

By the following morning I had made up my mind to try and establish if Aliza was still alive. I had thought before of approaching a former colleague in the Jewish Bureau, when Aliza had asked me to try and find out what had happened to Max, only to reject the idea. This time I knew that I had no choice but to do so and a few hours later I was able to make contact with him. Fortunately, I didn't experience too much difficult in persuading him to help me. We had always got on well, he was sympathetic when I took him into my confidence about Aliza being an old friend, and, as I had hoped, told me he had access to the information I was seeking.

19

Thuringia, East Germany, April 1944

'Otto, wake up, we're nearly there.'

I flinched and sat bolt upright. I was instantly annoyed with myself for nodding off. It wasn't something I usually did in the back of a car but it had been a long drive from Berlin and I had not slept well the night before.

I looked about me and could see nothing but trees on either side of the road. There was still snow lying in some places too and we were going uphill.

'How long have I been asleep for?' I asked my fellow passenger, Head of the Department of Film, Reichsamtsleiter Arnold Rastner, a quite jovial individual, with whom I got on well.

'Not long. Look, there are the camp gates, just ahead of us.'

I leaned forward in my seat and ahead of me saw that we had indeed reached our intended destination, Buchenwald concentration camp.

It was my first visit to this or any other such camp, having persuaded Rastner that I be allowed to accompany him. My discreet enquiries had finally borne fruit when I had received a telephone call from my former colleague informing me that Aliza Geisser was still alive and an inmate of this very camp. Had I not learnt that the Department would be filming there, I doubt that I would have been able to do anything more. But as soon as I knew, I just felt an increasing compulsion to satisfy myself that the conditions in which she was being held were not too terrible and she still had some hope of survival. Quite how I was going to find her in a camp holding thousands of inmates was quite another matter, but I had been given some hope when my former colleague had told me that the number of women being held in the camp was only a few hundred. Boldly, I also made up my mind that I was willing, if necessary, to resort to bribery to try and keep her safe from further harm.

In a matter of a few minutes we reached the Camp Commandant's house where our car pulled up and we both got out. I was pleased to stretch my legs, but despite the heavy overcoat that I was wearing, I immediately felt chilled by the freezing winter air.

'Welcome to Buchenwald, gentlemen, I trust you had a pleasant journey.'

It was the Camp Commandant himself, going out of his way to come and greet us at the steps of his house and to shake hands. As introductions were made I noted that the Commandant was an SS officer and also, by the look of him, in his mid-forties. But there, I hoped, any similarity ended for I was quickly struck by his cold and arrogant demeanour. His complexion was almost unnaturally pale and his features, especially his lips, too thinly drawn to be attractive.

'Can I offer you some refreshment?' the Commandant asked us once we had entered the warmth of his office. 'I still have some excellent coffee.'

'Thank you, that would be most welcome,' Rastner responded and I concurred.

The Commandant then offered to take us on a tour of the

camp and as soon as we had drunk our coffees he proceeded to do so. My first impression was that it was in good order and the buildings well maintained. There was also little sign of any of the inmates whom the Commandant confirmed were made up of a large percentage of communists and similar undesirables. However, I was increasingly struck by the sheer size of the place.

'How many persons does the camp currently hold?' I asked the Commandant casually.

'We now have about twenty thousand here; mostly men.'

'Really, that many?'

'Certainly, and that number is growing all the time. I am concerned about overcrowding with more Poles and Russians arriving.'

'The place seems very quiet to me,' I commented.

'That's because the majority of the inmates are at work in nearby factories,' the Commandant explained sharply. 'They are not brought here to be idle.'

'No, and nor should they be,' Rastner replied, just as brusquely.

'So it's just a work camp then?' I asked, trying to sound as indifferent as possible.

The Commandant eyed me somewhat coldly, I thought, before replying. 'That's its primary function, yes.'

'And the women you hold here are made to work as well as the men?' I also asked.

'Some of them, yes.'

After about twenty minutes looking around, the Commandant indicated that there was nothing more of interest to show us and began to lead us back to his house. In so doing we passed a nondescript wooden hut, much like so many others, but I happened to notice a woman looking out at me from one of its windows. She appeared young and quite pretty with un-cropped hair and I was close enough to her to judge that she was wearing lipstick, which startled me. The Commandant noticed her too and she immediately moved away from the window.

'That is the camp brothel,' he explained with a slight look of embarrassment on his face. 'Reichsfuhrer Himmler considered it necessary to introduce them into camps such as this to discourage homosexual practices.'

Rastner guffawed. 'Yes, I had heard that. And how many ladies do you have here?'

Again the Commandant looked embarrassed. 'I'm not sure, perhaps thirty.' I wondered if this was what he had meant by some women inmates being put to work.

'And with twenty thousand men they are kept very busy, no doubt?' Rastner responded with a lascivious grin on his face.

'They're not for the pleasure of any inmate, only those who have earned certain privileges. They receive regular health checks as well.'

'Very wise, I'm sure.'

Rastner looked at me as he spoke and we exchanged smiles. The Commandant, however, was clearly not so amused, and quickened his pace, his prickliness merely confirming my unfavourable impression of him.

That evening we had dinner with the Commandant as his guests and were joined at the dinner table by his rather shrew-like wife and also his lugubrious faced Deputy, whose name was Muhler. Conversation was at first constrained, but there were two good bottles of wine on the table, and as their contents were consumed tongues were loosened. Inevitably conversation centred on the war, the increasing number of air raids, and what was happening on the Eastern front.

'I fear we are losing this war,' Rastner confessed once we had finished our meal, to looks of consternation from the Commandant and his wife. I was in total agreement with Rastner but could tell from our host's reaction that he probably regarded such talk as treasonably defeatist.

'We have suffered some unfortunate reverses, nothing more,' the Commandant insisted.

'No, it is far worse than that,' Rastner retorted. "We were defeated in North Africa, we're on the defensive in Italy, and we're being defeated in Russia. Furthermore, we are increasingly unable to protect our cities from bombing from the air, and just as in the last war we shall soon have to contend with the full might of America.'

'Defeat is simply unthinkable,' the Commandant shot back. 'We are locked in a titanic struggle but our cause is just and we will triumph in the end!'

Rastner simply shook his head. 'Really, Commandant, I wish I had your confidence.'

I was used to Rastner's cynical tone but others round the table were simply shocked into an uncomfortable silence.

'So, what do you do for amusement in the evening in this place?' Rastner suddenly asked breezily after a few moments, looking straight at the Commandant, and apparently oblivious to any offence he might have caused. I knew as well that he was easily bored.

The Commandant hesitated to respond and it was his Deputy, Muhler, who did so.

'There's the mess. The beer is good.'

'Well, I'm all for a drink. Will you come, Otto?'

'I'm feeling rather tired.'

'Oh, come on, we needn't stay long.'

'All right then.'

Muhler offered to accompany us, and after perfunctorily thanking the Commandant and his wife for their hospitality, we made our way to the mess.

'I couldn't wait to get out of there,' Rastner whispered to me. 'The Commandant and his wife are such prigs, don't you agree?'

I nodded in confirmation. 'My thought entirely, Arnold.'

We soon approached our destination and I could hear the sound of singing coming from within. As we then entered the mess, I was struck by how crowded it was with an atmosphere thick with tobacco smoke. I noticed, too, where the singing was coming from as there were several men standing around a piano.

I couldn't help raising my eyebrows when I realised that there were three women with them as well, wearing make-up, and with long hair.

Rastner then nudged me. 'They're from the brothel, I assume.'

'Yes, they are,' Muhler responded. 'If the Commandant knew they were here there would be trouble but I've no intention of enlightening him.'

Muhler then gave us both a conspiratorial grin that belied the expression he had worn on his face over dinner. I was pleased to note that he seemed a far more personable individual than the Commandant. All the same, I still couldn't help wondering what atrocities the man might have witnessed, or even been responsible for against inmates of the camp.

I started to yawn, realising that I was feeling sleepy, and after one drink I persuaded Rastner to return to the Commandant's house where we were to stay the night before filming commenced the following day.

*****

It was as I was standing around in the morning sunshine waiting for filming to commence that my luck turned and I finally caught sight of Aliza

She was standing in line amongst a group of perhaps fifty women, from whom a roll call was being taken, but I still recognised her immediately. She was grimacing, too, her eyes somehow cold and distant, and I was conscious of how thin she was with her cropped hair and stripped inmates' uniform.

'My God,' I said under my breath.

'Are you All right?' Rastner asked me. 'You look shocked.'

'It's nothing, really.'

It was at that moment that she appeared to see me, too, for the first time. She was instantly startled and put her hand to her mouth.

'Otto, Otto.' It was Rastner speaking into my ear. 'You know that woman, don't you?'

'Yes, yes I do. It was before the war, a long time ago now. That she should be here, of all places.'

'I assume she's one of your old Zionist acquaintances, Otto?'

'Yes, that's right. We visited Palestine together. I must speak to her.'

'That could raise a few eyebrows, I expect. Don't worry, though, it's easily done.'

Rastner then turned and spoke to the Deputy Commandant. 'Muhler, The Baron here recognises one of the women inmates standing over there.'

'Yes, what of it?'

'He would like a word with her...in private. Is there a room here he could use?'

'There's an office nearby. But it would be thoroughly irregular.'

'So was allowing the prostitutes into the mess last night. I'm sure you can make some suitable excuse, can't you?'

Muhler hesitated. 'What, now?'

Rastner glanced at me and I merely nodded.

'Yes, if you would be so kind,' Rastner then replied.

'Oh, very well.'

I watched as Muhler went over to where Aliza was standing and I felt my stomach turn over. She was looking straight at me, her face expressionless, but her eyes, I sensed, full of pain. I rarely feel self-conscious in a crowd but as she began to walk towards me it was as if every eye was on us both and I coloured a little.

I muttered my thanks to Rastner. 'I'll only be a few minutes.'

'Take your time, Otto. We'll just get on with our job.'

Muhler then led us towards the office and within moments had left us on our own, shutting the door discreetly behind him as he left. I felt that my mouth was very dry and I realised that I was in a complete state of shock.

'It's good to see you again, Otto,' Aliza said, calmly enough. Her eyes though suggested that she was as fearful as a wounded animal and now that we were so close I could see how bloodshot they were. Nothing either could disguise how tired her face seemed, especially under the eyes and around the mouth.

'Aliza...I'm so glad I've found you. Have you been here long?'

'Just a few weeks; prior to that I was in Ravensbruck. My only consolation is that one of my children is still with me. That's Bathsheba, my oldest. She's now fourteen. Zara died in Ravensbruck nearly four months ago.' There was an almost hysterical edge to her words and tears started to well up in her eyes.

'I'm so sorry,' I responded gently.

'And have you also made enquiries about Max?'

I shook my head. 'No, but I could still try and do so.'

'Well, I expect he's dead by now,' she said bitterly, 'and even if you could, you'd still have to find a way to pass that information onto me.'

'That could be managed, I expect, but what's most important to me is that you're still alive. When I succeeded in tracing you and then discovered that the Department would filming here, just propaganda, of course, I asked its Head if I might accompany him. I feigned nothing more than idle curiosity but I really wanted to find you.'

'... Well, now you have,' she said flatly before staring at me coldly. 'You know it's your government and the policies that you support that put me here. I told you once before that you're the acceptable face of an evil system, and nothing has changed!'

I flinched. 'You have every right to hate me, I know.'

'Yes, I do, don't I, but I can't bring myself to. I was always too fond of you.'

'And I of you.'

She smiled a little. 'That was only too obvious. How it made your wife mad. Not that I blame her, of course. How is she by the way?'

'As well as can be expected, I think. The bombing raids on Berlin having been getting worse, but I managed to persuade her to take Leopold to the Black Forest. He's well, thank goodness.'

There was then an awkward silence between us and I felt lost for words.

'Well, I suppose I should be grateful that you decided to find me,' she said at last. 'You could very easily have decided to forget about me given what I've become. You could have me, too, now if you wanted me. After all, I've been raped before…'

'Aliza!'

'I'm sorry, but it's true.' With that her face became contorted and I could tell that she was on the verge of tears once more. I fumbled in one of my trouser pockets for a handkerchief and offered it to her but she refused it.

'I don't really cry any more, you know. I used to, of course, but I thought they had dried up. Look, I know I've begged you to help me before and I'm begging you now, again. Save me from this hell, please, save me!'

Clenching her hands together in supplication, she was now on her knees to me.

'Please, I beg you, please!'

Her voice had now become loud and demanding, and the tears were flowing. I felt embarrassed, imagining her cries being overheard. She was my temptress, my conscience, and I had come here in the hope that I might be able to do something to protect her.

'I'll do what I can, I swear it.'

She allowed me to lift her onto her feet and suddenly she was clinging to me. The warmth of her body shot through me like a bolt of electricity and I held her tight. I confess that I even felt an urge to kiss her but her face was turned away from me, resting on my shoulder.

'I'm sorry Aliza, really, really sorry.'

Still she clung to me, resisting my attempt to gently prise myself apart from her. It struck me what a wretched parody it was of how we had danced together all those years before. I felt almost completely overwhelmed and let my body sag

'I must go now,' I said to her at last. 'But I promise you, I'll do all I can to keep you safe.'

She nodded and stepped away from me. I thought I saw that old affection for me in her eyes, I momentarily touched her left cheek with my right hand, and then turned and walked from the room.

With my head bowed I quickly walked away, ignoring Rastner, who I knew had only meant well. I felt unnerved, emotional, almost in pain, and over and over again the same words kept echoing through my brain, *the acceptable face of an evil system and nothing has changed.*

Except that is that I had made her a promise; or at least a promise of sorts because I still really didn't know that I could do that much to protect her.

20

Later the same month

The Saturday of the annual reunion dinner of my wartime regimental battalion had arrived. It was an event I always looked forward to, bringing with it the opportunity to meet old comrades-in-arms with whom I had forged a special bond, albeit that a quarter of a century had now elapsed since the end of the supposed war to end all wars.

Because of the continuing bombing it was to be a lunch time rather than an evening affair. However, we were still able to use the same Berlin hotel in which we had been meeting for the best part of twenty years, and, despite the war, most of those who had been able to regularly attend every year had been able to do so this time.

As I had made my way to the hotel at around midday, I had noted that it was warmer than of late and that there was a feeling of spring in the air. Normally this would have given me pleasure, but on this occasion it merely accentuated my fear that an allied invasion of France might only be a matter of weeks away.

Upon entering the hotel the first person I set eyes on was my one time Battalion Commander, Conrad Wertheim, a tall, robust man, now a leading industrialist, and in his mid fifties.

We greeted each other with genuine affection and, as happened every year, I was quickly swept along in a round of salutations and handshakes with other former comrades.

As I'd anticipated, with a rapidly growing sense of dread, conversation was dominated by news of the current conflict.

'It feels just like nineteen eighteen all over again,' Conrad commented sadly as we drank aperitifs while waiting to be seated for our meal. 'Don't you agree, Otto?'

'I fear that it may be a lot worse than that, Conrad. At least that year began well.'

'With the defeat of the Russians, you mean?'

'Yes, of course, whereas this time…' I allowed my voice to trail away in gloomy introspection.

'This time we shall fight to the death,' declared Albrecht Voss, formerly an Oberleutnant in the company I commanded, who was standing next to me. He had always been a proud man, I reflected; fiercely patriotic, and driven literally to tears by the nineteen eighteen defeat. How many more might he now have to shed, I wondered ruefully.

'Yes, I fear that we will,' I replied.

'Enough of this defeatist talk, gentlemen,' Wilhelm Veits, another party to our conversation, insisted. Like me, he was a former Company Commander. 'If the Americans and British attempt to invade France they will be thrown back into the sea.'

'You were forever the optimist, Wilhelm. As I recall, you remained convinced that we would still capture Paris in 1918, even after we were forced to retreat back into Belgium.'

This kindly rebuke from Conrad brought smiles to everyone's faces and within moments, we were summoned to take our seats in the hotel's palatial dining room. At first the mood of the occasion seemed especially sombre to me. Of course there was the usual toast to our fallen comrades, which never failed to bring back sad memories, but this was deepened by the announcement that one member of our Battalion had been recently killed in an air raid. The toast to the Fuhrer and cries of *Heil Hitler* also struck me as being more muted than in past years. Soon the steady flow of alcohol then began to have its inevitable effect and voices all around me became louder and more animated.

After a while, I rose from my table to visit the lavatory and was immediately followed there by Conrad.

'Can I speak to you in confidence, Otto?' The words were almost whispered and I had to strain my ears to hear what he was saying to me. 'Not now,' he added, 'we must return to our table, of course, but later. It is important.'

My curiosity was naturally aroused. 'Why, of course, would you like to come back to my house? You would be welcome, and with Clara and Leopold presently in the Black Forest, as I mentioned to you earlier, the place is empty.'

'Thank you; that would be ideal.'

'Good luck with your speech by the way; it must get harder for you every year.'

'Yes, and this year in particular, I fear. Remember, though, that many of our company are too much in their cups by now to take in much of what I say and probably just as many will have largely forgotten anything I may have said in previous years.'

'True enough.'

In the event Conrad made a short, witty speech, which struck me as being fairly original, and made no reference to the dire straits in which our nation now found itself until the very end.

'Gentlemen, it has been an honour and a privilege to be in your company today and, God willing, I look forward to our all meeting again next year. The Fatherland is in peril, but it will prevail. *Heil Hitler!*'

With that Conrad gave the Nazi salute and everyone rose to do the same.

An hour later he was relaxing in front of a fire, in my study, with a glass of brandy in his hand.

'It's good of you to agree to this meeting, Otto. You know, I don't believe for a moment that our nation is going to prevail. That was just bullshit to encourage the troops. It's heading for disaster, I'm afraid.'

'You said as much before we had our meal.'

'…And you didn't disagree with me.'

'No, I didn't, but tell me what is it that you wanted to talk to me about in such confidence?'

'You're still a member of the SS?'

'Yes, although, as you may recall, I have only ever been a member of the Reiter Corp. That's never really been more than a social club and now we have very few members left.'

'…And still loyal to the Fuhrer?'

'Naturally, but why do you ask?'

'Don't you think that he has got this country into the mess it is in?'

I looked long and hard at my old Commander. 'It strikes me that what you are beginning to say has the whiff of treason about it. The Fuhrer is above criticism, as you well know.'

'Rubbish, Otto, no man is above criticism, and this country

faces nothing but catastrophe because that trumped up little corporal believes he is God almighty and Frederick the Great to boot. He has to be got rid of and quickly, don't you see that?'

'I could report you for talk like this, Conrad.'

'But you won't, will you?'

'No, not on this occasion as you are an old, dear friend, and I invited you here so that we could speak in confidence. However, if you wish to continue to take this conversation in the direction in which I believe you are travelling, I would prefer it that we brought it to an end and that you to left now. I will then forget what you have just said as I am sure will you.'

He sighed. 'I take it that you are not open to persuasion then?'

'Not on a matter of treason, certainly not.'

'I will leave then.' With that he gulped down the remainder of his brandy and got to his feet.

'He will be got rid of, you know,' he insisted.

'I do not want to hear this, Conrad, but this I will say, please, for God's sake, don't embroil yourself in treasonable acts against the State. You will end up being arrested and put to death.'

'I am not afraid to die; didn't we risk our lives enough in the last war?'

'Nor am I, and yes we did, but I am also loyal to the Party and to the Fuhrer and I will not become involved in any conspiracies against him.'

'If the Russians win this war you are the one who could end up being put to death, you know.'

I drew in my breath, my mind drawn to Eichmann's revelations. 'Perhaps, but I have done nothing of which I am ashamed.'

Conrad merely held out his hand. 'I'm sorry to have troubled you, Otto, really I am.'

'That's all right Conrad. As I say, our conversation is now forgotten. Just be very careful, though, I beg of you.'

'Don't worry about me Otto, I'll be fine.'

'Let me show you out.'

We shook hands and after Conrad had left I realised just how tired I was. I lounged back on a settee and had an urge to smoke as well so quickly lit a cigarette. The nicotine soothed my nerves a little but I still felt an overwhelming sense of lethargy. I reflected, too, on what a shocking state our country was in when one of my oldest friends was prepared to become involved in a treasonable conspiracy. The very idea made me shudder, not so much with fear as with horror that it should have ever come to this.

After a while I became conscious that the telephone was ringing. It startled me out of a semi-stupor and, getting to my feet as quickly as I could, I rushed into the hall and picked up the receiver.

'Hello…'

'Darling…'

'Clara…'

'You sound half-asleep, are you all right?'

'Yes, just a bit tired. I haven't long got back from the annual Battalion reunion.'

'Did many attend?'

'Yes, far more than I expected. Anyway, how are you?'

'…I'm bored, I want to come home.'

'There are still raids; it isn't safe. And how is Leopold?'

'He's missing you, of course. When can you come and see us?'

'Soon, I promise. I should be able to take a week's leave next month…'

We talked on for about another ten minutes about various inconsequential matters without making any mention of the war and all the while all I could really think about was the conversation I had just had with Conrad. It was what I wanted to talk to Clara about but I knew that my lips, on that subject, had to remain sealed.

'I will telephone you again next week,' Clara told me when our conversation had run its course.

'You know you sound awful; are you sure you're all right?'

'Yes, I've told you, I'm just tired. It's the effect of alcohol and good food.'

'I love you.'

'And I you; give Leopold a big kiss for me.'

'I will; goodbye, darling, keep safe.'

'I'll be fine, my love, really I will.'

With that she rang off. I was left feeling an overwhelming sense of loneliness and reflected that Conrad, too, had told me that he would be fine. Such reassuring words, but the truth, I appreciated, could well be very different. Our world was being gradually, inexorably turned upside down, and I feared that every man, woman and child in Germany was now in extreme danger.

Long and hard, I also pondered my conversation with Conrad. I knew that I was as disillusioned as he was with the Fuhrer and the state to which he had brought our country, but I had sworn an oath of allegiance to him and I am a man of my word. I feared, too, that it was already too late to change anything for the better by trying to overthrow the man. The country, I concluded, would just descend into civil war and chaos, the allies would still demand nothing less than unconditional surrender, and the Russians would run amok. Yet I realised as well, that defeat was still only a matter of time anyway and that by fighting on under Hitler the outcome of that unconditional surrender might ultimately be far worse.

Even though I did not feel able to be a party to it, I was therefore left hoping in my heart that any conspiracy against the Fuhrer would succeed.

21

Mid July 1944

I was looking up into the sky and saw, high above, a mass formation of bomber planes approaching. I was frightened and immediately sought shelter. At any moment I expected to hear the sound of explosions as bombs fell but none came. I entered a room and Aliza was there. She seemed relaxed, carefree.

'We must seek cover, quickly, quickly!' I implored her, but she seemed unconcerned, almost indifferent.

'Please, Aliza, please!'

The words seem to echo through my brain as I slowly came to and realized that I had been dreaming. It was morning and the sun was shining through the gap in the curtains. I still had the image before me of the planes approaching and then of Aliza's face. I felt, too, a sense of relief that I'd been able to spend another undisturbed night in the comfort of my own bed. There hadn't been any raids on Berlin now for some time and life was beginning to return to a kind of normality, albeit that a significant proportion of the city lay in ruins.

Clara had been pestering me to be allowed to return but I'd firmly resisted her appeals.

'The bombing will start again, Clara, it's only a matter of

time. For Leopold's sake, you must stay where you are,' I had said very firmly when we had spoken on the telephone only the evening before last.

'But it's been weeks since the last raid; you've admitted that yourself...'

'Yes, but it's only a temporary lull, nothing more, believe me. We are losing the war, Clara, the British and Americans have now invaded France and the Russians are advancing from the East. You are both safest where you are...'

'But I'm bored and lonely without you. Can't you at least come and see us again soon?'

'I'll try; I promise.'

Now as I got out of bed the image of Aliza's face remained in my mind. I continued to trouble me that I had not been able to do enough to help her despite the promise I had made her. I tried to comfort myself with the thought that, however degrading her existence had become, her life should not be in too much danger as there were no gas chambers at Buchenwald. However, I had increasing doubts about her fate, remembering that her younger daughter had already succumbed to disease.

When I returned from the camp I had, at least, not delayed more than a couple of days before deciding on a particular course of action. I'd stared at the telephone on my desk for several seconds before picking up the receiver.

I asked to be put through to Buchenwald concentration camp and after no more than a short delay I heard a woman's voice answer. I promptly asked if I could speak to Deputy Commandant Muhler.

'Who is calling for him, please?'

'Baron Otto von Buren. He should remember me from a

visit I made to your camp recently. You can tell him that it's a personal matter.'

'Please wait.'

After a couple of minutes, I heard the woman's voice again. 'I'm afraid he isn't answering his telephone. Can I take a message?'

I duly left my telephone number and replaced the receiver, feeling a tangible sense of relief that until my call was returned I'd been spared a difficult conversation. I was conscious, too, that if I had been informed that Muhler was no longer in post I would have had to abandon my plan anyway. I then tried to busy myself with my work and was somewhat taken aback when only about ten minutes later the telephone rang and I was informed that the Deputy Commandant was on the line. I took a deep breath.

'It's good of you to return my call so promptly,' I began, trying to sound as relaxed as possible.

'Not at all, Baron, what may I do for you?'

'You may recall that when we visited the camp there was an inmate who I recognised. Her name is Aliza Geisser. You were good enough to allow me to speak to her in private for a short while.'

'Yes, I remember very well.'

'And she is still with you then?'

'Yes, so far as I am aware.'

'We were acquaintances some years before the war, you understand, but I still have some concern for her welfare. May I ask a favour of you?'

'That depends on what it is.'

'Well, could you keep an eye on her for me and let me know

if you ever think her health is at risk or she is likely to be moved to a different camp?'

'The health of all our inmates is at risk.'

'Serious risk, I mean.'

'And what purpose will it achieve if I did agree to tell you?'

'Hum... to be frank I was hoping that you might see what you could do to keep her out of harm's way.'

'But I don't have that power and anyway it would be entirely out of order for me to seek to do so.'

'All the same as Deputy Commandant you must have some authority to...to...assign her and her daughter to lighter duties.'

'Perhaps, but I don't see why I should.'

'I could make it worth your while.'

I heard him draw in his breath. 'Baron, need I remind you that trying to bribe me is a matter for which I could report you.'

'I understand that but all the same I am merely suggesting that I could make you a gift in return for a favour. I am not expecting you to exceed your authority, or act in any way which is improper... Hello, Hello, are you still there?'

'Yes, I am....All right, I will see what I can do so long as it is understood that your gift, as you call it, will be sufficiently generous. I, also, cannot possibly promise the safety of this woman or her daughter.'

'I understand that, and I am most grateful to you. I will give you my home telephone number as well, if I may.'

After Muhler had rung off I ruminated on our conversation, feeling pleased with myself for having found the courage to do something to protect Aliza. Whether it was sufficient, however, was quite another matter, although even as my doubts grew I tried to comfort myself with the reflection that I had at least tried, and, so far as I was able to, kept my word to her.

In the course of the next few weeks it became clearer than ever that the war was being lost on all fronts and my particular fear was of a Russian invasion. It held out for me the prospect of a total bloodbath in which no one of whom the Bolsheviks disapproved would be spared, and I was aware that could well include not just Party officials and SS officers such as myself but anyone involved in operating the concentration camp system. In the ensuing mayhem I worried that even the inmates of these camps might be vulnerable.

Of course, I knew that if there was a successful coup against the Fuhrer such a catastrophe might yet be averted, and a day did not pass without my reflecting on the conversation I'd had with Conrad. I didn't intend to become involved in any acts of treason against the State but I couldn't help wondering if some attempt would soon be made. Finally, one evening, our housekeeper, Frau Solger, asked me if I had heard the news.

'No, what news?' I replied.

'There has been an attempt on the Fuhrer's life, sir. A Wehrmacht Oberst planted a bomb that went off but the Fuhrer was not seriously injured, thank God.'

'How have you heard this?'

'On the radio, sir; it seems the Oberst who planted the bomb along with other conspirators has been arrested. The Fuhrer is to address the nation shortly.'

'I see.' I immediately thought of Conrad and my heart sank. If he was one of those who were arrested then the chances were he would be convicted and executed.

'I'll be going home now, sir, if that's all right…'

I wasn't really listening. I was too lost in thought.

'Excuse me, Sir…'

'Yes, I'm sorry, of course. Have a safe journey home.'

'Thank you, Sir. I'll see you tomorrow then.'

As she let herself out, I realised that I badly needed a cigarette. The thought of one of my oldest friends being arrested by the Gestapo, no doubt put on trial and then hanged left me feeling profoundly shocked. Why had it had to come to this, I kept asking myself. Of course Conrad had been right and the Fuhrer was no more than a jumped up little Corporal with a gift for oratory, but that realisation was of little comfort now. One thing, of which I was certain, was that the invasion of Russia had turned into a total disaster. Worse, too, I couldn't reconcile myself to the mass murder of the Jews and I still shuddered to think of the repercussions of that policy. In time, I expected that every supporter of the National Socialist cause would be called to account for allowing it to happen. I inhaled the nicotine from my cigarette into my lungs but it failed to relax me. Instead, I ran my right hand over my neck and thought again of Conrad swinging from the end of a rope.

After this news I increasingly struggled to shake off a sense of depression bordering on despair, in common, I suspected, with many of my compatriots. This was compounded when only a few days later I received a telephone call from my sister, Freda, who lives near Hamburg, and is a few years my junior. The moment I heard her voice I knew something was wrong as she sounded tearful.

'It's Ernst… he's been killed! I just can't bear it!'

'Freda, I'm so sorry.'

She was crying, almost uncontrollably. Desperately, I did

my best to console her and after a short while gently managed to calm her down. Her husband Ernst had been a good man, perhaps rather strait-laced and unimaginative, but at least honest and full of integrity. I was aware that he had been serving in military operations in France as a Panzer Battalion Commander and between sobs Freda managed to explain that he had been killed in the fighting there.

'How are the children?' I asked her, referring to my nephew and niece, who were twelve and ten respectively. I knew that they would be as devastated as Freda by what had happened as Ernst had always been the best of fathers.

'Not very good. Irene has taken it worse than Franz as you know how devoted she was to her father, but it's hurting both of them terribly. Ernst's mother is in a bad state as well. She's upstairs now with the children. At least we've had each other's shoulders to cry on.'

'Look, I'm able to take some leave soon. I'm going to the Black Forest to be with Clara and Leopold but I'll come to you first of all for a couple of nights, if that's okay?'

'Of course it is. You would be welcome to stay longer. The children would appreciate it especially. You know they are both very fond of you.'

I could see myself becoming more than an uncle to them now that Ernst was dead. Also, I had already made up my mind to give as much support as possible to Freda, with whom I had seldom had a cross word.

'You must try and be brave for the sake of the children,' I told her encouragingly before she rang off. 'And I'll see you soon.'

I was as good as my word and I have since been able to see Freda, Irene, and Franz on a total of two occasions although not since before Christmas; and now… well, having lost her husband, she is now likely to lose a brother too.

I felt, after my telephone conversation with Freda, that a litany of bad news was being visited on me, starting with Conrad's likely arrest and execution, followed closely by her news of Ernst's death. Of course, having been through the last war, I was used to comrades-in-arms dying all the time, but I had hoped never to have to live through such an experience again. I had been as resentful as any man, of Germany's past humiliations, but now my faith in everything I had believed in throughout my life was, I realised, being inexorably shattered, piece-by-piece. The prospect of our country's utter subjugation at the hands of the Russians also caused me to feel an ever increasing sense of dread.

22

Later the same month

'Baron Otto von Buren, I assume?'
'Yes, that's correct, what do you want?'
I had been dozing in an armchair when I suddenly heard a loud banging on the front door. At first I imagined that Frau Solger would answer the door but it slowly dawned on me that she had gone home hours ago. I then glanced at my watch and was taken aback to see that it was now after midnight.

'I'm coming, I'm coming. Who on earth is it at this hour?' I called out irritably and upon answering the door realised that I was being confronted by a man wearing a uniform, which was familiar to me.

'I must ask you to accompany me to headquarters, Baron,' the man responded in answer to my question.

'Am I under arrest?'

'No, Baron, but I have that power should you refuse to accompany me.'

'I see. And what is so urgent that it can't wait until a more civilised hour?'

'I am not at liberty to discuss this with you, Baron. Now...'

'Just give me a few moments to put on my jacket, will you?'

'Of course, Baron.'

A short while later I found myself being driven through the night along the deserted streets of Berlin. We passed many ruined buildings that had an eerie, almost ghost like quality about them. I had never ,for a moment, imagined being taken for questioning by the Gestapo and I could think of only one reason why that should be happening to me. I knew I was extremely tense but did my best not to show it.

When we reached our destination in Prinz-Albrecht-Strasse, the tall edifice of Gestapo headquarters loomed above us in what I felt was a menacing fashion as we walked towards its entrance. I found myself wondering how long I might remain incarcerated within its walls.

I was quickly conveyed inside and taken to a nondescript room in the basement of the building. It was small, and without windows, with just a desk, a couple of chairs, and dimly lit by a single light bulb. The walls were also bare and somewhat grubby but there was an absence of any graffiti on them. I was asked to take a seat and, without another word being spoken, left on my own. And then I waited and waited, feeling increasingly fretful as the minutes ticked by with agonising slowness. If it was all part of some process designed to undermine my self-confidence, I determined to resist this and after a while, feeling increasingly sleepy, even began to doze off once more.

'Baron, good evening to you.'

Suddenly I was wide awake, sitting bolt upright, and I could see that a man wearing the uniform of a Gestapo officer, who I judged to be about forty, had just walked into the room. I also noticed that he was going bald and that he had an air about him of someone who was used to giving orders and being obeyed.

'You will forgive me if I don't introduce myself,' the officer went on. 'My identity is not really of any consequence and I hope this need not take too long. I also apologise for making you come here so late but in this job you will understand that we have to work anti-social hours. Would you like a cigarette?'

First the long wait and now the softening up process, perhaps. Was this all part of a standard interviewing technique? I had no way of knowing but my craving for nicotine was such that I was happy to accept the offer.

'Yes, thank you, I would.'

The officer proceeded to produce a cigarette case from his pocket and I was able to select a cigarette of my choice. He then produced a lighter and as I lit up and inhaled the nicotine I coughed slightly. The cigarette seemed particularly strong to me.

'Not the best quality, I'm afraid,' the officer remarked casually, 'but that's the war for you. Now to business, you are a friend of Conrad Wertheim, aren't you?'

'Yes, I had the honour to serve with him in the last war. He was my battalion commander.'

'He has been arrested for high treason…' I took a deep breath. 'You don't seem surprised!'

'On the contrary, I am deeply shocked. He's a true patriot, I'm sure.'

'He is implicated in the plot to assassinate the Fuhrer and yours is one of several names entered on a list that we have found amongst his papers. Have you any idea why your name should be on it?'

'No, except that I admit to being his friend. Anyway, I don't see what is so special about a list of names?'

The officer ignored this question. 'When did you last see your friend?'

'It was at our battalion reunion, earlier this year.'

'But not at all since?'

'No, unfortunately not.'

'And did he try to recruit you to the cause at this reunion?'

'No, certainly not.'

'But you did invite him back to your house afterwards, didn't you?' I felt the blood drain from my face. 'How on earth did you know that?'

'That's my business. So what did you talk about then?'

'Simply old times, nothing more, I assure you.'

'I don't believe you. He recruited you, didn't he?'

'No, absolutely not! I knew nothing of any plot against the Fuhrer and nor would I have ever contemplated being a party to any such plot. I swear that on my honour as a member of the SS.'

The officer looked at me coldly. 'I still don't believe you.'

'Oh don't you. Look, if this is all the evidence you have against me I suggest we terminate this interview now.'

I was becoming angry and stood up but the officer told me in no uncertain terms to sit down again. After that he opened up a file sitting on the desk in front of him and produced a small piece of paper.

'Here, this is the list.' With that he tossed the paper towards me. I tentatively picked it up and glanced at it.

'How many of those individuals do you know?'

'What, personally?'

'Yes.'

I studied the list with a growing sense of apprehension. 'None,' I answered flatly.

'Are you certain of that?'

'One or two of the names are familiar to me but I don't know them personally.'

'Have you ever met them?'

'I might have done; I have met a lot of people over the years.'

'Give me their names and tell me when you might have met them?'

Reluctantly, I did so. I was beginning to realise that his interrogation of me was likely to be a lengthy one. As an innocent man I ought to have had nothing to fear, but I sensed that in the prevailing climate of accusation I was still in danger of being regarded as guilty merely by association. The officer then changed tack.

'You are a supporter of the Zionist cause, are you not?'

I looked at him askance. 'I was once but that is many years ago now. If you have read my file you will also appreciate that I was simply pursuing official Party policy.'

'It was a policy that you advocated, though, wasn't it?'

'Yes, but at the time I was applauded for that and made head of the Jewish Bureau…'

'…A position from which you soon resigned..'

'Yes, but only when it was obvious to me that the policy I advocated was no longer going to succeed.'

'And you have never harboured feelings of resentment arising from what happened?'

I shook my head vigorously and adopted a sad expression. 'I can see where you are trying to take this conversation, but the answer is no. At the time I was naturally disappointed, who wouldn't have been, but it is years ago now and I have long since put that behind me.'

The interrogation continued as the officer returned to the

list of names and asked one probing question after another concerning my possible association with these individuals. Finally, he turned to precisely what I had talked about to Conrad when I had invited him home. I grew tired and increasingly irritated.

'Look, this interrogation is going nowhere, I have told you all I know, and I am innocent of any involvement in the plot against the Fuhrer.'

'I would prefer to be the judge of that,' the officer countered.

'Oh would you, well we can sit here going round in circles or you can accept that I have nothing more to tell you because there is simply nothing more to tell. I had one meeting, some time ago now, with Conrad that was entirely proper and we talked about old times. Perhaps, for all I know, he might have wished to sound me out, but if that was so he must have abandoned any such idea…'

'And why would he have done that?'

'You'll have to ask him, won't you, but it could well have been because I do recall telling him expressly while we were still at the dinner of my total loyalty to the Fuhrer and to the cause.'

'He voiced some criticism of the war then?'

'He asked me how I viewed developments; that was all. I told him that our nation faces a grave threat from the forces of communism but by putting our faith in the Fuhrer we will overcome it.'

I looked the officer in the eye with a steady gaze. I knew I had just taken a risk, for little of what I had just said was at all true, and if any interrogation that Conrad had been put under had resorted to darker methods he could well have confessed to having tried to persuade me to join the plot. Perhaps, indeed he already had, but I judged that if the Gestapo were serious about trying to implicate even those who had been approached, let alone agreed to participate, there might be few men left of any calibre to continue to wage the war.

The officer looked away, and proceeded to rummage through the file in front of him. I looked at him intently for any hint of what he might be thinking. Soon the officer stood up.

'If you will kindly remain seated here, I will be back.'

Again I was left to sit and wait and again time passed with an agonising slowness. Eventually, though, after more than half an hour, the officer returned.

'Baron, I am grateful to you for co-operation and I regret having had to trouble you but you will appreciate, I'm sure, that it is essential for the Fuhrer's sake that we identify anyone implicated in the plot against him. You are now free to leave and I have arranged for a car so that you can be driven home.'

For the first time since I had entered Gestapo headquarters, I permitted myself a smile.

'Thank you, I quite understand that you've only been doing your job.'

'That's gracious of you, Baron.'

I was delighted to smell fresh air again, even if a light drizzle was falling, but my pleasure at being released was tempered not merely by Conrad's fate but by the knowledge that it was really a lie for me to continue to profess loyalty to the Fuhrer. I wondered if in fact I had just become a spineless coward, intent on saving my own skin, and prayed, above all else, that I and every other German citizen would not be damned to eternity for the abominations being perpetrated in the concentration camps. Aliza's face came into my mind with a look that was full of reproach, and I bowed my head, realising that I was close to tears.

23

Early April 1945

'Please, please, don't go back to Berlin!'

Clara was literally wringing her hands as well as fixing her eyes on me with that fierce gaze that she could adopt whenever she was desperate to get her way. We were standing in the substantial kitchen of our house, deep in the Black Forest, that seemed such a sanctuary of peace and order in the midst of unfolding chaos. It was the evening of February 26, so more than six weeks ago now, and I had just announced my intention to leave the following morning.

'I have no choice, Clara. It's my duty…'

'Duty, don't talk to me of that. This country is finished, isn't it? You've said it often enough, haven't you? Surely, your first duty is to your wife and child?'

'But you are both perfectly safe here, you know you are?'

'…With American and British troops on the other side of the Rhine. Didn't you say just this morning that it can only be a matter of days before they manage to cross it? How can we then be safe if you're hundreds of miles away in Berlin?'

'I don't believe that either the British or Americans pose any direct threat to unarmed civilians, particularly women and children, and especially not here.'

'Those they haven't slaughtered already with their incessant bombing, you mean?' Clara's tone was now deeply sarcastic.

'That's in towns and cities, as you know full well.'

'And what about you? If you go back to Berlin I'm frightened I'll never see you again. Please don't go, I beg you!'

She was in tears and I immediately went to comfort her but she backed away and instead shouted at me. 'You don't care, do you!?'

'Of course I care, Clara, it's deeply unfair of you to suggest otherwise, but I cannot suddenly desert my post, especially with our nation now in such danger.'

'So you admit it then, your real intention is to return to Berlin to fight?'

'I remain an SS officer, I have been attached to the Volkssturm since November, our Fatherland is in the gravest danger, and needs every able bodied man who is willing to defend it.'

'But you aren't young any more and didn't you fight enough in the last war to last a life time?'

'I hoped that I had, but I am not yet in my dotage and can still remember how to fire a gun.'

'You'll be killed, I just know it!' Clara broke down in tears and this time she did not rebut my attempt to comfort her; rather she threw herself into my arms and sobbed quietly, laying her head against my chest.

'I'm sorry, my love, really I am,' I said soothingly, but she was in no mood to be comforted for long. Once again she broke away from me and made one more attempt to persuade me to change my mind.

'What difference can you make as one individual; how can it possibly matter?'

I shook my head sadly. 'If every individual thought like that...'

'Yes, I know that argument,' she interrupted me. 'But this is different, the country is finished, finished, do you hear, and I don't want you to die!'

'Please, my love, stop screaming, you will wake Leopold.'

'I don't care!'

'Clara....' Suddenly, we were plunged into darkness. 'Oh, shit!' The lights had gone out on us. It was yet another power failure and neither of us expected the lights to come on again that night.

'Let's go to bed, I'm tired,' Clara said miserably. 'It's getting late anyway.'

Perhaps she still hoped to use the comfort of the marital bed to continue to persuade me to change my mind but sleep overcame both of us too quickly.

In the morning I was first up and remained determined to leave while Clara now seemed resigned to the inevitable. It was only when the time came to say my farewells, particularly to Leopold, that I faltered somewhat. It suddenly struck me more forcefully than ever before that this might be the last time I ever set eyes on either my wife or son. Clara, sensing the hesitation in my manner, quietly but intensely, seized her opportunity.

'Don't go!'

I hesitated, but only momentarily, shook my head, and departed in the Mercedes as quickly as I could. It was snowing and I was reminded of another morning, only twelve years ago, although it might as well have been a lifetime, when the Fuhrer had not long come to power and I had felt so full of hope and self-confidence.

I reckoned that I would have just enough petrol for my journey back to Berlin. It has become a scarce commodity, of course, and that fact alone will make it more difficult for me ever to return to the Black Forest. It was a Sunday morning, cold but bright, and the roads seemed eerily deserted. I found it hard to throw off the sense of impending doom I still felt, and couldn't help wondering if I would ever come this way again.

As I travelled northwards, my journey brought me within half an hour's drive of Buchenwald concentration camp. I had heard nothing from Muhler since I had telephoned him and I felt a deepening urge to take a diversion in order to visit the camp. However, I resisted the idea. I decided that I hadn't enough petrol to risk it and didn't see that I had any real justification for simply turning up at the camp.

Yet even as I drove on towards Berlin there was a part of me that still wanted to turn the car round and head for the camp. Since that fateful night when I had met Aliza again she had seldom been absent from my thoughts for long. I even confessed to myself that part of my motivation for being so determined to return to Berlin was a vague hope that I might be able to see her again, so why, I asked myself, was I passing up what might be my only real opportunity?

I looked anxiously at the petrol gauge, made a quick calculation, and, as soon as I could, turned the car round and headed for the camp. I felt an odd mixture of fear and elation. Fear, that what I was embarking upon was just a waste of time that would leave me stranded without sufficient petrol to reach Berlin, and elation at the thought that I would soon be in Aliza's company once more, however briefly.

By the time I approached the gates of the camp, after twice

taking a wrong turning, and using up even more precious petrol than I could afford, I was extremely tense but had also made up my mind what approach to adopt. Admittedly, I wasn't in uniform, but I still had all my papers with me to prove my rank and position and I was confident that this should be sufficient.

'I am Baron Von Buren of the Reiter SS,' I informed the guard using my most authoritative tone of voice whilst waving my identity card under his nose. 'I was here earlier this year on a visit and wish to see the Deputy Commandant. I was in touch with him quite recently about one of your prisoners and as I was passing your camp decided that I would pay him a visit.'

'He won't be expecting you then, Sir?' the guard asked me respectfully.

'No, as I say, but I'm sure he'll be willing to see me.'

'Of course, Sir, do you know the way?'

'I'd be grateful if you could remind me?'

The guard did so and then came to attention as I drove past him. So far so good, I decided, and my luck continued to hold as, after only a short wait of about ten minutes, I was ushered into Muhler's office.

'Baron, this is an unexpected pleasure. You've come about Frau Geisser, I imagine?'

I sensed that the expression on Muhler's face was somewhat lascivious, but then dismissed the notion and tried to sound as relaxed as possible.

'Yes, indeed, I am on my way back to Berlin from my home in the Black Forest and as I was passing decided to see if she is still well?'

'So far as I am aware, she is. Since your call I have kept an eye on her for you.'

'Thank you. I have a small gift for you.' With that I put my hand into the inside pocket of my jacket and drew out my wallet from which I produced several Reichsmark bank notes.

'That is most kind of you Baron. I can arrange for you to see her again, if you wish?'

'I haven't long, I have to be back in Berlin tonight, but I would appreciate a few minutes. I am grateful to you.'

I hoped that my voice sounded matter of fact even though my heart was racing. I also still sensed the same expression on Muhler's face but I did my best to ignore it.

Less than half an hour later Aliza was brought to Muhler's office and as I looked into her eyes again, I felt a surge of love for her, which I sensed was reciprocated. Especially in the light of day, she admittedly looked even older and careworn than I remembered from our previous meeting, but not so much as to shock me, or diminish my feelings towards her in anyway.

'I have a matter to attend to elsewhere,' Muhler explained. 'I shall be about twenty minutes, if that's enough time for you, Baron?'

'Yes, most certainly, I'm much obliged to you.'

Muhler then discreetly withdrew and shut the wooden panelled door behind him. His office was on the ground floor but there was nothing overlooking its single window so I did not hesitate to go to Aliza and take her in my arms. She responded willingly enough to my embrace and smiled at me in that enigmatic fashion which I remembered even from our days together in Palestine.

'It's so good to see you, Aliza. Forgive me if I seem to have failed you yet again but please believe me that if there was any way I could have got you out of this place, I would have. At least I have been able to get Muhler to agree to keep you and your daughter as safe as possible. The war should now be over soon so you will be safe at last.'

'Are you really certain of that, Otto?' There was a sceptical edge to her question.

'Yes, definitely,' I reassured her. 'A few weeks, two months perhaps, but no longer: I expect the British or Americans will liberate this camp.'

'And what about you, Otto?' She asked me with a look of concern on her face.

'Oh, I am returning to my post in Berlin. The Reich will make a stand there against the Russians and I have a Company of boys and old men to command. I dread to think what the Russians will do to the entire population of the city if we cannot hold them at bay. My hope is that, if we can do so for long enough, the Americans and British will arrive, and we can surrender to them with some sense of dignity.'

'Otto, Otto, will you never learn?' She admonished me gently. 'Don't you see that ever since the days of the Kaiser it is hubris that has brought Germany to its knees?'

I felt chastened. 'Yes, I do see that, of course I do, but you have to understand that for a man of my class hubris is in our bones, our very being.'

'And if you cannot hold off the Russians?'

'Then I expect I will be killed or marched off to some Godforsaken hole in Siberia.'

'So I may never see you again?' she asked me hesitantly, her voice barely above a whisper.

'Probably not, but then perhaps that is for the best. The world needs to move on without dinosaurs like me still around.

We have done too much harm and will not be forgiven for it.'

'You are no dinosaur, Otto.'

'No, but I still feel like one.'

'And how are Clara and Leopold?'

'Still safe and well in the Black Forest. No harm can come to them there, I am sure.'

I looked closely into Aliza's eyes, wondering what would happen, if, by some miracle, I survived the war. I knew that I still cared for Clara, and then there was Leopold to also take into consideration as well. I reflected ruefully that my death would at least resolve the inner conflict with which my mind was struggling.

'What are you thinking, Otto?' Aliza asked me gently.

I managed a smile. 'I'm thinking what a beautiful woman you are and that I love you, have loved you in fact since we first danced together on the raging Moses all those years ago.'

She hugged me but did not bring her lips to mine. Instead she turned her head to stare out of the window.

'You know, I still hope that Max may somehow be alive, and you have Clara and your son.'

'Yes, I do, but then I accept that my love for you is just another of my many sins. I hope you can forgive me for it?'

'Of course I can, Otto, of course I can, because I love you too.'

'God, do you really, despite everything?'

'Yes, despite everything. You are still a good person, I believe, and there was always a certain chemistry between us, wasn't there?'

Once again I took her in my arms and this time our lips met.

*****

I returned to Berlin in emotional turmoil and as I reached the suburbs of the city I quickly realised that it was not as I had left it. Bombing raids had resumed since the New Year and it was obvious that there must have been a particularly severe one, even during the few days I had been away. Buildings, even whole streets, which had been untouched by the war when I had driven the other way, now stood in ruins. I flinched from the sight and prayed that I wouldn't find my own home reduced to rubble.

It was becoming dark but this couldn't disguise the extent of the devastation and as I turned into my road I saw that a house on my left had been struck by a bomb and was in total ruins. Other, nearby houses, although still standing, had clearly had their windows blown out and it was with an enormous sense of relief that I saw my own home remained intact.

But for how much longer? I asked myself gloomily.

When I travelled to the office the following morning, I wondered if the building I normally worked in would even still be standing. Part of me even hoped that it would not be, for I knew how increasingly pointless my work had become. As it was, the building was still intact and it was with a vague sense of disappointment that I passed through its familiar front entrance.

I hadn't been at my desk more than ten minutes when Arnold Rastner walked in.

'Good morning, Otto, I'm surprised to see you back.'

I raised my eyebrows. I knew Rastner was not one to mince words and the fate of those who had conspired against the Fuhrer had failed to deter him from proclaiming the Third Reich to be in its death throes.

'I said I would be back today, didn't I?'

'Oh come, Otto, with things the way they are no one would have blamed you for deciding to remain with your lovely wife. How is she by the way?'

'She's well. She pleaded with me not to leave her in fact.'

'And you refused to listen, I suppose?'

'No, of course I listened, but… well I considered it my duty to return. I have my Volkssturm Company to command, and I am neither a coward, nor a traitor.'

'I never suggested you were. It's just that we don't stand a hope in hell against the Russians and why waste your life for no good purpose?'

I chose to ignore this question. Instead I asked one of my own. 'So when are you intending to leave then?'

'I'm not, but then I haven't got a wife and child in the Black Forest.'

'No, but you still have your wife, Elga.'

'True, and she's scared shit of the bombing, too. The raid we had while you were away was terrible.'

'Yes, I couldn't believe the extent of the damage I saw when I came back yesterday.'

'Huh, that's nothing. You've seen Hamburg, haven't you, and you know Dresden was put to the sword two weeks ago. Our nation is steadily being bombed back to the Stone Age. If only that little bomb had sent the Fuhrer to his eternal rest last summer.'

'For Christ's sake, Arnold, keep your voice down.'

'Oh I know, the walls have ears, but I'm past caring. If it's not the Gestapo who get me, it'll be the bombing, or the Russians, so take your pick. You really shouldn't have come back, you know.'

'Old habits die hard, Arnold. It would have seemed too much like running away while other men are prepared to stand and fight.'

'Yes, but what's the point when defeat is inevitable?'

'If we can keep the Russians at bay for long enough, we can surrender with some sort of dignity to the British and Americans.'

'But they haven't even crossed the Rhine yet, whereas the Russians are no distance away at all. And what if there has been some agreement to carve up this country with the Russians being left to do what they like here in the East?'

'Then we must fight to protect our women and children, for if the Russians win they will spare no one.'

'But they aren't savages?'

'No, but they may still wish to wreak a terrible revenge upon us for starting this war in the first place.'

'Well, I still think you're a fool to have come back.'

'Think what you wish, Arnold. The fact is that I'm here and I intend to stay.'

With that Rastner shrugged his shoulders and walked out.

I just sighed. All I could think of was that final lingering kiss with Aliza before I had left her behind in Buchenwald, and the painful thought that I would probably never see her again.

24

'Baron?'
'Yes.'

I was sitting at my desk and the telephone had just rung in my office. Much of the time, the lines were no longer working and the ringing sound had startled me. The voice speaking to me was familiar but the line was crackly and I still struggled to identify it.

'It's me, Muhler, the deputy commandant at Buchenwald.'
'Yes, hello.'
'The Americans are closing in on us here. We are starting to evacuate. I thought that you should know that Frau Geisser is amongst those being moved to Theresienstadt. It's the camp in Moravia.'
'Oh yes, I've heard of it. And her daughter?'
'She's going with her.'
'Well, thank you for letting me know, I'm grateful to you.'
'I haven't found it easy to get through to you. I've tried several times.'
'You've done well to make the effort. Once again, my thanks.'
Even as I said these words, the line seemed to go dead on us. 'Hello, Hello.'
There was no response, but then I thought it something of a miracle that I had received the call at all.

*****

'What on earth?'

My office window had just been rattled by a loud thud. I leapt to my feet and went to the window to look outside. The street below was empty of both traffic and pedestrians. I judged that the noise could have come from an explosion some distance away. I assumed that it must have been a bomb going off. There had been no air raid warning but it was always possible that a hitherto unexploded bomb had detonated after being disturbed.

'What do you think it is?'

The question came from Rastner who had just walked into the office. I gave him the benefit of my opinion.

'I thought for a moment it was the Russians,' Rastner responded.

'It could still be, I suppose. In the last war we had this gun that could fire shells a hell of a distance.'

Rastner walked to the window and looked into the street below. Then he turned and grimaced. 'Well, they'll be here soon, that's for sure,' he remarked ruefully. 'I've just come from a meeting with Goebbels. He knows the country is finished. He talked of a red curtain falling across Europe with every nation that Stalin's armies have conquered becoming part of the communist Empire.'

'That makes perfect sense to me.'

'You know, you really should have stayed in the Black Forest while you had the chance.'

I felt irritated. 'We've had this conversation before, Arnold. I have a Volkssturm Company to command, and I intend to fulfil that duty to the best of my ability.'

'So what are you still doing here?'

'Clearing my desk, nothing more.'

'Well good luck to you, Otto.'

'And to you, Arnold.'

The two of us looked at each other intently.

'I am expected to report for duty as well, you know, Otto.'

'And will you?'

'I don't know. I certainly don't see myself as fighting material. I have never even fired a gun. I think I would be a liability.'

'But once… if the Russians enter the city?'

'I expect I shall have to find a good hiding place, a sewer perhaps?' He smirked nervously. Both of us understood that this was no joking matter, however.

'And what will our leaders do, I wonder?' I asked.

'The same, I imagine, unless they have the courage to fall on their swords. But you know it's the women and children I fear for most of all.'

'That is one good reason to stand and fight.'

Rastner nodded. 'Perhaps I will report for duty after all.'

'How is your wife by the way?' I asked gently.

Rastner gave me a bleak look. 'She's terrified. Some days I think the bombing has unhinged her brain. Your wife is well out of this.'

Now it was my turn to nod my head and the two of us then shook hands, realising as we did so that we might never meet again.

'Do you know yet which part of the city you are to help defend, Otto?' Rastner asked me. It was obviously an afterthought as he was already halfway out of the door.

'No, I've no idea, but I expect I shall soon find out.'

We both wished each other good luck once more and Rastner departed. The explosion and his sudden appearance had put any thought of Aliza out of my mind but not for long. As I left the office I was overwhelmed by a feeling of concern for her and cursed the fact that I was now more powerless than ever to help her. In a few days I would, after all, probably be dead; a grim reflection which I did what I could to suppress.

Outside it was cold and wet, and feeling thoroughly miserable I lit myself one of the last of my favourite brand of cigarettes. It offered me a small measure of comfort and I decided to try and concentrate my mind on the task of commanding a Company again for the first time in more than a quarter of a century. Certainly, I was under no illusion that it was going to be at all easy.

Later that day I inspected my men, amongst them members of the Hitler Youth who were at least smartly turned out in their uniforms. Their young, enthusiastic faces also reminded me of the previous war and many of my comrades who died on the Western Front before they were even twenty. The rest of the company simply wore their civilian clothes with armbands. From their demeanour it was clear to me that they had no illusions either about what lay in store for them.

I had as my Unteroffizier an old soldier who last held that rank in 1918, Joseph Leiberich, a plumber by trade, with a bluff, no nonsense disposition. We have discovered that we spent months fighting within five kilometres of each other on the western front. Others, too, amongst us have memories of that war along, no doubt, with the mental scars of that dreadful conflict. It makes me think that it is really just as well we do not have the power to see into the future.

'I don't want to be part of those forces that are required to hold defensive positions in open ground,' I confessed to Leiberich over a cigarette, after the parade was over. 'If that happens we'll just be an easy target for Russian artillery and superior firepower. It will be far better to be located inside a building somewhere as long as it isn't too isolated. From there we can expect to be able to inflict the maximum casualties and make the enemy fight for every metre of ground.'

Leiberich took a long puff on his cigarette and then glanced up at the sky.

'They'll come at us from the air as well, Sir, I expect,' he replied at length.

'And the Luftwaffe is finished.'

'All the more reason to be as much under cover as possible then.'

We looked at each other knowingly, both thinking that the most we could hope for was to delay a Russian victory.

'It's not just the mixed quality of the weapons that we possess that worries me but also the simple lack of ammunition,' I added. 'If it comes to it I've decided that we will have to take what we can from the dead.'

Leiberich merely nodded in response.

'And what's your view of the men's morale?' I asked. 'Will they fight?'

He shrugged. 'The young lads, Sir, God help them, yes, and those who remember how to fight from the last war will too, I expect. The rest, well, some will, but don't expect them all to.'

I smiled ruefully. 'I don't.'

*****

That conversation with Leiberich was just under a fortnight ago, on Friday April 14 1945. The Americans and British forces are still advancing on Berlin from the West, whilst the Russian army has encircled Berlin and yesterday began shelling the city centre.

I am looking sadly at the photograph of Clara and Leopold on my desk and feel a continuing sense of concern for the fate of Aliza and her daughter if they are now to be liberated, not by the Americans or the British, but by the vengeful Russians. With an assault on Berlin now underway, I don't rate the odds of my survival very highly. Admittedly, I have survived equally poor odds in the previous war but then I was a young man with well-armed and well-trained soldiers under my command. Now, in my late forties, I find myself in command of a motley group of individuals who are neither well armed nor well trained. Further, those who are also members of the Hitler Youth are for the most part sixteen or younger, whilst there are several men a good deal older than myself; in some cases over sixty.

I cannot believe we will be any match for battle-hardened Russian soldiers, but we should at least have some anti-tank weapons and a determination to fight. That thought makes me feel for my Luger revolver I now carry on my person at all times, and I wonder how long it will be before I have to use it in anger.

So now I've already sat here too long at my desk, thinking back over the events of the last dozen years. Tomorrow I shall go and take command of my men and face the Russians.

I began writing this memoir, in a frenzy of memory and words, on Saturday April 15 1945. It's now Thursday April

27 1945. My story has, in a sense, ended, but I dread to think what still awaits me.

PART 2

ESCAPE

25

28th April 1945

I could hear the sound of heavy guns being fired and it made me shudder. It reminded me too much of the trenches and of being under such heavy bombardment that the ground shook, the noise was deafening, and some men were driven even to madness. Berlin was now completely encircled by the Russians and they had begun to shell the city with a ferocity that seemed to be totally indiscriminate.

My company and I were occupying an office building in the darkness. From where I was standing, behind a bricked-up window on the first floor, with a gun loophole built into it, my view of the outside world was limited, but I could just make out part of the Moltke Bridge over the river Spree. Leiberich was standing next to me.

'I just hope the bridge has been well mined,'.

'If it hasn't, sir, we'll have the Russians swarming all over us tomorrow.'

'Well, if that happens, we'll be ready for them. We must be prepared, too, for an attack under cover of darkness. My main worry is still our lack of ammunition.'

Leiberich appeared unconcerned. 'I think we've got enough to put up a decent fight, sir.' He dropped his voice to barely more than a whisper, having turned his back to the three other men in the room so they could hear his words.

'The rations we have with us, sir, will barely last a day.'

I nodded. 'Noted, Unteroffizier. If necessary, we will just have to scavenge for more.'

Leiberich grunted in response and peered outside again,

I feared that it was going to be a long night, and already I was feeling tired. Part of my brain was also telling me that it would make sense to surrender and put an end to so much death and destruction. But then I thought of what the Russians might do, not just to German soldiers, but also the women and children of Berlin, and my resolve hardened.

'Well, I can't see any sign of the Russians, yet, sir,' Leiberich told me. I could see the pensive expression on his face as he spoke and after a few moments silence he coughed and spoke to me again. 'You know, sir, the thing I disliked most about the last war were the hours spent just waiting for something to happen.'

'Even more than the fighting itself?' I asked.

'To be frank, sir, yes... well, perhaps not to begin with, but as time went by. It just made me more and more depressed and anxious. The worst of it was when we just had to lie low while we were being shelled. I used to feel so powerless.'

I smiled a little. Leiberich certainly hadn't struck me as being the anxious type. 'The Russians will attack soon enough, I expect, if not tonight then early tomorrow,' I replied.

Only a second or two later there came the noise of a loud blast striking a building very near our own, followed instantly by the sound of falling brickwork and glass. The floor we were standing on shook and both of us instinctively ducked.

'Christ, that was close,' I hissed. 'What did you say about feeling powerless under shellfire? At least in those days we were well dug in!'

I could feel my heart racing and braced myself against further blasts. I had not been under fire like this since November 1918 when the last fearsome conflict ended and I remember praying that it would never happen again.

'*Plus ça change*,' I muttered to myself, half aloud.

'Did you say something, sir?' Leiberich asked me.

'Nothing of any consequence.'

Before I could recover my equilibrium another blast struck the building next to our own and this time I wondered if my nerves could stand much more of this pounding.

'I fear it will be our turn soon enough,' I muttered to Leiberich. 'But at least it only appears to be the upper parts of the buildings that are being damaged and we've got five floors above us. Let's go and offer the men some encouragement.'

'Yes, sir.'

What I hadn't said, of course, was that the blast might start fires and bring ceilings crashing down on top of us, but I was doing my best to put any such thought to the back of my mind. Half the trick of commanding men, I remembered very well, is to appear unruffled even in the face of extreme danger. You might be so scared that all you want to do is shit yourself but you must never show it. I felt desperate, too, for the calming affects of nicotine, but that would have to wait until I'd completed this task.

'Ready to give those Russian bastards a good thrashing, Hans?' I asked one lad while putting a hand on his shoulder. I knew he was barely sixteen, and looked completely terrified.

'Of course, sir,' was his rather limp response.

'Good man.'

It was bad enough that the last war had killed so many young men who were still only eighteen, but now, to see sixteen year olds and younger, facing the prospect of an early grave made me want to weep. Instead, I smiled at the lad, squeezed his shoulder, and move on.

A dozen times I repeated this exercise, before pausing to look outside in the direction of the bridge. I could just make out the heads of some helmeted men in German uniforms.

'I think our engineers may be about to blow the bridge, Unteroffizier!' I said excitedly to Leiberich. Up until now I had been striving to remain calm, to keep my voice measured, even relaxed, but this time the true level of my emotions betrayed me.

'Not a moment too soon, if you don't mind me saying so, sir.'

I grinned ruefully, both of us understanding, only too well, that the destruction of the bridge offered us a small but vital lifeline.

Meanwhile, artillery fire continued to rain down on buildings all around us. I was then deafened by a bang that almost lifted me off my feet. In the same instant, I felt plaster falling on top of me.

'Shit, we've been hit!' Leiberich shouted.

I dusted the plaster off my uniform and looked up. There was a large crack in the ceiling.

'Order two men to go up the stairs to check that there's no fire blazing.'

'Yes, sir!'

I looked outside once more. I could see rubble, from above, scattered across the street in front of me. After that I glanced towards the bridge, which was deserted. Almost immediately, there was a loud explosion, and the bridge disappeared from view behind a cloud of dust. When this gradually settled, though, my heart sank. I could hear, too, one of my men groan with disappointment and I turned around. Leiberich, having given the necessary order, was by my side again.

'The bridge is still intact,' I informed him lamely.

'But I heard the explosion…'

'It's caused some damage, as you would expect, but nowhere near enough.'

'So tanks could still get across it, sir?'

I sighed. 'I fear so, yes.'

The men sent to investigate the damage to the upper part of the building soon reported that they had not been able to get past the third floor but hadn't detected any fire.

'It probably took the roof off, sir.' Leiberich suggested.

I merely nodded in response, agonised that time seemed to pass so slowly, as the bombardment continued. More buildings, some nearby, were hit, some for a second or third time, but fortunately not our own. Eventually, I noticed that it was completely dark, the shelling had stopped, and I was unable to suppress a yawn. I felt increasingly bored and also sleepy. I searched for my cigarette case and offered a cigarette to Leiberich, which he gratefully accepted.

As I lit up, the nicotine helped to relax me a little and I began to doze off. Then, I came to with a start. glanced at my watch and realised that it was approaching midnight. I peered outside once more and what I saw made my heart race. On the opposite bank of the river I could just make out a few Russian troops and also a slow moving T34 tank.

'They're here,' I said quietly to Leiberich. 'Tell the men to stand ready, but that no one is to fire until I give the order.'

'Of course, sir.'

For the first time that day I took out my Luger revolver. It seemed a very meagre weapon in the face of what was now advancing towards us but it was still capable of killing a man provided I could aim it properly. I was doing all I could to remain calm and focused but it was a struggle. Images of Clara and Leopold kept flashing across my mind and then of Aliza, too. I had always recognised that I was incredibly fortunate to survive the previous war and now I really felt my chances of coming out of this situation alive were terribly slim.

The Russian tank was soon on the bridge and coming closer. To my annoyance my men and I had ended up without any anti-tank weapons, but German forces defending the bridge itself were better equipped, although far more exposed. I could see a bazooka being fired and then a flash as its well aimed missile struck the tank, penetrated its turret, and brought it to an immediate halt.

One of my men, standing to the left of me, let out a shout of triumph, which I thought was highly premature. I could see the Russians were now bringing up light artillery and I decided that the time had come to give the necessary order.

'Tell the men to fire at will, Unteroffizier.'

I made no attempt to fire my Luger yet, knowing that it would be a waste of ammunition to use it at such extreme range. However, for those of my men armed with rifles and machine guns it was a different matter as they began to inflict heavy casualties. Indeed, not just my men, but also German troops in several other buildings overlooking the bridge, were now putting the Russians under intense fire. I saw several Russian soldiers fall to the ground, either dead or wounded, and, in the case of the latter, I heard their screams. It was a sound that brought only flashbacks of the previous conflict to mind, which I did my best to suppress.

Yet, for all their losses, the Russians managed to get two light artillery pieces into position, load, and fire them. They aimed, too, at the lower storeys of the buildings we were defending and I sensed that it could only be a question of time before their superior firepower and numbers gained the upper hand.

From where I was standing, I couldn't make out directly how much damage was being inflicted by the artillery shells, but I could hear them crunching into the walls of nearby buildings, and as the noise died away, I spoke again to Leiberich.

'Tell the men to cease firing. We'll need every round we possess once the Russians get across the bridge.' Leiberich looked at me askance but I meant what I said. 'You heard me; they're bound to get over it eventually, whatever we do.'

It was now apparent to me that another Russian tank was approaching the bridge. It would have to manoeuvre around the one that had been knocked out and would be just as vulnerable to anti-tank fire. However, more than one Russian machine gun was firing on our emplacements defending the bridge. I could see the tank, slowly but inexorably, advancing, all the while firing its own gun at these emplacements.

'Shit,' I exclaimed, half under my breath, as I saw a German soldier first aim his bazooka at the tank and then fall back, a victim of well directed machine gun fire. It's been sheer luck, I thought, that the first tank had been knocked out so easily and there now seemed nothing to prevent the second tank successfully crossing the bridge.

German troops, in buildings closer to the bridge than ours, were still directing fire against the advancing Russians, and whilst some of them were able to shelter behind the advancing tank, others continued to fall dead or wounded. One of the Russian machine guns was knocked out, but this didn't prevent others from continuing to offer cover to their advancing troops whilst their light artillery did the same.

The Russian tank now seemed unstoppable while another one came up behind it. No doubt many more were following.

'Look, sir!' Leiberich cried out. 'It's one of ours! It's a Panzer!'

In the same instant, the leading Russian tank, having only just crossed the bridge, was hit and came to an immediate halt. A shell fired by the much larger Panzer tank had easily penetrated its armour with deadly effect.

I felt my spirits rise, daring to hope that there was still some possibility of preventing the Russian advance, after all. Excitedly, I tried to see if the Panzer was merely the first of several, but there appeared to be no sign of any others. I grimaced, knowing that one tank, however powerful, would not be enough.

'Surely there must be more than one Panzer?' Leiberich asked, echoing my thoughts.

'Not necessarily, I'm afraid.' Then I groaned. The Panzer had been struck by an artillery shell, which quickly set it alight. The surviving members of its crew immediately tried to evacuate, but I could see that one of them was on fire. The man, having leapt off the tank, was desperately trying to remove his burning jacket. Then he tensed, suddenly, before falling to the ground.

It seemed evident to me that he'd been shot as his body didn't stir despite the fact that his clothes were still burning.

'Poor bastard,' Leiberich muttered.

I preferred to say nothing, the bullet that killed the man had really been a blessing, saving him further misery. So often, while serving in the trenches, I thought the same. Those who die quickly are really the lucky ones. I looked towards the bridge once more, only to see more T34 tanks approaching it. With a flash of light, almost instantly, I saw one of them being struck before bursting into flames.

'It must be our own guns, sir!' Leiberich cried out excitedly. 'They've got their range.'

Yet more of their tanks were disabled by the artillery fire that was brought to bear on them, stalling the Russian advance. We could pride ourselves on having won a small victory and as the firing died away I was increasingly confident that the Russians would not attack again until after dawn. My men and I could now rest, however fitfully, but sure enough, as it once more began to grow light, I was able to make out yet more tanks approaching the bridge. I still feared that it could only be a matter of time before they managed to get across.

26

'Fire, fire at will!'

The Russians were now across the bridge, their infantryman sheltering as best they could behind their tanks. Otherwise, they would have made easy targets, reminding me of how vulnerable we had been in No Man's Land during the last great conflict.

I put my finger to the trigger of my Luger and fired it repeatedly until, having run out of ammunition, I had to pause to reload. I'd seen two men go down, a testimony to the fact that I could keep a steady hand and was still a good shot, while the street in front of me was quickly littered with the bodies of dead and dying Russians. All the same, I knew the game was up.

From where I was standing I could tell the leading Russian tank was in a position to start firing at the building we were defending. Worse than that, as I looked towards the bridge, I could see the Russians were now manhandling their light artillery pieces across it.

I expected that we could still inflict significant casualties upon the Russians, but nevertheless once their artillery was brought to bear on us, in little time at all we would all be blasted to kingdom come. It left me wondering whether or not I should order a retreat? Leiberich then echoed my thought.

'Do we fight to the bitter end, sir?'

'No, I don't think so.'

The words had barely left my mouth before the Russian tank fired its gun. A split second later I heard a scream as the shell punched a hole through the wall of the room next to us. In the time it would take the tank crew to reload, I knew that it could be my turn next.

The orders I'd been given were to assist in the defence of the bridge, and to do so at all costs. The bridge having been lost, it seemed inevitable to me that if we didn't retreat, we would be either be killed or captured.

The building we were in had a back entrance leading out into the street behind it. There was still time left to retreat but this was fast running out as more Russian troops managed to cross the bridge. At any moment the Russian tank would fire its gun again.

'Unteroffizier, I want all the men out through the back entrance apart from the two machine gunners on the ground floor – I'll speak to them, all right. They're to act as a rearguard and keep fire on the Russians until everyone else is out of the building. Then get out as well.'

'Yes, sir!'

As I gave this order, I backed away from the window from which I had been directing my fire on the advancing Russians. Leiberich was ahead of me, shouting to the others to follow him.

I was last to leave the room, and as I entered the hallway outside, leading to a flight of stairs, there was another explosion. The building shook, I heard more screaming, and I found myself covered in plaster falling from the ceiling.

'Unteroffizier!' I shouted out. I was at the head of the staircase and could see Leiberich at the bottom.

'Yes, sir?'

'Walking wounded only, to be assisted; understood?'

'Very well, sir.'

'And Unteroffizier…'

Leiberich looked at me anxiously as I ran down stairs towards him. 'Yes, sir?'

'I'll stay by the back door to help the machine gunners. Lead the rest of the men towards the Tiergarten, and I'll follow when I can.'

Leiberich glanced at me uncertainly.

'That's an order. If anything happens to me, you're in command, understood?'

Leiberich merely touched his cap while I went to the two machine gunners.

'Keep firing,' I told them. 'I'll be at the back door. When you hear me shout that the building's been cleared, retreat as well.'

'We'll soon be out of ammunition, anyway, sir,' one of the two men, who looked at least sixty, replied grimly.

'Well, fire every last round you have, if necessary.'

'Yes, sir.'

I looked out at the street and glimpsed approaching Russian infantrymen. I sensed there was a risk of one of them coming close enough to lob a grenade. Plaster showered down on me as a Russian shell hit the building two floors above me.

'Sir! It's Leiberich.'

'Yes, Unteroffizier, I thought I told you to lead the men out of here!'

'Two men are too wounded to move, sir.'

'I told you! Leave them. Is there anyone else left in the building?'

'No, sir!'

I turned to face the machine gunners. 'Just give them one more burst of fire men and then let's all get the hell out of here!'

A few seconds later I was the last man to leave the back entrance of the building, just as another shell struck the front of it, this time only just above street level. The blast was powerful enough to shatter windows even at the rear of the building, so, as I ran clear of it, I was cut on the right hand by falling glass. Blood trickled from the wound, but I could tell it was superficial, so ran on, ignoring it as best I could.

As I looked around, it seemed to me as if most of my men had also managed to get out of the building alive, but what I was supposed to do with them now I really wasn't sure. Essentially, the battle we were ordered to fight had just been lost, and I had an image of the Russians making similar advances all over the city so that before long there would be nowhere left to retreat to.

I began to feel disorientated from the smoke. It seemed to be swallowing us all up, until it briefly cleared. I had a sudden glimpse of armed soldiers and, for a moment, thought that they must be Russians. I opened my mouth to shout out a warning but then recognised, from their helmets, that they were in fact on our side.

'It must be a counter-attack, sir,' Leiberich asserted.

'Yes, I suppose it must be.'

'You're bleeding, sir,' Leiberich added, pointing to my wounded hand.

'It's nothing, just a cut.'

I could now make out an officer advancing towards me, armed with a sub-machine gun. He was gesticulating in my general direction, and looked to still be in his twenties, his face contorted in anger.

'Get out of here,' the man screamed at me, 'unless you all want to be killed!'

I bristled with annoyance. I'm unaccustomed to being shouted at in this fashion by anyone, let alone by a junior officer who was young enough to be my son.

'Don't address a senior officer in that fashion, OberLeutnant. My men and I are withdrawing in good order, I assure you.'

The young man's face dropped. 'I'm sorry, sir, it's the smoke, I couldn't see you properly. I'm afraid you and your men are in danger of being caught in cross-fire.'

'You are counter-attacking, I take it?'

'Yes, sir, and there are 88 mm guns not far behind us.'

'Well, good luck.'

'Thank you, sir.'

As I led my men towards the Tiergarten's open space, the smoke that was still drifting around began to clear once more. It enabled me to glimpse the Reichstag, not all that far away. This was clearly the building that the Russians most wanted to capture.

'If the Reichstag is taken, they've won,' I told Leiberich, although in my heart I know full well that they had really won a long time ago; perhaps on the very day when Germany committed itself to a war against Russia that it did not have to fight. Otherwise, they had certainly won on the day when the actions of Japan at Pearl Harbour had brought America, the most powerful nation on earth, into the conflict.

A truck hauling an 88 mm gun drove past us and was quickly swallowed up by the smoke. The gun was an effective anti-tank weapon as it had already demonstrated that morning but its use could only delay the inevitable. I felt completely dispirited and, above all, extremely tired.

Spring had come to the Tiergarten and the trees were in leaf. It seemed like an oasis of peace in the midst of hell. It made me want to weep for my beloved city that was slowly but surely being utterly destroyed.

'What do we do now, sir?' Leiberich asked me.

'We stay together as a disciplined group of men, and try to seek further orders.'

'I have to say, sir, that I think the men's morale is broken,' Leiberich said quietly, looking about him as he spoke.

I glared at him. He was right, of course, but as far I was concerned that wasn't the point. The men were still under orders and no one had told me to surrender.

'I'll personally shoot the first man who tries to desert!' I shouted out. 'Even now our regular troops are counter-attacking so all is not yet lost.'

The men stared at me. A few looked resentful but no one tried to dissent and with a wave of my hand I led them on in the direction of the Reichstag. As we approached it, I could make out a number of 88 mm guns placed directly in front of the building along with troops, many with machine guns, dug-in behind sandbags. We were then confronted by an anti-tank ditch, which had been filled with water. I contemplated trying to go round it before deciding it was narrow enough to simply leap.

'Come on, we can get across this easily enough,' I declared confidently, and, with one bound, just about managed to do so.

The men followed me, but, for a couple of them, it proved

too difficult a task and they managed to fall into the water. Several of their comrades either jeered or laughed, bringing a flash of comedy to an otherwise grim experience.

I was now intent on finding a senior officer to whom I could report, and looking around spied a man who I thought I vaguely recognised. He was dressed in the uniform of an SS Sturmbannfuhrer. Making straight for him, I gave the Nazi salute and introduced myself.

The Sturmbannfuhrer looked at me sceptically through gaunt eyes and I decided that, after all, we had not in fact ever met.

'I hope you and your men are ready to die for the honour of the fatherland, Hauptmann?'

'We are, sir,' I responded hesitantly.

'Good, for you're of no value to me if you're not. Our purpose is simple; to defend this building to the last man.'

With that the Sturmbannfuhrer stretched out his right hand, as if to encompass the impressive proportions of the Reichstag. At that moment it's gloomy eminence, with its windows and main entrance bricked in, seemed to me to be the very embodiment of the doomed Third Reich.

'Where do you want us to take up position, Sturmbannfuhrer?'

'Here will do well enough for now. If necessary, we're prepared to retire inside the building itself.'

'Very well, sir.'

Again, I saluted, and then returned to my men, informing Leiberich quietly of what the Sturmbannfuhrer had said to me.

'I don't believe the men have got the stomach for this, sir,' Leiberich responded bluntly.

'Well, they'd better have, because if they haven't they're as likely to be shot as deserters as they are by the Russians.'

We stared at each other and it was Leiberich who first looked away.

With sullen expressions, my men then joined the troops defending the Reichstag. They only had the tank trap and sandbags to protect them and, as I reflected on our position, I was more convinced than ever that my life was close to its end.

Behind me, I could hear the sound of firing and I thought it was coming nearer. I turned round and saw a few German soldiers running for their lives.

'The counter-attack has failed,' I said gloomily to Leiberich. Not that he looked at all surprised. After nearly four years of bitter conflict we both appreciated that the Russians had fought their way from the outskirts of Moscow to the very heart of Berlin. They were hardly going to be denied final victory now and, with a dreadful inevitability, it wasn't long before their tanks and infantrymen came into view.

We, the defenders of the Reichstag, still possessed some 88 mm anti-tank guns. Yet, for every tank they destroyed, more appeared. It wasn't long, either, before the Russians brought up their own artillery and, as they began firing, I felt like a helpless observer. Then the ground seemed to shake, I was lifted half off my feet, and felt a searing pain down my right leg.

27

I was almost delirious with pain and I felt reality spinning away from me, although in a strangely detached way I was still able to grasp the thought that I might be dying. I was moaning loudly, too, although barely able to comprehend that I could be making so much noise.

'Sir, sir!'

The voice calling out to me seemed at first to be far away but then came closer. I was lying on my back and recognised Leiberich crouching over me as I tried to lift my head.

'I'm going to get you out of here, sir!'

I tried to reply but felt such a stab of pain from my leg that all I could do was cry out in agony.

'You must get up, sir. Here, I'll help you.'

Leiberich put his arms around me and, with a supreme effort, I managed to stand. Again though, I was crying out in pain and but for Leiberich's support I would have simply collapsed once more.

Placing all my weight on my left leg, and with Leiberich's right arm around me, we moved slowly in the direction of the Reichstag.

With an effort, I managed to find my voice. 'Are we going inside?'

'Yes, sir.'

I looked down. 'I'm bleeding to death!'

'You'll be all right, sir. I'm going to find you a Doctor.'

'Good.' I was still too confused and in too much pain to question his assertion. Then I remembered the rest of the men under my command.

'Have there been other casualties?'

Leiberich seemed to ignore my question as we struggled on. 'Unteroffizier, I asked...'

'Don't you worry about that, sir. The men are falling back with us.'

I glance around. I could see men running in the direction of the Reichstag but I didn't recognise any of them. I gasped.

'Unteroffizier, you're bleeding too!'

'It's just a graze to the head, sir. Nothing serious.'

In fact he looked awful and I realised that he probably hadn't told the whole truth about the men either. We were both very lucky to still be alive while others, I suspected, had been killed, or so severely wounded that they would never stand up again.

Leiberich and I carried on as best we could, while the air was full of the sound of explosions and gunfire. I sensed that at any moment we might be killed and I had the conviction that I'd descended into the same hell-like 'No Man's Land' from which I had been so fortunate to escape all those years ago on the Western Front.

The entrance to the Reichstag was just ahead of us but completely bricked-in, as were all the ground floor windows. I assumed that there must still be some way into the building via a back or side entrance and I could only pray that there were some medical facilities inside. With every metre of ground we covered, however, there came a dawning realisation that the building was a death trap and that once inside we'd never come out again alive. I managed to mutter my fear to Leiberich.

'Don't worry, sir, I agree.'

I was now leaning more and more heavily on him and certain that I must be continuing to lose a lot of blood. Desperate fatigue and waves of faintness were threatening to bring me to my knees. Still we somehow struggled on, with Leiberich managing to bear my weight, past the Reichstag, and on, instead, in the direction of the Brandenburg Gate.

'I'm going to try to get you to a hospital, sir,' Leiberich told me, which only made me think that they could all be in ruins, or so overcrowded that their staff could no longer cope. I remembered Leiberich telling me, though, that he knew Berlin like the back of his hand so I hoped that if anyone could get us to a hospital that was still intact, he would be able to do so.

'I'm sure I can remember the whereabouts of one, not far from here,' he added in confirmation of his talents, so we struggled on as best we could.

'There it is! It's a hospital, sir, we'll be there soon,' Leiberich suddenly cried out. 'I knew it was somewhere close.'

By now I was completely exhausted and fighting to remain conscious. Everything just seemed to be swimming before my eyes and becoming a blur until I had this vague awareness that we'd entered a building and a lot of people were moving around in a seemingly chaotic fashion. After that I must have lost consciousness.

When I woke up I was lying on a pallet in a long corridor with a blanket over me. I felt incredibly thirsty and tried to sit up. This was a mistake, however, as I hit a wall of pain that made me cry out.

'It's all right, sir, just lie back,' Leiberich told me gently.

'Water, I need water.'

'I'll get you some, sir, don't worry.'

I stared up at the ceiling. The pain was easing a little and I was aware that my injured leg has been bandaged and that I was wearing just a vest and pants. I could also hear other men moaning in pain and I wondered how much time had passed since we entered the hospital. I could feel that I was still wearing my watch but, as I brought it up to eye level, I saw that it had stopped. The corridor was dimly lit and, although from where I was lying it appeared windowless, I sensed that darkness had fallen.

Leiberich seemed to be gone hours, although in truth it was probably no more than fifteen minutes.

'Here's a glass of water, sir. I'm sorry it took me so long. It's chaos everywhere.'

'Thank you, Leiberich, thank you.'

I drank the water greedily, and all too quickly drained the glass, my thirst far from sated. I grimaced with disappointment.

'I can try and get you some more, sir?' Leiberich suggested.

'Could you?' I tried to smile and looked up at him. 'Are you all right?' I asked, becoming aware of his bandaged head for the first time. I felt a wave of gratitude towards him.

'Yes, I'm all right, sir.' He coughed and a look of discomfort crossed his face. 'There's something you should know, sir.'

'What's that?'

'The Russians are here, sir. There are guards on the front doors; I imagine the building is surrounded.'

'I see.' I could sense from Leiberich's tone of voice that he was frightened. 'And what time is it?' I asked, almost casually.

'It's nearly midnight, sir.'

Almost the 1ˢᵗ of May I thought but did not say. Springtime had truly arrived and with it a new beginning. I felt drowsy and wondered if Leiberich was still by my side.

*****

I woke with a start, conscious as I did so of a familiar sensation in my bladder as well as a throbbing pain in my leg. I could hear the sound of firing but it seemed to be quite distant. Then I remembered that the Russians had come and I looked around. Leiberich was slumped next to me, obviously asleep. I sensed that it was still night time.

I felt another wave of gratitude towards Leiberich. Yet again an individual, from a lower station in life, whom I'd only met through war, had been prepared to sacrifice everything for my welfare. It made me want to shake my head at the massive paradox that is human nature. Instead I crawled towards him and then nudged him awake.

'Shhh…' I whispered as with a startled look he opened his eyes. 'We have to get out of here!' He stared at me as if I was mad.

'If we don't the Russians will imprison us or worse. We may never see our families again!'

'But I told you, sir, this building is guarded. There may even be Russian soldiers inside the building. We can't just walk out, your trousers had to be cut off you at the knee, and even if we could you're in no fit state either…'

'All right! Perhaps we could hide somewhere.' Leiberich looked at me sceptically but I persisted. 'This place is huge, isn't it? There must be attics, cellars…'

'I've no doubt we could find somewhere for a few hours, but after that we'd need to eat and drink. I'm sorry, sir, but I think we're trapped.'

I allowed my head to sink forward and felt a sense of desperation. Behind me I could hear someone stirring. They, along with most of the men lying in the corridor, might well have overheard my fierce exchange with Leiberich, but I really didn't care.

'It's still the middle of the night, isn't it?'

Leiberich looked uncertain. 'I expect so, sir.'

'I need the lavatory; will you help me?'

Leiberich nodded and with a wince of pain I managed to stumble to my feet. It took us a few minutes to find a lavatory and by the time we did I had made up my mind what we were going to attempt.

'First, I need to get dressed, and then, I tell you, we've got to get out of here.'

'But sir…'

'No buts, Leiberich. I can just about walk and there must be plenty of back and side entrances to this place. The Russians surely aren't going to be guarding all of them that closely in the middle of the night. By the sound of things there's still some fighting going on as well so that should be giving them something more important to think about.'

Leiberich still looked sceptical. We both appreciated that I was asking him to take a risk of being shot at.

'Come on; it has to be worth a try. Can you fetch my clothes and boots for me? They're next to where I was lying, aren't they?'

'Yes, sir.'

'I'll wait here.'

A few minutes later Leiberich returned and I required all his support to be able to put on my trousers, or rather what was left of them. It was a painful exercise as well, and more than once I had to clench my teeth to prevent myself from crying out. The bandage around my leg was also blood stained and in need of changing. It was fortunate that I'd only suffered a deep flesh wound but I could tell that it had still gone well into my calf muscle, lacerating it in several places and, I suspected, leaving some tiny pieces of metal embedded in the muscle.

The nurse, who'd hurriedly dressed the wound before bandaging it, had done her best, I was sure, but there is no getting away from the fact that it would need further attention.

Leiberich shook his head at me in sheer disbelief at what I was trying to do. 'This won't work, sir. Suppose we do get out of here, where are we going to go, and how are you going to get treatment for that leg of yours?'

'Whatever fighting is still going on out there can't be all that far away. We'll find our own troops and with luck there'll be some medical auxiliaries who can help me. Come on, I'm not staying here. Are you with me or not?'

Leiberich merely nodded and, trying to ignore the pain I was in, I limped into the corridor outside the lavatory. It then took the two of us some ten minutes to find our way to a nondescript back entrance to the hospital by which time I was barely able to walk at all. On our way we'd also passed medical staff, some of whom had given us curious glances, but no one had made any attempt to stop us, or even speak to us.

I was fearful there would be one or more Russian soldiers guarding even this small single door, but as we approached it

I could see no one. Of course, it might have been locked, in which case I thought we would just have to try and find another door in the hope of being luckier a second time.

'You go ahead,' I whispered to Leiberich. 'Try to open it as quietly as you can.'

Drawing in my breath, as a wave of pain from my leg made me want to cry out, I watched as Leiberich turned the handle and the door slowly opened. After a moment's hesitation he stuck his head outside.

I tensed myself, expecting a cry of alarm from a Russian soldier but instead there was only silence.

'We're in luck, sir.'

'Indeed we are, Leiberich, come on!'

There could, though, be no question of hurrying and our only source of protection was the fact that it was still dark. Dawn was, however, no more than an hour away, and I realised that if we couldn't find our own troops by the time it grew light, our only hope would be to find somewhere to hide, and quickly. Otherwise, we'd either be captured or shot in no time at all.

We were in a small back street that seemed almost eerily deserted and the immediate question that confronted us was the direction in which we should travel? There was the noise of firing, which seemed to be coming from the direction of the Reichstag, but I immediately decided that it really made no sense to go anywhere near a building which must, by now, be totally surrounded by large numbers of Russian troops.

'We need to find a viewpoint,' I whispered to Leiberich, who again looked at me as if I'd taken leave of my senses. 'I mean by the time it gets light. It may give us some chance of seeing where our own troops are.'

'In my opinion, sir, those who haven't already surrendered must be completely surrounded by now.'

I drew in my breath at this bluntness from Leiberich and decided to ignore it. As we then turned a corner, I could see several buildings on fire and heard the crackling of flames. Rubble was also piling up across the street from buildings that had already collapsed, while the atmosphere was full of dust and smoke and the pungent smell of burning.

'What was that?' Leiberich asked anxiously.

It was the sound of voices and running feet, Russian voices too, and coming rapidly closer. I seized Leibreich's arm and together we shrank back into the shadows of a shop doorway. I didn't so much crouch as collapse in a heap, biting into my sleeve as I do so, from the pain in my leg, rather than cry out, which would have given us away.

The booted feet of at least a hundred Russian soldiers went past us, followed immediately afterwards by several tanks. With every passing second, I feared that we would be spotted. Yet the darkness still served as our protector and ,within a short while, the street was silent once more apart from the sound of the burning buildings.

Now we were within a short distance of the Tiergarten. I could recall passing large concentrations of our own troops at its western end when my men and I marched to the Moltke bridge to take up our position overlooking it. I decided that if German troops were still holding out in significant numbers anywhere in the city centre, the Tiergarten had to be the most likely place.

Informing Leiberich of my intention, I hobbled to my feet

and we set off once more. Our progress was extremely slow and several times we were forced to halt completely because I was in too much pain. Eventually, though, the open space of the Tiergarten came within sight. Dawn was just breaking.

I had my precious viewpoint in as much as I would soon be able to see some distance across the Tiergarten, even indeed as far as the Reichstag and the Brandenburg Gate, but I and Leiberich were now losing the measure of protection that darkness had afforded us. If there were still un-captured German troops in the vicinity, I knew we would have to catch sight of them very quickly, while, even then, reaching them might be impossible if they were engaged in actual combat. The risk, too, of being captured, or simply shot down by Russian troops, was also now immense.

We moved on tentatively from one shattered doorway to the next, hugging the shadows that the still dim light afforded us, until the Tiergarten stood opposite us across a road littered with burnt out vehicles, rubble, and the bodies of the dead. Most gruesomely, I could also see the figure of a man hanging from a lamppost. It was far from being the first time, though, that I had witnessed such a sight, and I assumed that, like so many others, he had been summarily executed by the Gestapo for not being prepared to stand and fight the Russians.

'Sir, those armoured vehicles over there are ours and still intact!' Leiberich whispered excitedly into my ear, pointing as he did so.

I nodded in agreement, but a brief moment of euphoria was soon replaced by one of fear as I heard the sound of Russian voices coming from behind us and getting closer. Realising that it might already be too late, we set off immediately in the direction of the armoured vehicles whilst I continued to curse the pain I was in. If there was ever a time to be able to run, this was surely it, but I knew it was totally impossible. Instead, all we could do was keep our heads down and remain in the shadows of the ruined buildings.

'You go on,' I urged Leiberich, 'don't wait for me.' However, my stubbornly loyal Unteroffizier merely shook his head and stayed by my side.

We were soon tantalisingly close to our destination and I could see the face of the driver of one of the armoured vehicles. I wanted to wave at him but restrained myself, anxious not to alert the enemy. Then I heard the sound of the vehicle's engine come to life, and also of the other vehicles close to it, and realised that they must be about to leave. I panicked, and shouted out.

'Wait, wait!'

I held up my right hand as well and waved frantically. The driver, whose face I'd seen, clearly now saw me, and I could sense his hesitation. I waved again.

'Help us,' I cried.

The driver held up a hand to me in response and a door to the vehicle began to open. I smiled in gratitude, but Leiberich and I still had thirty metres of exposed ground to cross, and before we were even halfway we heard the sound of firing.

I stumbled. Leiberich, however, saved me from falling, and although we both feared that at any moment we'd be gunned down, we somehow reached the still open door in safety. An outstretched hand then helped me climb on board, Leiberich was able to follow me, and the vehicle immediately sped off.

'Thank you for waiting for us,' I said, gratefully looking into the eyes of the young, unshaven soldier, sitting next to me.

'You were lucky we did. Another minute and we would have been gone.'

I then introduced both Leiberich and myself.

'I'm Leutnant Max Helm of the Muncheberg Panzer Division,' the young man replied. 'I can assure you that we have no intention of surrendering to those Russian pigs,' he added with a grin.

He looked down at the bandaging around my injured leg that had largely turned from white to red. 'We still have an ambulance with us. One of the medical auxiliaries ought to be able to change that for you.'

I nodded in thanks, but I soon began to feel dizzy, and everything seemed to be slipping away from me. I opened my mouth to speak but the words wouldn't come. I was just overwhelmed by sheer pain and exhaustion and began to pass out.

28

I regained consciousness slowly. I was extremely thirsty and called out for water before I even knew where I was.

'Here, sir, drink this.' It was Leiberich's dependable voice, offering me an immediate sense of reassurance.

I took the flask that was offered to me and drank from it thirstily. It was only having done so that I began to realise we were no longer in the armoured car but rather under canvas. 'Where are we, have I been out for long?' I asked anxiously.

'A few hours, sir.'

I looked at him incredulously.

'You've had a fever, sir. You've been delirious. This is a small field hospital. The nurse here has been able to re-dress your wound.'

' … And the Russians?'

'We're still holding out against them, Sir.'

I tried to lift my head but then started to feel faint, even nauseous.

'I don't think I've eaten a morsel since yesterday; any chance of any food?'

'I'll get you some bread and cheese, sir. I am afraid that's all there is.'

With that Leiberich disappeared and I lay my head back, conscious as I did so that I was lying on a stretcher with merely a thin blanket over me. I felt cold as well as hungry and I could hear the familiar sound of firing too. It seemed dangerously close. Fear of capture began to come back to me and I cursed under my breath at the very idea. Yet what could I possibly do to avoid it, if I couldn't even stand up without feeling ill?

Leiberich returned after a few minutes with the promised food and I greedily ate the bread and cheese he handed to me. It was gone all too quickly without satisfying my appetite but still helped to revive me.

'There's talk of surrender, sir,' Leiberich then confessed to me. It made me think of the words of the young officer in the armoured vehicle and I wondered if he was even still alive. 'The Russians have taken the Reichstag,' Leiberich added. 'And it's being said that the Fuhrer is dead. Suicide apparently.'

'Better that than become a prisoner of the Russians. Are we completely surrounded here?'

'I don't think so, sir.'

'Then I tell you I'm not being taken prisoner by the fucking Russians, Leiberich! We escaped from that damn hospital and there has to be some way out of this situation, too.'

I don't usually resort to swearing. I've long thought of myself as being too civilised, too urbane, to have to stoop to such coarse use of language, but I was now too tired and too angry to resist the temptation. I tried to sit up but my head began to spin and I collapsed back onto my stretcher.

'You need to rest, sir, to get back your strength,' Leiberich said comfortingly.

I simply closed my eyes and didn't respond. After a few minutes I opened them again and realised that Leiberich was still watching over me.

'I'm extremely grateful to you for all your support, Leiberich.'

'It's nothing, sir.'

'No, it's not; you could easily have deserted me. Look, you've a wife still in the city, haven't you?'

'Yes, sir, I have.'

'Then go to her, man, while you've still got the chance. You're not wearing any proper uniform, after all.'

'I am still on duty, sir.'

'Sod that, Leiberich, It's every man for himself now. The Fuhrer's dead, this city has been overrun by the Russians. I'm sure she needs your help more than I do.'

'I might not be able to get through to her, sir, while there's fighting going on. She could already be dead, sir… or worse.' Leiberich's voice trailed away even as he spoke.

'But, it's still got to be worth a try, and better than standing around here looking after me.'

Leiberich still hesitated. 'Only if you're sure, sir?'

'Of course, I am. Just go and take my best wishes with you for what they're worth.'

With that I held out my hand and Leiberich shook it warmly. 'Good luck, sir.'

'And you Leiberich, and you. Perhaps, we'll meet again in better times.'

'I do hope so, sir.'

I watched Leiberich depart, and for a moment regretted having encouraged him to do so. After all I was now alone, still incapacitated by my wound, and more than likely to spend the next few years of my life a prisoner of the Russians. In fact, I knew that if I was sent off to some Godforsaken prison camp in Siberia I might never come back at all. Yet, it would not have been fair to the man to keep him hanging around when he still had the chance to slip away and find his wife. Then I thought of Aliza, Clara and Leopold and with a sigh, closed my eyes.

I slept on and off, remembered asking for and being given water, and at some point being able to eat some bread and cold sausage. I was still in pain but far less so than I had been and the following morning, the 2nd May, I was woken by the sound of talking.

'It's official,' a man was saying. 'The surrender will take place today.'

'God help us then.'

The response had come from a woman whose voice I recognised as being that of the nurse who'd been looking after me. I felt a wave of panic. I was determined as I'd ever been not to be taken prisoner and immediately tried to stand up. I winced in pain but didn't feel any nausea or faintness. Once more I realised that all I had on was a shirt and pants and I desperately looked around for the rest of my clothes.

'Where are you going?' the nurse asked me, hurrying to my side.

'I'm getting out of here. I need my jacket... and my trousers, and shoes...'

'You're not well enough.'

'I feel well, better than I did anyway. Please, my clothes.'

'I'm afraid I've thrown away the trousers you were wearing.'

'You've done what?'

There was a note of anger in my question, but the nurse was unflustered by it.

'Don't worry; we've treated a lot of men who are now dead. You can have one of theirs. I'm sure I can find you a pair that will fit you.'

Her matter-of-fact tone slightly shocked me. Nurses had to be tough, of course, but looking at her face properly for the first time I thought how young she was and also how vulnerable. If she was taken by the Russians I didn't like to think what they would do to her.

She quickly brought me my jacket, shoes, and three pairs of trousers.

'I think these will fit you,' she suggested, holding up one of the pairs.

I reflected briefly on the fact that I was about to step into a dead man's trousers and almost shuddered at the thought. Also, with my heavily bandaged leg it didn't prove that easy a task and I required the nurse's support, but once I'd got them on I decided that they fitted me reasonably well.

'Yes, they'll do, I'm sure. Thank you.'

At first glance I might now have passed for a man who was unwounded but the moment I tried to take my first step I started to stumble and felt a searing pain in my leg. The nurse came to my aid but I gently shunned her away.

'No, no, I'll be all right,' I insisted and took another step. This time I was able to maintain my balance and the pain was bearable but I could still only walk with a severe limp. I realised that I was not going to get far and that capture by the Russians was inevitable unless I could hide somewhere. But, by itself, that would not be enough. I'd need a supply of food and water and sooner or later further medical treatment. I took a few more steps and then turned and looked at the nurse.

'My advice to you is not to hang around here until the Russians come. You won't be safe in their hands, I'm afraid,' I told her bluntly.

'I have my duty to these poor men to consider,' she answered me bravely, spreading out her right arm as she did so as if to enfold all of the wounded men in her care.

'Yes, I suppose you have. Good luck to you, anyway.'

'And to you as well.'

Once outside I felt desperately exposed and alone. I was prepared to contemplate suicide in preference to capture by the Russians but I'd been without my revolver since entering the hospital. Then, by luck, I saw Leutnant Helm and his crew standing by their vehicle barely fifty metres away and hobbled towards them as quickly as I could.

'Leutnant,' I called out as I got closer. 'Are you and your men going to surrender to the Russians?'

'No, sir, not if we can help it. The plan is to attempt a breakout and, if we make it, to head west.'

'Even if whoever is left in command of this city orders you to surrender?'

'It would have to be done at gunpoint, Sir. Otherwise, we're going and soon.'

'Will you take me with you?'

'With respect sir, you've been wounded. I'm afraid we are only prepared to take able bodied men.'

'You'll try and head out through Spandau, though, won't you?'

'Yes, certainly.'

'Well, my house is there. If it hasn't been destroyed or isn't already crawling with Russians, I still have a car in the garage with a tank full of petrol. At least take me that far with you.'

The Leutnant still seemed doubtful.

'Look, you don't have to take me to the front door. Anywhere within half a kilometre will do and I'll manage to walk the remainder of the distance.'

'All right, sir, it'll be a pleasure.'

'Thank you, Leutnant, I'm extremely grateful to you.'

'I should really obtain my commanding officer's permission, of course, but… well… in the circumstances…'

The two of us shook hands and within an hour I found myself being driven through the shattered streets of Berlin, the vehicle I was in being the last of a convoy of five armoured cars. At any moment I expected that we might find our retreat blocked by Russian tanks or infantry, but this threat failed to materialise. The city had fallen strangely silent and our only difficulty was caused by having to manoeuvre around debris that had fallen into the streets from destroyed buildings, the bodies of the dead, and the occasional wrecked or burnt out vehicle.

Nobody spoke but I was conscious of a palpable level of tension around me, which I shared. Surely, we were not going to be able to escape this easily? Still the minutes ticked by and although our progress was slow I reckoned we must have travelled more than a kilometre before we finally encountered any Russian troops.

'They're only infantry, put your foot down!' Leutnant Helm shouted at our driver. However, the amount of debris on the road made it virtually impossible. From where I was sitting I had very little view of the outside world, but I could hear the sound of shots striking the walls of our vehicle and bouncing off. I instinctively ducked, shut my eyes, and prayed that these wouldn't be followed by something more deadly, such as a hand grenade or an armour piercing shell, but this didn't happen.

'We're past them!' Helm shouted out excitedly and I breathed out slowly in sheer relief. Finally, I dared to glance outside again and I was able to recognise the ruins of a church that I'd long admired although I'd never been inside its now burnt out walls. I also realised that we're barely a kilometre from my home.

'You can let me out soon, Leutnant,' I said in as matter-of-fact a voice as I could muster.

'We don't have to, sir. You're welcome to stay for the ride if you want to…'

'But you said…'

'Yes, but now you're with us, well, I'm hardly going to throw you out. Here, fancy a cigarette?'

Leutnant Helm grinned at me mischievously and, as soon as I was able to light up, I was grateful to imbibe the shot of nicotine that the cigarette gave me. It relaxed me a little but I still couldn't help wondering if it was really wise to remain where I was for very much longer. I had a sense that the vehicle I was travelling in could become my funeral pyre as it would only take one well aimed shell to incinerate all its occupants. Would I still be better off making my way home, I wondered? Changing out of my uniform for good, and using my own car, assuming it was still intact, could be my means of escape.

Of course, I knew that the car might be just as, if not more, vulnerable to enemy fire, while, with my injured leg still hurting me as much as it was, I might even struggle to be able to drive the vehicle. I'd also be entirely on my own, although not completely unarmed, as, despite the loss of my Luger. I had another one with ammunition that I kept in a locked drawer in my study. There was also another incentive for taking this option that, up until now, I'd been putting to the back of my mind.

'More Russian troops, I'm afraid, sir,' the driver of our vehicle suddenly shouted out and almost instantaneously there came the sound of firing.

I was just able to make out the vehicle in front of us, swerving to avoid some obstruction and then seeming to disappear behind a cloud of smoke which rapidly swallowed up our own vehicle. A shell, or it could have been a rocket, had struck the walls of a building, bringing it down onto the road, and scattering a great cloud of dust everywhere.

The firing continued, but once again we managed to elude danger and continue on our way. Even so, I'd made up my mind now.

'Leutnant, I'm grateful to you for your offer to let me stay on board, but we're now very close to my home and I've decided to make my way there.'

Leutnant Helm shrugged his shoulders. 'As you wish, sir. You'll have to make a quick exit, though. We can't risk hanging around, you know.'

'Of course, Leutnant, I fully appreciate that.'

29

I was feeling exposed and isolated as I waved farewell to Leutnant Helm. For a brief moment I stood my ground, watching the convoy of armoured vehicles continue on their journey westwards towards the River Halbe. If they were lucky they might succeed in crossing it and surrendering to either the Americans or the British, while, if they were not, at least they'd had the courage to try.

I began to look around me and was immediately struck by how eerily quiet it had become after so many days of constant bombardment of the city. I could also see no sign of anyone, but I was acutely conscious that at any moment either Russian soldiers or Russian vehicles might appear.

As I limped in the direction of my home, I flinched with pain and, although I would like to have been able to walk faster, I knew that this was simply impossible. In happier times it would have been inconceivable to me that taking this all too familiar route, of a few hundred metres towards my own front door, would be such a frightening experience. Nonetheless, as I turned into my own avenue, still lined with trees in the bloom of spring, I dared to hope that I'd reach my destination undetected.

Then I thought of my keys and, with a rising sense of panic, rummaged in one of the pockets of my jacket.

'Thank Christ.' I thought to myself. If necessary I'd have had to force entry but that would have been both time consuming and noisy.

I managed to reach the entrance to the driveway safely and with a sigh of relief, I gave thanks that my luck had held. I could see, as I approached the front door, that it was still shut and, even more importantly, the doors to the garage were as well. I knew it could only be a question of time before Russian troops arrived to loot a house as palatial as mine, but by then I hoped to be well gone.

As I turned the lock and entered the hallway, I immediately thought I could hear a noise. I wondered if it had come from behind me and glanced outside. There was no sign of anyone, however, so I shut the door, assuming for a moment that I must have imagined the sound.

'Baron, is that you?'

I jumped with shock and then recognised the voice.

'Yes, Frau Solger, it's me, but what are you doing here?'

She was coming towards me now, looking distraught. She had obviously been crying.

'Baron, thank God it's you, I thought it might be the Russians.'

'They'll be here soon enough, I expect. But why aren't you at home?'

'It's just a ruin… and…'

At that she burst into tears and I consolingly took her in my arms.

'We were in a shelter, and then the Russians came. They started to rape us, they were like animals, I…'

She placed her head on my shoulder and sobbed.

'It's all right, it's all right,' I tried to assure her.

'I just didn't know where to go… I had my key, I was so hungry…'

'Yes, of course, I understand…'

My mind was now racing. This was a complication I could do without. I had always liked Frau Solger. She was a decent woman who had served me well over many years. She had also been a widow since the last war, although I was aware that she had a daughter who lived not all that far from her. I struggled, though, to recall her name.

'What about your daughter and her family?' I asked her gently.

She looked up at me nervously and at that precise moment I saw the face of a small boy standing at the door of the kitchen. A moment later his mother also appeared. She was so much like a younger version of Frau Solger that no one could have failed to recognise they were related.

'Please forgive me, sir, but my daughter and her son are also homeless.'

'Yes, yes, don't worry, you did the right thing.'

I smiled at her reassuringly and also at her daughter and grandchild, my mind racing with uncertainty even as I did so. What was I going to do with them, I asked myself, pack them in the car and take them with me? No, they would represent too great a liability and were probably as safe in my house as anywhere, until that is any Russian soldiers arrived.

I glanced behind me and had a view through the hall window of the drive up which I have just walked. I half-expected to see Russian soldiers marching into sight but for the time being at least all remained quiet.

'Frau Solger, I need to get out of this uniform. It'll only take me a few minutes. You know that you and your daughter are still at risk if the Russians come?'

'Yes, sir, we do.' She was beginning to shake with fear at the very mention of that dreaded word.

'I suggest that you all be prepared to hide in the cellar. Do you know where the key is?'

She shook her head, so I quickly found it for her. Then I limped upstairs to my bedroom and painfully changed into civilian clothes as rapidly as I could. The very act of divesting myself of my uniform for the last time gave me a palpable sense of relief, but I remained anxious to dispose of not just the uniform but also anything else that could identify me as an SS officer and member of the Nazi party. Having to take such a step gave me mixed feelings, though. In many ways I still did not believe that I had, personally, done anything to be ashamed of; indeed I considered that I'd always sought to act honourably. However, I still felt damned, if only by association, and couldn't escape a strong sense of collective guilt for the sins of the Party. Above all, I feared the treatment that I could expect to receive at the hands of the Russians.

I also sensed the clock ticking against me. It was, though, now late afternoon and I had decided not to make any attempt to escape until darkness falls. I had also worked out an escape route that might just avoid road blocks.

'Frau Solger,' I called out. 'I need your help, please?'

I limped back down the stairs and into my study where I proceeded to search quickly through my desk. After that I asked Frau Solger to light a small fire.

It was risky, of course. If Russian troops were nearby and saw smoke coming out of the chimney it could draw them towards the house like a magnet. Yet I had already taken enough risks in the last two days to almost be beyond caring. Next, I asked Frau Solger if she knew of the whereabouts of a pair of clothing scissors.

'I need to cut up my uniform,' I explained to her.

'I'll do it, sir,' she responded, scurrying off upstairs. I was left continuing to chuck any incriminating paperwork I could think of onto the fire. I remained reluctant, however, to destroy my diaries and above all my memoir and decided that it was pointless trying to destroy everything I'd ever written about my life as a member of the Party. Instead I took my diaries along with my memoir down to the cellar where I hid them under the stairs in an old box. I resolved that if I should be fortunate enough to survive and ever be able to return to this place, I would add a chapter or two about my experiences over the last few days and also no doubt some more chapters as well about what was to come.

I then returned to my study where I managed to smile wearily at Frau Solger's grandson, who was standing by the door, watching me shyly. I could also hear the child's mother, whose existence I'd barely even acknowledged, sobbing. The child turned away, no doubt wishing to offer her comfort, but the sobbing continued unabated.

I decided that the whole situation was positively surreal and turned my face towards the fire, while willing what I've thrown on to it to burn as quickly as possible. I would have liked to burn my uniform as well, but realised it wasn't a sensible option. Instead, I decided to bury it in the garden and hope it would rot away to nothing before it was ever disturbed. Then I remembered that I had a spare uniform hanging up in my wardrobe.

'Frau Solger!' I shouted. I was already limping towards the stairs as I opened my mouth.

'Yes, sir,' she called out in reply.

'Have you found the scissors yet?'

'Yes, and I've started to cut up your uniform.'

'I'm afraid there's a spare one as well. I'm going to bury both of them in the garden. There isn't time to cut up both of them. If you can just remove the insignia then that'll have to do.'

Barely five minutes later I limped into the garden with Frau Solger alongside me, carrying the two uniforms. I was immediately struck by how tranquil and undisturbed everything seemed. The Third Reich was in its death throes, its cities in ruins, Russian troops surely very close, yet the signs of spring were still everywhere, a symbol as always of new life and a new beginning.

I hurried as fast as I could towards the shed where I knew I'd find a spade and I soon set to work to dig a hole. But for my wounded leg it would've been an easy and quick enough task. As it was however…

'Let me do it for you, sir,' Frau Solger insisted.

I felt helpless and cross at my lack of physical capacity but this was no time for hubris so I handed the spade to her with muted thanks.

'You need to rest, sir,' she admonished me gently.

'Just as soon as you've finished this task for me, Frau Solger.'

'Are you in a lot of pain, sir?'

'I've known worse. Don't worry about me, I'll be all right.'

The hole that Frau Solger managed to dig was only a shallow one but I decided that it would have to do, and, throwing the uniforms into it, I urged her to cover them up.

As the earth closed over them, and we then made our way back indoors, I felt a grim sense of satisfaction. I was now no more than a civilian at home with his housekeeper and her family who has been made homeless by the bombing. It was a lie that could still, all too easily, be exposed, of course, but at least I thought I ought to be at less risk of being marched away to imprisonment in Siberia.

Once back inside the house, I felt able, at last, to give some thought to what had encouraged me to return here in the first place. I made my way back into my study, still as much a sanctuary of civilised elegance as ever, and searched under the Louis XVI clock that stood proudly on the mantelpiece. As I did so, I noticed that it had stopped and I couldn't help thinking that this was rather appropriate. Then I placed my fingers around the key that I was looking for, went to my desk, and opened one of the drawers, from which I took out a bag and looked inside.

I thought paper Reichsmarks must now be worthless, but gold was quite another matter. It is always bound to retain some value, in parlous times perhaps even a considerable value, and I was confident that if I could ever get to Zurich I could get a good price for the coins in the bag. They were Kaiser Wilhelm twenty-mark pieces, about fifty in all, which held their value even during the disastrous period of hyper-inflation in 1923, and which I'd always regarded as my final reserve in case such an era, or something akin to it, should ever return. There were as many again at my home in the Black Forest, which Clara was free to make use of, as well as an account in a Zurich Bank with a healthy balance, so I took some comfort from the fact that her financial future ought to still be reasonably secure.

Next, I looked around me and saw that the maps I owned were still in their usual place on a shelf next to the window. I needed to plan a route that would avoid as many main roads as possible, but the more I thought about it, the more I wondered if there was really any realistic chance of successfully escaping from Berlin. Seeking to do so on foot would have been an alternative, of course, but I was still too badly wounded for that. There was also another consideration that continued to trouble me.

In the last few days I had tried not think too much about Aliza, but now she was once again at the forefront of my consciousness. If her camp was liberated by the Russians I still feared for her safety, and even if that fear was groundless, I couldn't help feeling an unshakeable compulsion to go to her aid. I recalled that Theresienstadt wasn't all that far from Prague, which before the collapse of the Reich, I would have been confident of reaching by car in less than five hours. However, to get there would mean travelling in a slightly South Easterly direction, whereas my home in the Black Forest lies to the South West. Prague too, might well have fallen by now, just as Berlin had, and there could, indeed, have already been a general capitulation following the Fuhrer's death. I decided that, above all, I needed to have some idea of what was going on outside Berlin and decided to turn to the radio.

Music was playing, although not anything that I recognised. I turned the dial, searching for a station that for so long had been forbidden listening; the voice of the BBC. It was close to the hour and with luck I hoped to be able to hear a news broadcast. Sure enough, I was soon listening to the well modulated tones of the news reader. What is said confirmed that Hitler was apparently dead. It told me too that Admiral Doenitz had now become Fuhrer and what I knew already, namely that Berlin had fallen. But what of Prague? Russian forces were advancing in its direction but apparently it was still in German hands. This news helped me to make up my mind.

'Sir, can I get you anything to eat?' Frau Solger asked me, putting her head around the door. She asked the question in such a matter-of-fact tone that it might have been just another day rather than one in which our whole world was continuing to fall in around us and the Russians could be on our doorstep at any moment.

'There isn't much, I'm afraid. Some rather stale bread and some sausage and, oh yes, a little cheese.'

'That would be very nice, thank you, but what about you, and your daughter and grandchild?'

'There's enough to go round, sir. I don't think my daughter is in any state to eat at all, and I don't feel much like eating anything either.'

She quickly disappeared in the direction of the kitchen and I continued to study my maps. The food she soon brought me was enough to satisfy my hunger and she provided a bottle of beer as well. The combination of alcohol and nicotine from one of my few remaining cigarettes relaxed me considerably, and also helped ease the pain in my leg, but I still couldn't help feeling that I was about to embark on a suicide mission. I even began to half-wish for the Russians to turn up and put a halt to my plans.

I went in search of Frau Solger and found her sitting at the kitchen table, comforting her grandson, while her daughter sat opposite her, looking just as traumatised and tearful as before.

'Frau Solger,' I said gently. 'I'm going to try and escape from Berlin tonight if the Russians don't come first. My car is still in the garage and it has a full tank of petrol. It's going to be very dangerous, I'm afraid, and I could well be killed; captured anyway. You're welcome to stay here, of course, but you will continue to be vulnerable…'

'Can we come with you, please?' Frau Solger's daughter asked me, pleadingly.

'I don't think so…'

'Please, sir, please don't leave us here?'

'No, I'm sorry, it's too dangerous.'

'But if the Russians come we will be raped again!' She was now almost hysterical and I wavered a little.

'There's the cellar, you can lock it from the inside…'

'That won't stop them!'

I wavered again but only for a moment. 'I'm afraid you'd still be taking a far greater risk coming with me. You'd never forgive me and I would never forgive myself if your child was shot. And even if I do escape, I intend to head South towards Czechoslovakia.'

'Why, sir?' It was Frau Solger who asked this question.

'There is something I must do there and it's really for the best if I go alone.'

'But the Russians…'

'According to what I have just heard on the radio they haven't captured Prague yet.'

Frau Solger's daughter was now sobbing again so she sought to console her while I returned to my study. There I opened the locked drawer of my desk and took out my spare Luger together with a box of ammunition. I knew it would give me no protection at all against machine gun fire and I contemplated putting it back. Instead, though, I took it with me to the garage where my car was waiting for me.

I paused for a second or two to admire it. The vehicle had served me well, I reflected affectionately. It was reliable, fast, and built to last. I was, however, about to put it to a very stern test indeed and could only hope that it wouldn't let me down. Opening the boot I put the Luger and the ammunition inside and then returned to the house.

I'd made up my mind not to attempt to leave until after midnight. Two or even three o'clock in the morning would be ideal, as any Russians manning road blocks, or simply patrolling the streets, would be likely to be at their least alert, but I had a long way to go and needed the maximum cover of darkness.

As the evening drew on my sense of impatience began to mount. I would have liked to have had a rest, or even a sleep, but I was both too restless and too tense, still expecting, even as it began to grow dark, that Russian troops would come marching up the drive.

30

3rd May 1945

It is only as I drove out into the night that the real enormity of what I was about to attempt began to strike home. My wounded leg made the very act of driving painful, there were no street lights, it was pitch dark, and yet there could be no question of putting my car headlights onto full beam for fear of announcing my approach long before I actually arrived. It was also extremely quiet and at first the engine of my car seemed loud enough to waken the dead.

Frau Solger kissed me on the cheek and wished me 'God speed' before I departed and I hugged her in return. She gave me some bread and cheese that she had wrapped and I took some bottled beer and water for the journey as well. I dared to hope that we might meet again in happier times but I feared that the prospects of that happening were remote.

I had remembered to take some of Clara's clothes with me in the hope that Aliza and her daughter would be able to wear them, as, if I was to rescue them, they would certainly need to change out of their camp uniforms. I thought it as well that Aliza and Clara were not so different in height and could only hope what I had chosen for Aliza's daughter wouldn't swamp the girl too much.

I decided that my best chance of eluding the Russians lay in the fact that Leutnant Helm and his men had already helped me escape from the centre of Berlin and that my house stands close to a large expanse of wooded land that is criss-crossed by many small roads and pathways. There are just two roads of any size through it, one to the West that runs partly along the banks of the river Havel, and an autobahn to the East, but I was determined to avoid the former as much as I could and to ignore the latter completely. I also knew the woods well but trying to drive through them at night on dipped headlights would still be a challenge.

To my relief I managed to turn onto one of the minor roads leading through the woods with surprising ease and set off down it at a cautious speed of about thirty kilometres an hour. I reckoned, too, that if I could travel that far before dawn I should then succeed in reaching my intended destination. All the same, every kilometre was still going to be fraught with danger and I had more than two hundred to travel.

I found it hard not to be completely unnerved by the total uncertainty of my situation. At any moment I might find my way blocked or that I'd simply run into a concentration of Russian troops encamped by the roadside, some of whom would be awake enough to fire at me if I didn't halt immediately when commanded to do so. Yet, the road remained eerily deserted, lined only by somnolent trees looming out of the darkness, so that the further I travelled, the more I allowed myself to believe that I might really be able to escape.

By the time I reached the southern end of the wood I had left the main part of the city, but not its outer suburbs. I knew, too, that I had no choice but to join the road system that passes through them. The route I'd planned enabled me to skirt Potsdam to the West and Tretlow to the East. For a few kilometres I would be forced to travel through a built up area that I realised must have been overrun by Russian troops as they encircled the city. The question was how many of them still remained there and to what extent had they sealed off the roads?

I kept thinking that what I was attempting was the sort of madness that the Russians were probably prepared for. However, it was now one o'clock in the morning, and they had just won the war, so their guard might be down a little. I pressed on, and began to drive along a deserted road lined by houses that, even in the deep gloom of a moonless night, I could tell were mostly ruined. At least, the road was passable and there was still no sign of any Russian troops.

I could tell that I was not far from Wannsee Railway station, as likely a place as anywhere for there to be Russian troops about, and I'd already planned to avoid this. It meant driving along a series of back streets that I was only vaguely familiar with and, in the pitch dark, I grew more and more anxious that I might take a wrong turn and become lost. Worse, that I might even start travelling back towards the city rather than away from it. Gripping the wheel ever tighter, I could feel sweat trickling down the back of my spine.

If I could just cross over Potsdammerstrasse safely, I knew I'd be into another wooded area and once there perhaps be able to relax a little. Yet, the road I was on was so dark I wasn't at all sure I was going the right way. Then I heard a sudden thud as something struck the body of the car. I looked around in fright, instantly thinking the worst, but quickly came to the conclusion that it must have been some rubble lying in the road, which had been kicked up by the car's wheels. I could just see a junction ahead of me and prayed it was the one I wanted.

It was only as I reached the junction that I realised, with a curse of annoyance, I had made a mistake. As rapidly as I could, I reversed the car and went back the way I had just come. I decided I must have taken a right hand turning when I should have taken a left. Thankfully, it took me barely more than a minute to get back on the right road, or so I hoped, but then again every minute was so precious.

Now I was approaching a junction again and this time to my relief I was certain it was the right one. A split second later, however, I noticed a uniformed figure and then another standing on the corner of the junction with what had to be rifles slung over their shoulders. They both turned and looked in my direction and my foot immediately hit the accelerator.

The men were barely ten metres away and taken completely by surprise. As I sped past them one of them shouted out, and I think I saw one of them begin to take his rifle off his shoulder, but there could be no question of my stopping, and my one intent was to get across Potsdammerstrasse.

The road leading into the woods was now immediately ahead of me but to my horror I could also see a Russian tank. It wasn't, thank God, quite blocking the road, but in order to get around it I was forced to mount the pavement and almost lost control of the wheel. I fought to regain it and even as I succeeded, and sped off into the night, I could hear shouts behind me, and then also shots ringing out as well.

I instinctively ducked and heard yet more shots followed by the sound of breaking glass. My rear windscreen had been shattered and the bullet, which had inflicted the damage, had also gone through the front windscreen, missing my head by no more than a few centimetres. I was so shaken that at first I could only breathe in short, sharp, fearful bursts, but I was still alive and still driving on, if only into a wall of darkness.

I looked anxiously into the rear mirror, expecting that I'd be followed but I could see no lights. I could afford to concentrate on the way ahead, realising nervously that I'd have to join a more major road quite soon and that one significant obstacle still lay ahead of me, the Teltow canal. If all its bridges were down, or completely blocked off, then I might well still be trapped and all my efforts to escape have come to nothing.

As I approached the more major road I thought I could hear the sound of vehicles moving along it and then saw approaching headlights. My foot hit the brake, sending a searing pain up my leg, and in almost the same instant I switched off both the headlights and the engine. I was still some distance back from the junction; enough, I hoped, for my presence not to be too obvious. Anyone glancing in my direction and catching a glimpse of my vehicle might simply have assumed that it had been abandoned and was of no consequence. I lowered my head whilst retaining a view of the way ahead. If necessary, I might still have time to put the car into reverse, but then I remembered what I had just escaped from and wondered if anyone had decided to pursue me after all.

I was sweating again, really totally exhausted, and running on nothing more than adrenalin. The headlights ahead of me grew brighter, a convoy of about a dozen vehicles drove by, but no one appeared to take any notice of my car and very soon they had passed. I waited for about five agonising minutes, still worried about what might be approaching from behind, and then started the engine again.

Driving down the road the convoy had been on made me intensely nervous. I knew, as well, that I was now very close to the canal and that the chances of finding any bridge both intact and unguarded were very slight. I rehearsed a plan in my head. The way over the nearest bridge, if it is still standing, was quite familiar to me. I began to accelerate as I got closer to it, travelling now at forty and then an even noisier fifty kilometres an hour.

The bridge was now in sight and appeared to be intact. Further, nothing appeared to be obstructing access across it, but as I accelerated to an even faster speed I could see the dark figures of a couple of Russian soldiers standing next to it. One of them shouted at me and then raised his rifle, but by now I was so close to him that by the time he tried to take aim I was already speeding past him onto the bridge.

A shot rang out from behind me and I heard the bullet strike the roof of my car above my head. Ahead of me I now saw another Russian soldier begin to raise his rifle, but I was travelling so fast in his direction that the man abandoned his intention and instead leapt to one side to save his skin. Again, as I sped off into the night, I was pursued by more shots, but I heard none strike my car, and allowed myself to believe in miracles. I had now truly escaped from Berlin!

31

Sooner or later I knew I was going to have to find somewhere to stop. If I didn't, I would simply fall asleep at the wheel and crash the car. Yet I was convinced, as well, that I had to make the most of the cover of darkness and achieve the maximum amount of progress before dawn came up. Also, I had no idea whether or not I was driving into territory already occupied by advancing Russian troops so the need for vigilance remained paramount. Above all, I realised that wherever I halted, if I then fell into too sound a sleep, I would be as vulnerable as any new born infant.

By the time dawn broke I had managed to travel about seventy kilometres south of Berlin without much incident. Twice I had seen the lights of vehicles approaching in the distance, but on both occasions I had just had time to be able to turn off the road I was on, switch off my lights and engine, and wait apprehensively for the vehicles to pass me. I concluded that the drivers of the vehicles must have seen my lights as I had seen theirs, but if they wondered why they didn't pass anything, it didn't cause them to stop. Whether they were friend or foe I had no idea.

Once I saw the lights of a vehicle following me, so, despite the pitch dark and my unfamiliarity with the road I was on, I instantly accelerated from a modest thirty to more like fifty kilometres an hour. The light of the vehicle faded into the distance and then, even as I slowed down somewhat, disappeared, so I assumed that the vehicle either halted or turned off in another direction.

My leg continued to cause me considerable pain but even this couldn't prevent me from beginning to nod off. My tiredness was in fact becoming overwhelming and as the light steadily improved I was determined to find a quiet spot where I could rest, eat and drink, and perhaps even allow myself to fall asleep for a couple of hours. Visibility was also now good enough to enable me to switch off my headlights, but within seconds of my doing so I thought I could hear the sound of distant artillery fire coming from the East.

I was more than a little encouraged by this as it could only mean that German troops were still fighting and that I was now behind their lines. That should also mean that Dresden and just as importantly Prague had not yet fallen to the Russians. There was still every chance, therefore, that I could reach Theresienstadt in time to rescue Aliza. Yet again, though, my head nodded forward and with a start I realised I had been asleep for a split second, which was long enough to begin to steer too far to the right. I hastily corrected my mistake and started looking around anxiously for somewhere safe to stop.

I was now driving through a large wooded area and before too long noticed that I was approaching a small turning in the road. As I came up to it I slowed almost to a halt and could see that it was no more than a narrow un-signposted lane. I decided to take it, stop after no more than about a hundred metres, switch off the engine, and examine the map. I was quickly convinced that it was taking me even deeper into the wood, so that if I continued along it for a little while longer I should soon find what I was looking for.

Sure enough, after progressing no more than another kilometre, I spotted a track leading off the lane. It was clearly not intended for motor vehicles, being narrow and muddy, but I reckoned that there was still just enough width to be able to drive along it. Above all it appeared to quickly veer to the right behind some tall trees. Once again I halted and this time got out of my car to reconnoitre. I found, to my delight, that the track actually widened out somewhat and I was satisfied that the ground was firm enough for there to be no risk of getting bogged down in it. Most importantly, I decided my car should be invisible to anyone coming along the lane.

When I turned round and approached my car I almost gasped. This was the first time I had been able to appreciate just how "shot up" it was. I counted several bullet holes through the bodywork and realised how lucky I was the bullets had not only missed me, but also failed to hit either the petrol tank or the wheels. With a sense of relief I got inside and greedily drank the beer I had brought with me. I also thought about eating something but didn't really feel that hungry. I was too tired and rapidly fell asleep.

****

I woke with a start, wondering at first where I was. I could hear a droning sound and realised it came from an aircraft flying overhead. I couldn't see it, but the noise was all too familiar to be coming from anything else. Still barely conscious, I blearily looked at my watch and groaned with dismay. It was almost ten o'clock in the morning and I'd been asleep for all of five hours, twice as long as I had intended. My leg was also throbbing with pain and I felt a pang of hunger as well. I also suspected that it was this combination more than the noise of any plane that had finally woken me.

Anxious to be on my way as soon as possible, I ate about half the food I had with me, attended to a call of nature, and within a few minutes of waking started the engine. I felt a tinge of anxiety as it spluttered a little but it was an expensive car, which had always been reliable and it did not let me down. Soon I was able to reverse onto the lane and drive back towards the road that I knew led to Dresden.

Signs of spring were bursting into bloom everywhere and at first the countryside appeared to be empty, but not for long. Civilians started coming into view, walking in the opposite direction; old men, women and children, carrying a few precious possessions. As I drove past them I was struck by how dispirited they seemed, and the further I travelled, the more crowded the road became with these pitiful refugees, until I was nearly brought to a complete standstill.

I began to grow frustrated and to worry not just about the time I was losing but also the amount of petrol my car was consuming.

'Dresden's in ruins. Don't you know that?' a woman in her forties called out to me from the side of the road.

'The Russians are coming too,' another older-looking woman, standing next to her, added, 'I'd turn round if I were you.'

I ignored them and as the crowd of fleeing refugees thinned out a little, I was able to pick up speed for the first time in more than ten minutes. I had come too far to turn back now and anyway Dresden was not my final destination.

It was my intention ,as well, to bypass the city, if I could, and I was well aware that it had been devastated by allied bombing more than two months previously. It brought to mind the conversation that I had had with Arnold Raether when I had last returned to Berlin from the Black Forest. I wondered if he was still alive and then I thought, too, of Clara and Leopold.

I was still trying to convince myself that I had done the right thing coming this way in order to try to rescue Aliza and her daughter. By doing so, I understood full well, I was putting their interests before Clara's and Leopold's. Worse still, I realised, too, I was motivated above all else by a desire to see Aliza again and I accepted my actions were essentially selfish. My only excuse, I supposed, was that I was compelled by a desire to make some amends for her suffering, as well as by the love that I felt for her.

Although I also doubt if I would have succeeded in getting out of Berlin at all by any other route than the one I had taken, I knew I had long since ignored the opportunity to turn west in the direction of the Black Forest. At least, though, I was still behind German lines unless, of course, the woman who had just called out to me was right and the Russians had broken through everywhere.

Within moments I saw an armoured vehicle coming towards me and began to panic. I looked around me, desperately hoping that I could turn around before it reached me, but then I noticed that the vehicle had the familiar swastika markings on it. I sighed with relief and saw that the vehicle was the first of several. Quickly, I got out of my car and, as the leading vehicle came closer, I waved in the direction of the driver.

'Hullo, can you tell me what's happening? I'm trying to get to Prague.'

In response to my question a fresh faced young man sitting next to the driver stuck his head out of the window of the vehicle.

'I wouldn't bother if I were you. We're on our way to surrender to the Americans or the British, if we can. I expect the Russians will be in Prague very soon.'

'But I heard the distant sound of gunfire to the East. Some of our men must still be putting up a fight, surely?'

By now the vehicle had driven past me, however, and the young man has already put his head back inside its window. I cursed under my breath in frustration but by now the second vehicle in the convoy was almost alongside me, so I tried shouting out much the same question.

'I'm trying to get to Prague… is the line still holding?'

'As far as I know it is.' This time the response came from a much older looking man, whose face had a lined, war hardened look about it, and was smeared with dirt. 'But I don't suppose it will for much longer. I'd follow us if I were you. We're heading west.'

'Thank you but I need to get to Prague… it's important.'

'Suit yourself.'

I continued to stand by my car as the remainder of the convoy drove past me and I felt that familiar urge to smoke. The nicotine, at least, helped to soothe my nerves a little and with a grim sense of fatalism I was soon driving slowly south once more.

Then I heard the sound of planes coming from the east. The noise of their engines was loud and menacing and getting lower. I looked up and could just make out a fighter plane approaching at only a few hundred metres.

My stomach tightened with fear as I realised the pilot's intentions. I hit the brakes hard, almost instantaneously switched off the engine, and threw open the door, but it was already too late for such measures. The plane had already begun its attack. The bullets, though, were aimed not at me but at the convoy of vehicles I had just passed.

Even so, I still abandon my car as quickly as I could and hobbled away from it, taking cover under a roadside tree. From this vantage point I could make out three aircraft attacking the convoy, and I heard an explosion, presumably from one of the vehicles catching fire. Seconds later I saw a cloud of black smoke rising up from the air and I wondered if the men I had just been talking to were dead or wounded.

I felt relieved not to have taken up their offer to follow them, although I still felt intensely vulnerable to the possibility of attack. After all, my car had to be fully visible from the air, and if they wished any one of the pilots above me could decide to shoot it up. However, they chose not to do so, perhaps because it was obviously not a military vehicle, perhaps simply because they wanted to conserve their ammunition. In any event, my luck was continuing to hold, and once the planes had disappeared I felt free to continue on my way.

After that incident, my journey south was comparatively uneventful, if slow, as the road continued to be crowded with refugees heading in the opposite direction. By early afternoon I was approaching the border with Czechoslovakia and felt increasingly confident of reaching my destination before the end of the day. This was just as well, as I had now eaten all of the food, and drunk all the beer, which Frau Solger had given me.

I had a growing sense of unease, too, about the car's petrol consumption. Certainly, I was beginning to doubt if the contents of my remaining spare can would be anywhere near enough to get me as far as the Black Forest. I reckoned, though, that what I had in the tank would still get me as far as Theresienstadt and before anything else I preferred to focus my mind on my endeavour to reach there.

When I finally reached the border with Czechoslovakia, I felt a certain sense of elation, knowing from my map that I now only had a comparatively few kilometres to travel in order to arrive at my destination. Although I'd never been there before, I knew of its reputation and that it was an old fortress situated near a small town of the same name. My map even marked its exact location so I was sure that I'd be able to find it quite easily.

Increasingly, I thought only of Aliza, and prayed she and her daughter were safe and well. Fearing that they might not be, and that something might still go dreadfully wrong, darkened my mood a little and made me feel strangely tense. I had come, at much personal risk to myself, wounded and still in pain, to offer her salvation, and I believed that I could count on her gratitude. That this also extended to her love, as she had assured me when we last met, carried with it complications that I preferred not to dwell upon. Those were for another day and my one priority was now, I believed, within my grasp.

32

Evening had come by the time I finally approached Theresienstadt concentration camp via a long, tree lined drive. The weather was fairly pleasant, with sunshine breaking through the clouds, and giving a faint feeling of warmth. In the last few kilometres of my journey I had felt an increasing amount of pain in my leg and I was hungry as well as thirsty. An overwhelming sense of tiredness was also once again creeping up on me, making it difficult to keep awake, and twice I had lost my way, before eventually, to my intense relief, I saw a signpost telling me that I was nearly at my destination.

My stomach was gripped with apprehension as the gates of the camp come into sight. They stood open, which rather surprised me, and I could see no guard on duty. I also began to make out people walking around inside the gate quite freely and to my shock noticed there were many gaunt looking figures sitting or even lying by the trees. It was all too obvious that the camp guards must have have gone and I almost groaned at the thought that Aliza might also have already left.

I parked my car just outside the gates and with a grimace of pain tentatively got out. I could see a man walking towards me from inside the camp. He was dressed in a white doctor's coat and looked about sixty.

'Can you tell me what is going on, please?' I asked him, anxiously.

'We're Red Cross,' he answered me in fluent German but with a distinct Swiss accent. 'We've been in charge here for a couple of days now. As you can see the conditions are grim and I'm afraid typhoid is rife.'

The man spread out his hands as he spoke while looking me straight in the eye. 'And may I ask you what business brings you here?'

'I'm looking for a woman who I believe has been incarcerated in this place. Her name is Aliza Geisser. She has her daughter with her.'

Even as I opened my mouth to speak, however, I was seized by fear. Was Aliza already dead or dying? To what was I also exposing myself just by coming here?

'Theresienstadt holds thousands of inmates,' the man answered me, shaking his head as he did so. 'Many of them are too sick to move. You can look around if you wish but have you ever been vaccinated against typhoid?'

'No, I don't believe so.'

'Then if I were you I would turn around and leave immediately.'

'I've come too far. It's important.'

The man shrugged his shoulders. 'As you wish but I really must get on with my work.'

The man began to walk away but I stepped in front of him.

'Have you any vaccine?'

'We have some but it's too precious to waste on just anyone. A jab won't give you immediate protection, either.'

'But it would still be better than nothing.'

'I'm sorry, but I'm too busy.'

I remembered the Luger I had left in my car and for a

moment contemplated forcing the man to give me an inoculation, but then I thought better of it. If my bluff were to be called, there would be no question of actually shooting the man. Then another important question occurred to me.

'Have you heard if the Russians are coming?'

'Not as such but it can only be a matter of time.'

'And when they do?'

'They'll take charge, I expect, but until then we will continue to do what we can. Now, if you'll excuse me please…'

'Yes, of course.'

The man swept past me, leaving me at something of a loss as to where to go next.

'Just remember,' the man called out after he had walked about twenty metres away from me, 'don't eat or drink anything while you're here and don't use any of the toilets. Then you'll probably be all right.'

With a deepening sense of dread at what I might find, I began my search as best I could. My leg was aching terribly, however, forcing me to move at a torturously slow pace. I was determined anyway to be as systematic as possible, moving from room to room within the fortress, and in each one calling out Aliza's name.

The scenes of human suffering which confronted me were ghastly and above all the stench was overwhelming, so that after a while, the sheer enormity of the task began to defeat me. I was increasingly tired as well as hungry and thirsty and, stepping outside into the courtyard to escape the awful smell, virtually collapsed onto the ground against a wall. I then closed my eyes.

'Are you all right?' The question was asked in German but the female voice had a particularly strong Swiss accent. I looked up to see a plain faced, middle-aged woman in a white Red Cross nurses' uniform peering down at me with a concerned look on her face.

'Yes, I'm just very tired. I've come a long way to try and find someone but it isn't easy.'

'Perhaps I can help.'

I stumble to my feet and explain who I am looking for.

'And what do you want with these persons?'

'It's a long story. I have known Aliza Geisser for many years. I want to rescue her and her daughter from this place. I feel I owe her that.'

'You know that Theresienstadt is rife with typhoid?'

'Yes, one of your colleagues has already told me.'

'And did he tell you that we are operating a rule of quarantine?'

I was startled. 'No, he did not.'

'Not that we have the means to enforce it, of course, if people are determined to leave, but when the Russians come…'

'Which is precisely why I'm here. I have witnessed what they have done in Berlin, raping, slaughtering…'

'There is no reason for them to harm anyone here.'

'Perhaps not.'

'So what does she look like?'

'She's dark haired, quite tall, strikingly attractive, and in her late thirties.'

She smiled at me a little. 'Then I think I know where she is.'

'Really?'

'Yes, follow me.'

With that she set off across the courtyard at a brisk pace while I did my best to keep up with her.

'You're in pain, aren't you?' she asked me gently.

'Yes, I was wounded in the leg in the fighting in Berlin. It's nothing serious though. It's well bandaged.'

'How long ago?'

'About…' I hesitated in my reply, realising how much had happened in such a comparatively short period of time. '… Thirty six hours ago, I think.'

'The bandaging will soon need changing then. You don't want the wound to become infected.'

We were now approaching a part of the fortress into which I had not yet ventured, and I could see a door directly ahead of us.

'If I'm right that it's her, there are some stairs to climb,' the nurse told me. 'But don't worry, just wait here, and I'll bring her down to you.'

'But if it's not her?'

'Then you'll have to keep looking, won't you. Who shall I say has come for her?'

'Tell her it's…' I was about to say *Baron* but then thought better of it. 'Tell her it's Otto von Buren.'

The nurse looked at me rather askance and then disappeared inside. I was feeling extremely tense and would have liked to pace up and down, or, even better, to be able to light a cigarette. Instead, I realised I had left my last few cigarettes in my car, so I merely leant against the wall of the building, feeling utterly exhausted, my face turned away from the door.

'Otto, is it really you?'

I turned round and was instantly struck by the radiance of her smile, like a ray of light in a dark world. She almost stumbled into my arms and as I held her I had the same old memory of us dancing together on Board the raging Moses. I could see as well just how careworn her face was and how streaked with white her hair has become but I didn't care. With a surge of pleasure I simply beamed at her and our lips met.

'I managed to escape from Berlin,' I told her. 'It wasn't easy, of course, but now I'm here to take you and Bathsheba away from this place. I know I've let you down in the past but not this time.'

'Thank you, Otto, thank you.'

'I have a car, petrol…money and clean clothing for you and Bathsheba to wear. I hope they'll come close enough to fitting you both.

'But it's getting late. It will be dark soon.'

'I am concerned that the Russians could arrive at any time. I don't want you to fall into their hands.'

'We could leave at first light in the morning, but where is it that you intend taking us?'

'Into Bavaria, and then to my home in the Black Forest. I expect that American or British troops will have advanced into the area by now but you have nothing to fear from them.'

'And you?' she asked me perceptively.

'I have merely served my country. That is all.'

She hesitated. 'I don't know that I should go with you, Otto. You have your duty to Clara and Leopold to consider and if the Russians come it will be as liberators. Why should I fear them?'

I felt totally crestfallen. 'You have not seen what they have done in Berlin; I still believe that they could behave badly here. I really think you would be safer coming with me.'

Still she looked at me sceptically.

'For pity's sake, Aliza, I've risked life and limb coming here when I did not have to. Come with me, please, at least as far as Bavaria. You will regret it if you don't. Life will be harsh under the communists, of that I am certain.'

Her expression softened and I immediately sensed I had persuaded her.

'Very well, but not until the morning.'

'Agreed, but we must leave by six a.m.'

She nodded and I smiled warmly at her, feeling an intense sense of relief. I then remembered how hungry and thirsty I was, that I had exhausted all my supplies, and had been warned not to eat or drink anything in Theresienstadt. At this moment, too, the nurse reappeared.

'Frau Geisser and her daughter will be coming with me,' I told her, expecting her to object but she made no attempt to do so. 'We shall leave at six tomorrow morning. I can sleep overnight in my car but I need something to eat and drink. I suppose any hotels or restaurants in the vicinity are likely to be closed?'

'Probably, but we have some supplies…'

'Your colleague told me not to eat or drink anything here.'

'We have bottled beer and food that we have brought with us. It's quite safe, I hope.'

'I can pay for it.'

'There's no need although I can't give you much.'

I expressed my gratitude to her and, turning to Aliza, affirmed I would fetch the clothing I had brought with me and then be back for her in the morning at the agreed time. Briefly, we embraced once more, and, after squeezing her right hand in a reassuring gesture, I followed the nurse. By coming here I truly believed that I had not only acted out of love but also helped lift the weight Aliza had been on my conscience. Yet I feared that I might never be totally free of a sense of guilt for the suffering my Party's policies had inflicted on too many people.

I passed an uncomfortable night in my car and slept only fitfully. Even so, I had reason to be grateful to the nurse for having dressed my wounded leg and providing me with both food and beer. As I made my way to collect Aliza and Bathsheba I also felt a mixture of relief and anxiety that although no Russians troops had arrived overnight, they might yet do so at any time.

It was ten to six when I reached the door leading to Aliza's quarters and by five past she had still not appeared. Only my wounded leg prevented me from pacing up and down, and I was about to go inside in search of her, when she suddenly appeared along with Bathsheba. She was holding one suitcase for both of them.

I almost gasped, as Bathsheba, who I realised must now be approaching sixteen, looked so much like her mother.

'Quickly,' I said to Aliza, anxiously recovering my voice. 'We are late already. What kept you?'

Aliza flashed me an angry look. 'Bathsheba is tired.'

I looked at the girl again and could see how thin she was. Her eyes especially also lacked any vitality and seemed resigned and disinterested. It made me think of Leopold and the many childhoods the war had stolen. Worse, too, even than that, of how many lives had been lost even before they had properly begun.

'I'm sorry,' I respond lamely. 'I've had a bad night worrying if the Russians might come.'

We set off towards the gate, and almost reached it when from behind I heard a voice call out.

'Where the hell do you think you're going?'

I recognised it as the voice of the same man who I had met upon my arrival the previous evening.

'This place is under quarantine. No one is allowed to leave!'

I groaned, wondering why the man was even awake at this hour of the morning.

'Keep walking, just ignore him.'

The man though began running towards us and soon caught us up.

'I said no one is allowed to leave!'

'Well, we're going anyway. Come on Aliza…'

The man made a grab at Bathsheba but I shoved him away.

'I've risked my life coming here and I say we are leaving. Is that clear?' I shouted at him.

The man swore at me and shouted out in the hope of alerting some of his colleagues, but by now we were through the gate and the car was only a few metres away. I had left my Luger in it and made a swift decision to threaten its use, if I had to. As needs must I was even prepared to fire it over the head of anyone who tried to stop us driving away.

Running to the car was impossible and even quickening my pace was painful, but as fast as I could I bustled Aliza and Bathsheba towards the car and, after fumbling for my keys, opened the doors.

'Get inside as fast as you can.'

I glanced over my shoulder, and noticed the Red Cross man was now just standing by the main gates, watching me. He had clearly given up any hope of stopping us leaving so I was simply able to drive away.

33

'Stop the car! I'm sorry but Bathsheba isn't at all well. She's going to throw up.'

We had only driven a few kilometres when I heard the girl begin to retch. Acting as quickly as I could on Aliza's command, I drew into the side of the road, immediately fearing that the child might have typhoid.

Between us, Aliza and I then managed to bundle Bathsheba out of the car and she proceeded to be sick into some bushes.

'Does she suffer from car sickness?' I asked, more in hope than expectation.

Aliza cast me a worried look. 'No, normally she doesn't. This could be something more serious. She's rather feverish.'

I frowned. 'We need to keep going.'

'She may need a doctor.'

'We must get into Germany first.'

We drove on for about thirty minutes in a south westerly direction. I had been able to pour the last of the spare petrol into the tank of the car the previous evening, so it was almost full, but if there was any deviation from my planned route we could still run out.

'I've seen a road sign to Prague. We could find a doctor there, surely?'

It was Bathsheba who had asked the question, sounding as well as looking so much like her mother. She had barely uttered a word before.

'No!' I snapped at her. 'It could already be under attack by the Russians. I had a hard enough task getting out of Berlin.'

'Otto, don't be so cross,' Aliza responded reproachfully.

'I'm sorry, but I've just seen our capital city reduced to a pile of rubble and I don't want us to get trapped in Prague while it goes the same way.'

I drove on, putting my foot on the accelerator. It was a bright enough morning and the road still deserted. I was determined to keep as near to an optimum speed as possible to conserve petrol but after I had travelled only a few kilometres Bathsheba started retching once more.

'I'm sorry, Otto, you'll have to stop again!' Aliza insisted.

I cursed under my breath. I was half-inclined to keep going but then Bathsheba retched again.

'For pity's sake, Otto!'

I slammed on the brakes and once again we bundled Bathsheba out of the car although not before she was sick over the back seat. I wrinkled my nose at the smell and went to the boot of the car where I knew I would find a rag as well as my last packet of cigarettes.

'Don't worry, I'll clear up the mess,' I told Aliza. 'Just look after her.'

Once I had cleaned the back seat as best I could, I lit a cigarette, which at least helped to soothe my nerves a little, although unfortunately Bathsheba was continuing to be sick by the roadside. I wanted to pace up and down with frustration but still couldn't' help but feel concern for the child. She was clearly in a poor state.

'She's pretty bad, isn't she?'

Aliza merely nodded at me and hung her head.

'We really must keep moving; at least until we are out of Czechoslovakia. As soon as we are, I promise that I will stop in the first town we come to and see if we can find a doctor.'

We were soon on our way again but the smell of sickness was pervasive and Bathsheba was frequently complaining of stomach ache. The sun at least was now shining cheerfully through the clouds and for a few more kilometres I was able to make good progress. However, when I arrived at a junction with a more major road I found it was already crowded with fleeing refugees. I assumed they must all be of German extraction and with the same intention as we had of escaping from Czechoslovakia.

The road rapidly became so busy that to my annoyance I soon found my way was blocked completely. We were reduced to travelling at no more than walking pace and I cast an anxious eye at my fuel gauge.

'Have the Russians attacked Prague yet?' I asked an elderly man dressed in a suit that had obviously seen better days, and who was walking alongside us.

'Not that I know of, but it can't be long before they do. There's trouble brewing inside the city as well. Many of the Czechs have got arms from somewhere and are threatening to rise up against the garrison. They're out for German blood, I reckon. I decided I wasn't going to hang around any longer to find out.'

I glanced around and caught Aliza's eye. She had Bathsheba in her arms and it remained obvious to me just how unwell the girl had become.

'Otto, we must get her to a doctor quickly,' Aliza appealed to me.

I said nothing in response, my mind dwelling on the possibility that I might soon have two sick women on my hands.

'Otto, please answer me!' Aliza snapped.

'I'm sorry, but what can I do? We can't go forward except at a snail's pace and the road is just as congested behind us. We're trapped!'

My sense of frustration now began to mount. I fidgeted in my seat, cursed under my breath, and tried unsuccessfully to keep my eyes from straying towards the petrol gauge. I was rapidly coming to the conclusion that my best hope was to merely get us over the border into Germany. Once there, we would be safe from any unfriendly Czechs or, hopefully, any advancing Russians. I thought it possible, though, we would come across American or British troops, but this did not particularly concern me. What was important was that it ought not to be too difficult to find a doctor, or as needs be a hospital, which could offer Bathsheba treatment, as I reckoned, of anywhere in the country, Bavaria's infrastructure should still be fairly well intact.

I tried to explain this thought process to Aliza but she was tetchy with me.

'I can't hear what you're saying, Otto. Can't you speak up!'

I repeated myself but she still seemed unwilling to listen.

'Bathsheba is getting worse by the minute. She needs treatment immediately.'

'Aliza, please, there's nothing I can do while we're stuck behind all these people.'

'Look, there's a road junction coming up,' she responded. 'At least get us off this road, Otto.'

'Not if it will get us lost. I've only got a very basic map and we are beginning to run out of petrol.'

As we came closer to the junction I was able to make out a road sign and the name Prague. It wasn't the only place name but none of the others meant anything to me.

'Turn off, Otto, please!' Aliza appealed to me.

'Just because I take another road doesn't mean that it is going to be any less congested.'

Bathsheba was moaning once more and I thought for a moment she was about to throw up yet again. I was seized by a sense of panic and the realisation that despite my best endeavours the whole venture was turning into a nightmare.

'Take it, Otto, for God's sake!'

'No, Aliza, no! If we go into Prague we may never escape. I might as well have left you in Theresienstadt, don't you understand that?'

'All I know is that Bathsheba could die if we don't act quickly. I've been through hell and back protecting her and if you really care about me you'll do as I ask. The sign says Prague is only twenty kilometres away. If we carry on towards the border it must be double that distance at least. I just don't care about the Russians. Bathsheba's life is more important!'

I cursed, more in frustration than anger, yanked on the wheel, and as I turned in the direction of Prague I saw the way ahead was fairly clear. There were some refugees on the road but, not surprisingly, they were all heading away from the city.

As we drove down the road I felt evermore convinced that I'd been unwise to give into Aliza and I decided to voice my concerns in no uncertain terms.

'Aliza, don't imagine Prague is going to offer much help to Bathsheba. It's a big city, and, if that old man I spoke to is correct, its population is turning increasingly hostile as well.

I've also only ever been there once and I certainly don't know my way around; do you?'

'No,' she replied in a grudging tone.

'If the Russians attack it we could easily all be killed. I was in Berlin, I know what a hell on earth that became. Unless you had seen it with your own eyes you really couldn't comprehend the extent of the devastation.'

'So you say...'

'Yes, I do say!'

'Surely hospitals will still be open. All I ask is that you try to find one.'

'All right, I'll do what I can,' I responded in a bad tempered tone. Then I winced from the pain in my leg and had an image in my mind's eye of the seemingly chaotic scenes that had greeted me and Unteroffizier Leiberich when we first entered the hospital in Berlin. In fact, it had quickly become apparent that a surprising amount of order was still being maintained within its walls, and I could only hope that it would be the same in any hospital I managed to locate in Prague.

As we came ever closer to the city, the road leading to it, that we were travelling along became more crowded with refugees fleeing the place. They were strung out across the road as well, impeding our progress, and those who gave us any attention at all seemed to me to be looking at us as if we were mad. Finally, as I approached a road junction at the very edge of the city, I could make out the uniforms of German troops standing by their armoured cars and jeeps, which were parked along the roadside.

It was a sight which gave me an immediate sense of comfort and I decided to find out from them what was happening inside the city. Even as I slowed down to do so, however, an officer stepped out in front of me and held up his hand, signalling to me to halt

'Where do you think you're going?' the officer called out to me, curtly.

'I am Baron Otto von Buren of the SS. I have my wife and daughter with me and I'm afraid my daughter is seriously ill. I was hoping to get her into a city hospital as soon as possible.'

This lie as to the true identity of Aliza and Bathsheba slipped off my tongue with an ease that I could only hope would sound convincing. Meanwhile, they were both huddled together on the back seat of the car, and if the officer's attention was caught by anything it was no doubt the unfailing allure of Aliza's dark eyes.

'I wouldn't advise it, sir,' the officer told me, adopting an altogether more courteous tone. 'We have word that fighting has broken out in the city.'

'Is it the Russians?'

'No, Sir, although they can't be far away. It's Czech partisans.'

'I see. My wife and I will consider the matter. If we decide to continue, I take it you will not seek to prevent us from doing so?'

'I have no orders to that effect; I am merely offering advice. If you ignore it you do so at your own risk, of course.'

The officer walked away and I turn to face Aliza. I thought I saw a hint of regret in her eyes.

'I still want to go on,' she told me emphatically.

'But you heard what he said. If we drive on into Prague we are putting all of our lives at risk and may never get out again. Is Bathsheba really so unwell that a few hours spent getting across the border into Germany will make any real difference?'

'I don't want to take that chance, Otto. She needs to see a doctor urgently.'

'Yes, so you say, but even supposing we can get her to a hospital quickly, who knows how long she might then have to wait to be seen, let alone treated.'

'But if we turn around now, the roads won't be any less crowded so you'll just run out of petrol in the middle of nowhere.'

I glanced at my fuel gauge and sighed before turning to face Aliza once more.

'I'll ask the officer if he can spare any petrol,' I told her.

She looked at me sceptically, but I knew I had one commodity in my possession that might prove to be persuasive. Without another word to her, I got out of the car, went to its boot, opened it, and rummaged in a bag to find what I was looking for. After that I strolled over to where the officer was standing talking to his men.

'Hauptmann, is there any chance you could let me have some petrol? I'm running short?'

He looked at me as if I was asking for the earth but then noticed what I was holding in my hand.

'I can pay in gold. It's real, I assure you, and half a canister would be better than nothing.'

'Are you seriously trying to bribe me?'

'That's putting it a little bluntly. I am just offering you a small inducement. But if you've none to spare…'

With that I turned round and began to walk back towards the car.

'If you've any more where those came from, I could be

persuaded,' the officer called out to me.

'I've got a couple of more gold Marks in the car, that's all.'

'Make it five and you can have a full canister.'

I smiled ruefully to myself at the thought that petrol was literally coming close to being worth its weight in gold.

'Very well, Hauptmann, you have a deal.'

*****

'We should still try and find a hospital in Prague,' Aliza insisted once the canister had been handed over. 'I think Bathsheba is getting worse. She's complaining of a headache and she's started shivering more.' Aliza then put a hand to her daughter's brow. 'She's hot too. Look, Otto, she is definitely not well, and we are now so close to the city. Let's at least see if we can find a hospital. If not we can drive out again, can't we. Please, Otto…'

'All right, Aliza, all right, but don't blame me if this turns out to be a death trap.'

34

Even as we entered the outskirts of Prague, I was convinced I could make out the familiar sound of gunfire. I imagined myself back in Berlin, while my hands tensed on the wheel of the car as I thought how unwise I was to have allowed myself to be persuaded to put my head in the noose again. Doing my duty as an officer of the third Reich in defending our capital city against the forces of communism was one thing, but to have agreed to this – well, I feared it was just sheer madness. But then, the moment I turned south towards the Czech border when I could so easily have turned to the west towards my home, I had known I was taking a huge gamble, it was a joy to have been reunited with Aliza, and Bathsheba was undeniably very unwell. I couldn't help but shake my head at the tangle I had weaved for myself.

'Are you all right?' Aliza asked me anxiously.

'No… I mean yes. Can you hear the sound of gunfire? It's getting closer all the time.'

'I can hear a sort of crackling noise.'

'Well, I can tell you that it's the sound of bullets being fired. The Hauptmann was right.'

'What do you intend to do?'

'I'm going to ask the first person I can, the way to the nearest hospital. It's just a pity the officer who gave me petrol had no idea.'

I was now about to turn a corner and as I did so I could see the road ahead was blocked by a couple of tanks. This forced me to apply my brakes and as I came to a halt the commander of one of them shouted at me from the conning tower.

'You'll have to turn round. There's fighting in the city centre and we are not allowing anyone through!'

'I have to get to a hospital. Do you know where I might find one?'

'Wait, I'll ask if any of my crew know.'

With that the commander disappeared inside his tank only to emerge again a few seconds later. He proceeded to give me some rather garbled directions which I was not totally sure I understood but I still thanked him for his assistance, and, turning my car around, I headed off down a road I hoped would soon bring us to a hospital. Ten minutes later, however, I feared that I had become completely lost.

'We are going to have to ask again, I'm afraid.' I informed Aliza.

The road we were now on was deserted so we drove on more slowly, looking out hopefully for someone we could speak to. I then spotted the head of a man looking out from what was apparently an entrance to a small hotel.

'Hullo,' I called out, 'can you help me?'

The man eyed me suspiciously, saying nothing, and then merely withdrew his head out of sight. 'Damn him,' I cursed under my breath before pulling into the curb immediately opposite the entrance.

'I don't know why he wouldn't answer me, Aliza. I'm going inside. If he can't help me, perhaps someone else will be able to.'

'Be careful,' she urged me.

'Of course.' Not that I could really see there was anything to be careful about, however, although it half-crossed my mind to go to the boot of the car and get out my Luger. However, I rejected the idea as totally unnecessary.

As I entered the hallway of the hotel, I had an immediate sense of genteel decay. I then saw a man standing in front of what was obviously the reception desk. He had his back to me but suddenly turned. It was the same man who had been looking out of the hotel entrance. He was in his forties, I suppose, tall, gaunt, and with dark, rather bloodshot eyes.

'We're closed,' he said frostily in broken German.

'I just wanted to ask, can you…'

'Can I what?' The man interrupted me, his manner now thoroughly aggressive as I took a pace towards him. I recall Aliza's words of warning as being prescient indeed and began to regret my decision not to carry my Luger with me.

' … Just tell me where I might find the nearest hospital, please? I was given some directions but…'

'Why should I give you any help? You German scum are about to get what you deserve in this city and when the Russians come…' A faint smile crossed the man's face and he drew the fingers of his right hand across his throat.

'I have a sick, innocent girl with me,' I protested. 'She needs a doctor. Please, just give me some directions; it's all I ask?'

'All right, you're quite close to one. Simply carry on the way you were heading, take the second turning on the right, and you'll see the hospital on your left within a few hundred metres.'

'Thank you.' I was already on my way out of the door as I said this and it was with a sense of relief that I took the wheel of the car again.

'You look shaken,' Aliza said.

'Do I really? Let's just say he wasn't the most charming of individuals. Anyway, we're nearly there apparently. Just two turnings on the right…'

I then heard the sound of gunfire. I couldn't be sure where it is coming from but it seemed quite close so I instinctively put my foot on the accelerator. As I did so, we passed the first right hand turning and I realised, almost too late, that I was in danger of missing the second turning. I braked sharply, and heard Bathsheba groan.

'I'm sorry, I nearly went too far…'

I then swerved to the right and headed down the road I had been directed to take. I could only pray that the man hadn't told me a load of bullshit.

The sound of gunfire now seemed to be following us and it was with an intense sense of relief that I saw a building coming up on our left-hand side that had to be a hospital as there were two ambulances parked outside its entrance.

'We've made it,' I declared triumphantly. 'Quick, let's get inside. I don't like the sound of all that shooting. It's far too close.'

The scene that greeted us as we entered was in stark contrast to the one that had greeted my arrival only a few days previously when I had hobbled into the hospital in Berlin. There chaos had appeared to reign whereas here all still appeared ordered and relatively quiet.

'It's as well that we've arrived when we have,' I remarked to Aliza. 'With that amount of shooting going on, I imagine it won't be long before casualties start pouring in.'

Carrying gold in my pocket, I quickly located a nurse, and

anxious to be gone as soon as possible, did not take kindly to being told by her, albeit in excellent German although by her accent she was a Czech, that Bathsheba would have to wait to be seen.

'I'm afraid we're extremely busy and you'll have to take your turn.'

'But I can pay handsomely.'

She sniffed at me disdainfully. 'I'm sure you can, sir, but you will still have to wait. There are others ahead of you and they can pay as well.'

'But this is urgent…'

'So are the cases ahead of you. The doctor is already dealing with one gunshot wound. You will have to wait!'

She was clearly losing patience with me, and, feeling the restraining weight of Aliza's hand on my arm, I merely grunted and turned away.

Precious time, a commodity that I was fast coming to appreciate I had run out of, ticked by inexorably as we began the long wait for Bathsheba to be examined. Meanwhile we could hear the sound of gunfire echoing across the city, some of it threateningly close. Bathsheba was also deteriorating before our eyes and I worried, too, for Aliza, who looked exhausted.

'Are you all right?' I asked her anxiously.

'Yes, but what about you? I can tell you're in pain.'

'It's nothing really. I've got used to it.'

'Even so, you should ask to have your dressing changed.'

'I will.'

'And then you should go.'

'We should go, don't you mean?'

'No, Otto, Bathsheba is too ill to travel anywhere. I may soon go the same way.'

'But…'

'Listen to me, Otto, I will always be grateful to you for coming to the camp to rescue us and I know how much you love me but…'

'You love me as well, don't you? After all you admitted that when we last met in Buchenwald.'

'Yes, I did and I do, but we will be safe here.'

'But the Russians…'

' … Cannot possibly harm us here.'

'I still can't just desert you. Where will you go once Bathsheba is better?'

'I don't know, but the war has totally dispossessed us anyway and we will surely be in good company. We have our marks as well, you know.' With that she bared her arm to me and I could see her prison number clearly. 'That will stay with me for the rest of my days, I'm afraid. It will be the same for Bathsheba, of course, but at least we will surely be treated as victims, even by the Russians.'

'I'm not leaving either of you, Aliza, not after having come this far.'

'Then you care for us more than for Clara and your son and have chosen to desert them. That's the truth of the matter, isn't it?'

'Yes… I suppose to an extent it is,' I confessed. 'You're completely under my skin, Aliza, and in a way you have been ever since we first met.'

'I see that, but we were so much younger then…'

The clear signs of age creeping up on us both were all too

apparent as we looked into each other's eyes. I also noticed that Bathsheba appeared to have fallen sleep, which I decide was just as well.

'If you leave today you should still be able to escape over the border,' Aliza told me firmly. 'After all, you now have enough petrol,' she added with a smile.

'Yes, and that's enough for the three of us,' I insisted stubbornly.

She shook her head. 'But I told you Bathsheba is simply too ill to travel.'

I hung my head in dismay and there was an uneasy silence between us before Aliza spoke again.

'You know, Otto, your place really ought to be with Clara and Leopold. You owe it to them both, although please believe me when I tell you that I am really grateful to you for what you've done. If we had still been in the camp, Bathsheba would have stood far less chance.'

'Perhaps you're right. But I still don't regret coming. It had to be done and I could not have lived with myself otherwise. You do understand that, don't you?'

I could see a smile playing on her lips and her eyes seemed full of fondness for me. 'Yes, of course I do,' she said softly.

'And I'm prepared to leave Clara,' I blurt out, 'You are more important to me!'

'But you must think of Leopold. Perhaps one day, when the war is far enough behind us all.'

It's a suggestion that was left hanging in the air as Bathsheba yawned, clearly now awake once more. The hospital also at least had a canteen providing tea and simple hot food, so we decided to assuage our thirst and hunger although Bathsheba was now too ill to accept anything but liquid past her lips. After that all that we could do was continue to wait, while in my mind I continued to wrestle with myself and, every few seconds, glanced at the clock sitting high on the wall opposite to where were sitting. The day was slowly but surely ticking by on us and still I was going nowhere.

At last the call came from a nurse and we were shown into a room where the doctor, wearing a white coat, was sitting with a pen in his hand, in front of rather than behind a desk. It was piled high with scattered notes. He was bald and looked as if he was at least seventy. As we entered he didn't even look up at first, preferring to continue writing, although he must have been aware of our presence. When he deigned to do so his face displayed barely any emotion.

'Herr Doctor,' I hastened to explain having established he was German, 'I am Baron Otto Von Buren and I have with me an old friend, Frau Geisser, and her daughter, who's unwell. I would be grateful if you would examine her.'

At first the doctor said nothing in reply. Instead he merely looked us up and down, which began to make me feel angry. When I had first arrived I had toyed with the idea of pretending that Aliza was my wife and Bathsheba my daughter but had firmly rejected the idea. I did not need to tell any falsehoods or owe any individual in this building any explanations either, however suspiciously the Doctor might now be eyeing me.

'Very well,' the doctor finally said. 'What's wrong with her?'

Before I could open my mouth Aliza began to explain. Her voice was immediately gentle and persuasive. It was obvious to me that she was instinctively bringing her feminine charm to bear on the doctor, whose demeanour towards us grew rapidly more relaxed.

Once he had examined Bathsheba, his manner became grave, however. 'I'm afraid she has symptoms of typhoid fever. She will need to be isolated.'

'But have you no drugs you can give her?' I asked him.

'None that will cure her, I'm afraid. There is a vaccine but we have no supplies. I can admit her, though. We have some free beds available in an isolation ward. You are both at risk as well, of course.'

'I doubt if I am,' I responded. 'I helped Frau Geisser leave Theresienstadt concentration camp this morning. Before that I was in Berlin.'

'I see.' The doctor now looked at me as if all his worse suspicions had been confirmed. 'It is, however, a highly contagious disease.'

Now I felt real dismay. I had come so close to achieving my objective, had escaped from Berlin against the odds, driven all this way, rescued Aliza, or so I thought, only to have all my hopes dashed. My leg had also been aching badly for hours and the pain suddenly became so intense I grimaced and couldn't prevent myself from crying out.

'I'm sorry, doctor. It's my leg, I've been wounded.'

'Let me see…'

'It just needs dressing again, I expect.'

'Well, I'll get a nurse to have a look at it.'

'Thank you, doctor.'

*****

'I can't leave you now, Aliza. Bathsheba has been admitted and you've nowhere to go. The nurse also told me I need to rest my leg and with the pain I am in I don't think I could drive any distance at the moment. I need a decent night's rest, at least. So do you.'

Once more Aliza had tried to persuade me to make my escape but I remained stubbornly reluctant to agree.

'Very well, but you should still leave in the morning, really you should.'

I shook my head vigorously. 'No.'

'At least think about it. You don't have to make an immediate decision.'

'Perhaps, but don't expect me to change my mind. Look, let's go back to that hotel. The man I spoke to said it was closed but offering to pay him in gold might well change his mind and I need a good night's sleep. So do you, I'm sure.'

'He was rude to you, wasn't he?'

'Yes, he doesn't like Germans, but I can't blame him for that. If he isn't to be persuaded we'll have to come back here.'

'I don't like leaving Bathsheba.'

'No, of course not, but she'll be well taken care of. The hotel is also no distance away.'

'And we are more than just friends now,' Aliza said softly.

'Yes, I believe we are… my love.'

I held out my hand and she immediately took it. The sudden intimacy of the gesture sent a thrill through my spine and I gently squeezed her hand.

'Yet, you know I have been through such hell, Otto, such hell. And it was your ideology and your government, which has been responsible for that,' she declared with sudden vehemence. She did not however seek to withdraw her hand from mine.

'Believe me, I'm truly, truly sorry.'

'Yes, I know you are. I would not be walking out of this building with you now if I thought otherwise.'

As we stepped into the early evening sunshine the sound of gunfire was louder than ever. I was almost indifferent to it but it made Aliza flinch.

'The shooting sounds so close, shouldn't we go back inside until it has stopped?' she asked me, nervously.

'We'll be all right in the car. We're not going far, after all.'

She still hesitated and I could see the look of fear in her eyes.

'Come on, we'll be there in a couple of minutes.'

Again I held out my hand and she not only took hold of it but also squeezed it tightly.

35

With Aliza seated beside me, I proceeded to drive towards the hotel. The moment, however, I turned left into the street in which it was located, I sensed that I had made a serious mistake. The sound of gunfire was not merely intense; bullets were actually being fired in our general direction from more than one location. There could be no question of reaching the hotel either, as a barricade had been thrown up across the street completely blocking our access to it. Aliza, too, had begun to scream.

'Please, please, get us out of here!'

'Duck, duck! I'm going to reverse!'

As I turned my head I caught a glimpse of a helmeted German soldier behind a machine gun. This was obviously trained on the barricade and I realised that I had driven right into the line of fire. In desperation, I carried out my intended manoeuvre as quickly as I could, intense pain shooting up through my leg even as I did so.

'We're safe now,' I said and turned to look at Aliza but she had slumped to one side. Her blood seemed to be everywhere and I screamed.

'Aliza, oh my God, Aliza!'

I wrenched at the wheel of the car and within seconds I was driving back the way that I had just come. I felt as if I wanted to throw up but more importantly I knew that I had just one chance to save her life.

Please don't die, Aliza, please don't die I kept repeating in my head.

There were tears running down my cheeks as I raced up to the entrance of the hospital, slammed on the brakes, and rushed to try and carry her inside. Yet, in that very instant, it dawned on me that the act of seeking to move her out of her seat might of itself prove fatal, and anyway I lacked the strength to do so on my own.

'Help me someone, help me!' I cried out without even knowing if anyone could hear my appeal. I looked around and saw only an elderly couple with their backs to me entering the hospital. I followed them as fast I could, half tripped over myself, and ended up almost falling through the hospital doors. As I did so, I spotted the same nurse who had so recently dressed my wound.

'Nurse, nurse, help me, please! The woman I was with. She's outside in my car. She's been shot.'

Between us we managed to get Aliza out of the car and onto a stretcher while I struggled desperately to control my emotions. I had seen so much blood, so much suffering in my lifetime, that I imagined that I had become inured to it, but as Aliza's lifeblood appeared to drain out of her in front of my very eyes, the tears were flowing freely, and all I wanted to do was scream out in a mixture of rage and grief.

I kept thinking too that this was all my fault; that I should have just driven west towards the Black Forest and never come anywhere near Theresienstadt.

Then none of this, none of it all, would have happened! You selfish, stupid bastard! I said to myself before catching my breath in an attempt to stop myself breaking down altogether.

I tried to concentrate on bearing the weight of Aliza's limp body on the stretcher and getting her through the hospital doors. She was moaning with pain and I found myself clinging to this sound like a man clinging to a piece of wood in an attempt to save himself from drowning.

Another nurse was now rushing forward to assist us and Aliza was carried to a treatment area where a doctor appeared. He was obviously much younger than the one who had so recently examined Bathsheba and his whole demeanour was far more anxious and concerned.

'She's been shot in the back of her right shoulder, doctor,' one of the two nurses told him.

'Another one, eh. Well, get her on the table where I can examine her. Gently now.'

I helped in this task whereupon the Doctor gently squeezed my arm.

'Is she your wife?'

'No, a personal friend. I…'

'We'll do what we can for her. I suggest you wait outside.'

'Of course…'

I withdrew but not before casting a fearful eye over Aliza. She was still moaning and looked deadly pale. I wondered if I'd ever see her alive again.

The wait that followed was torturous. My acute sense of guilt was heightened above all else by the realisation that I'd have to tell Bathsheba what had happened to her mother. I feared she would blame me; probably hate me, indeed, if I had to give her the worst news of all. It would be all that I deserved, I thought, even though I was prepared to go down on my knees and beg her forgiveness, not just for my own folly, but for all the misery that the Nazi cause has visited upon her family and countless others across the continent of Europe and beyond.

Finally, the doctor came to find me. I had practically fallen asleep with sheer exhaustion, both mental and physical, so I was taken by surprise when he nudged my shoulder.

'She will live, I think,' he told me quietly. 'The bullet missed any vital organs. I have managed to operate on her and remove it. We had some of her blood type, too, and she's had a transfusion. She's asleep now.'

'Thank you, thank you so much. I am so grateful to you.'

The doctor merely smiled modestly and said nothing.

'Can I see her, please?'

The doctor nodded. 'You can sit by her bed if you wish but do not make any attempt to wake her.'

We shook hands and I was taken by one of the nurses to Aliza's bedside. Tears again welled up in my eyes at the sight of her. I had been so fearful, wondering if I could ever bring myself to face Bathsheba. Even now it would not be easy, but at least I could assure her that her mother was going to get better. Should I then slip away though, I wondered, seeking to escape from Prague much as I had escaped from Berlin? Aliza had after all entreated me to go and while she and Bathsheba remained sick in their hospital beds I was powerless to do anything for them, whether for good or ill.

I was certain of only one thing and that was that I would make no attempt to leave that night. I was too tired and in need of sleep even if that just meant only being able to curl up in the chair in which I was sitting. In the morning I would think again.

*****

And when the morning came, I was stiff, cold, and still completely undecided as to what to do for the best. I feared that I had brought Aliza nothing but ill fortune, which alone would be a good ground for leaving, but equally I felt that I simply couldn't do so without speaking to her first and certainly not without speaking to Bathsheba. I had also made up my mind that whatever happened they had to have the benefit of some of my gold marks.

Seeking out the ward that Bathsheba was in, as I entered it I quickly saw that she was well enough to be sitting up in bed, looking bored.

A stern-looking nurse rushed to meet me. 'What are you doing coming in here?' she asked me crossly. 'Didn't you read the sign? This is an isolation ward.'

'I have to speak to Bathsheba Geisser; it's very important.'

'Are you her father?'

'No, I'm a friend of her mother. She's been shot but she will live. She's in another ward of this hospital.'

Even as I spoke I could see Bathsheba looking at me. The expression on her face seemed to be resentful of my presence. I dropped my voice.

The nurse reluctantly allowed me to approach Bathsheba's bed. The girl merely stared at me coldly.

'Bathsheba… It's about your mother. I'm afraid she's been shot…'

Bathsheba gasped in horror.

'But she's all right, truly she is. The surgeon has operated. The bullet has been removed and she's out of danger. I expect you'll be allowed to see her soon.'

'How did this happen?'

'We had just left here after you were admitted. We were caught in crossfire. I'm sorry…'

'Why did you ever come to take us away from Theresienstadt?' she asked me angrily.

'To save you and your mother from the Russians but I'm sure you will be safe enough here so it may well be for the best that I leave. There's something I want to give you, though.' With that I produced some gold Marks.

'I don't want your money.'

'Take them all the same.'

'Why not give them all to my mother, if you are so insistent?'

'They're for you both…'

'Well I've told you, I don't want them.'

I sighed deeply. However painful it might be, I could fully understand her hostility towards me.

'Very well, I'm going to visit your mother now, but, if she 's asleep as I expect, then I'll return and leave the Marks here on the cabinet next to your bed. What you do with them then will be up to you.'

My words were met with nothing more than a morose silence so I simply turned away and left the ward.

True to my word, I went immediately in the direction of Aliza's bedside. I did so, however, with even more apprehension than I felt when I had visited Bathsheba. Part of me hoped that she would indeed be asleep, and the other part that I'd find her as awake as Bathsheba, but without the seething sense of resentment. She would, though, I thought, have every reason to feel anger towards me as it was through my unasked-for intervention in her life that she had come so close to being killed.

As it was, I found her in a feverish state, drifting in and out of consciousness. It made me fear once more for her life and I was even more in two minds as to what to do for the best. The nurses at least allowed me to sit by her bedside but I doubted if she was aware of my presence. I would have liked to be able to go down on my knees and beg her forgiveness, liked to ask her, too, if she really thought it best that I should go, but she was in no fit state to communicate with me.

Her hair might be turning grey, she might be ageing before her time, but I still found her beautiful, and I reflected that in my heart I'd lived a double life all these years; secretly loving her and thereby betraying Clara. Yet in the end I feared that I'd betrayed them both, not so much by my decision to try and rescue Aliza and Bathsheba from Theresienstadt, but by my very participation in a regime that had brought Germany to its knees and made it a pariah amongst nations.

In the end I stood up, looked lovingly at Aliza's face, and left the ward. I returned immediately to Bathsheba's bedside and, without a word passing between us, put down the gold marks, before walking straight out of the ward again.

I then returned to Aliza's bedside and continued my vigil. Time passed slowly and I began to doze off until suddenly I was aware of her voice calling out to me.

'Otto, Otto, can you give me some water, please?'

'Of course, Aliza,' I responded, looking lovingly into her eyes. 'Please, please, forgive me.'

'I was shot, wasn't I?'

'Yes, I'm so, so sorry.'

'You don't have to be, there's nothing to forgive, really there isn't. You just acted out of love, after all.'

I hurried to give her water from the cup sitting next to her bed and she smiled up at me limply.

'How long have I been unconscious for?' she asked.

'About eighteen hours, I suppose. They operated on you and removed the bullet.'

'I'm lucky to be alive then.'

In response I simply squeezed her hand and felt close to tears.

'And how is Bathsheba?' she then asked me anxiously.

'She seems better. I've been able to speak to her.'

'That's good news. And what are you going to do now, Otto?'

I looked at her intensely. 'Stay with you, of course. How could I do otherwise?'

'I still think you should try and return to Clara and Leopold while you have the chance.'

'But I may never see you again!'

'Perhaps, but I still believe that you should do what is right for Leopold. You can't simply desert him or Clara; not now. One day in the future, if you still have feelings for me and we are in touch…'

'I will always have feelings for you, Aliza, you know that.'

'And I will for you.'

'All right, I'll think about it.'

'But not for long, Otto; I'll survive and it's best that you go, you know it is… I expect the Russians will be here soon… I really don't want you to be captured.'

Her voice was trailing away and I could barely make out the last few words she had spoken. She then closed her eyes and was soon asleep again. I put my head in my hands and wondered what I should do. She was right, of course, the honourable thing to do was to return to Clara and Leopold and hadn't I always striven to be an honourable man?

'Aliza, Aliza,' I put my face close to hers and gently shook her uninjured shoulder. She opened her eyes and smiled at me.

'I will always love you, Aliza,' I told her and then put my lips to hers. She kissed me in return and smiled into my eyes.

'So, Otto, you've decided to leave?'

I remained conflicted, of course I did; still feeling that I shouldn't desert her when I was by no means convinced that she was bound to live, yet fearful of the Russians and with my conscience constantly pricking me that my first loyalty was to Clara and Leopold.

'I... I suppose so...'

'Yes, you must. I insist.'

'Oh, very well.'

She squeezed my hand. 'Good luck then, Otto, and thank you.'

'I've left money for you as well, just here by your bed. They're some of the gold Marks. Bathsheba has some too.'

She thanked me once more; I looked one last time into her eyes, and then turned and walked away. There were tears in my eyes.

*****

As I climbed into my car I was aware once more of the sound of gunfire. It was one thing, I knew, to have made up my mind to leave Prague, quite another to seek to accomplish that objective.

There could be no question, of course, of attempting to leave the way I had come, but then that was unnecessary anyway. Instead of turning left at the nearby crossroads, I would simply drove straight on in a westerly direction. After that, if I was lucky, I would be out of the city within a matter of minutes, on my way to the German border and safety.

Even as I drove off, however, I began to feel that something was wrong with the steering. I carried on as best I could towards the crossroads but the problem was getting worse to the point that I felt I had no choice but to stop. It had already occurred to me that one of my tyres might be flat and on a quick inspection that proved to be the case.

I cursed and cursed again. Of course, I had known it was bound to happen sooner or later. It was little short of a miracle indeed that I had kept my car, shot up as it was, on the road for so long. Quickly, I checked to see if the spare tyre I carried in the boot was still intact and to my relief found that it was. I then set about substituting it for the flat one as patiently as I could. It was, after all, a task I had performed often enough in the past but never when so incapacitated by an injury. The sound of gunfire also seemed to be getting ever closer and nervously I looked back up the street the way I'd come.

A handful of German troops were running in my direction, clearly in full retreat. Beyond them I could see men advancing, firing their rifles at the fleeing men as they did so. They were wearing civilian clothes and were obviously Czech partisans. I heard a bullet whistle past me and instinctively ducked. One of the German troops then collapsed within metres of me, blood pouring from a gunshot wound to his back, while another sought cover behind my car.

'I'd get out of here, if I were you. Do you want to be killed?' the man hissed at me before raising the rifle he was carrying to his shoulder and taking careful aim at one of the advancing partisans.

I felt like a cornered animal. I was in no condition to run anywhere and I decided instead to take cover inside my car where I knew I still had my Luger. Even as I attempted to do so, however, I felt a terrible pain in my left arm. I had been shot. I screamed in agony and collapsed against the side of my car. I sensed with a visceral terror that my life blood was flowing out of me and that I was finished. It had been such a cruelly sudden end with everything snatched away from me after being so tantalisingly close to completing my escape. I thought of Aliza, of Clara, above all, of my son, Leopold.

Then I calmed down a little and realised the bullet must have only winged me; barely ripping through muscle. Naturally, though, I was still losing blood, but I reasoned that the flow was more than capable of being stemmed. It was also just as well that I am right-handed. I managed to get inside my car, where I kept my head down, and extract my Luger from the glove compartment. It was already loaded. I then extracted a soiled handkerchief from my trouser pocket and, with some difficulty, succeeded in wrapping it around my wounded arm and tying a makeshift knot. Of course, I was still going nowhere but I felt some reassurance at having the means to defend myself.

I took the risk of raising my head a little. I could see the German soldier who had taken cover behind my car was still firing at the partisans and I had the impression that their advance must have been temporarily halted although surely not by any one man's efforts alone. Other German troops must be fighting back as well, I thought, and I became certain that I could hear the sound of machine gun fire, which I was sure was being directed at the partisans. In the ebb and flow of battle, this time it was their turn to fall back.

For a short while, at least, I felt I was relatively safe but I still had to tighten the bolts on the replacement wheel before I could even attempt to drive away. Also, I had no idea what other damage the car might have suffered in the last few minutes since I was shot, while my wounded arm was throbbing and still dripping blood.

As German troops began to move forward I decided I must take a chance. I opened the car door and climbed out, looking around as I did so for the spanner I had dropped when I tried to take cover. I then quickly tightened the wheel's bolts as best I could before taking my seat behind the wheel of the car. It was time to re-start the engine and to my relief it fired up the moment I turned the key. *Good boy,* I said to myself. *Good boy.*

Five hours later, having escaped from Prague, I reached the German border and began to feel safer. I knew I had been very fortunate to survive but I feared that I might never see Aliza again. I had to concentrate on getting treatment for my wounded arm, after which I was determined to reach the Black Forest. I tried to be positive, thinking of a world that would soon surely once more be at peace and looked forward, above all else, to being reunited with Leopold.

EPILOGUE

King David Hotel Jerusalem, Spring 1963

I struggle to believe that thirty years have passed since I last set foot inside this building. At this moment it seems to me that it could just be yesterday. I remember with such vividness the walk that I and Aliza took together into the old city, her smile, her intoxicating laugh, more regrettably Clara's recriminatory anger when we returned.

When I think too of what followed, above all the horrors of war, of the so called Final Solution, and all that it led to, I still want to weep. But I draw much comfort from the rebuilding of Western Germany as a rich nation that is gradually coming to terms with its past, for all that many scars remain. There is irony as well in the thought that so much of that prosperity is thanks to American money, which was instrumental in destroying the Third Reich in the first place, but then, of course, I must be eternally grateful for the mistakes of Versailles not having been repeated. Some lessons are learnt from history, albeit the hard way. But then again, as time moves on, circumstances are never quite the same.

In my mind's eye I can see Joseph Goebbels wagging his finger and ranting with an appalling sense of self-righteousness that, of course, he was right all along and that his prediction of an Iron Curtain falling across Europe has become such a brutal reality, causing the Fatherland to be deeply divided with the East of it, apart from West Berlin, a mere satellite of the Communist Russian Empire. I can also imagine him expressing indignation that nearly twenty years after the war ended so many British and American tanks remain on German soil and that we remain an occupied nation. But then again, those of us who survived are all good democrats now, and I for one, can only give thanks for the security that NATO, along with its nuclear deterrent, have given those of us fortunate enough to live in the West.

My journey here, in fact I like to think of it as my pilgrimage, makes me realise, too, how proud Aliza must be of the nation that Israel has become. The Zionist cause truly seems to have triumphed, albeit through force of arms against its Arab enemies. I have been determined to see the fruits of that victory and, I must say, that what I have seen so far has impressed me. The Palestine I came to in 1933 was still little more than a poor backwater, just emerging from centuries of rule by the old Ottoman Empire, whereas so much of what I have seen since I flew into Tel Aviv airport yesterday is clearly modern and prosperous.

But I have not just come to see Israel. No, in my heart, I have come for a far more important reason and that is to see Aliza again. I do so in some fear and trepidation, for it is now nearly twenty years since we last set eyes on each other, I am now into my sixties, while she must be in her late fifties. I can only hope, too, that I will still recognise her and that she will recognise me.

I can also only sigh with sadness, as I remember Clara. But

for her death nearly a year ago from cancer, I know that I would not be here now. We were married for more than thirty years and I came to love her more as the years passed. I will always be grateful indeed to Aliza for persuading me to return to Clara and Leopold, who I have been fortunate enough to see grow to manhood and become a father himself, making me the proud grandfather of a grandson, whom I adore. Aliza, meanwhile, remains a widow.

The immediate aftermath of the war was completely chaotic. Yet, even though it meant going behind Clara's back, I became increasingly determined to see if I could find out what had happened to Aliza, knowing that I simply couldn't rest until I was satisfied that she was alive and well. Finally, in early 1946, I decided that I had to act. I engaged an enquiry agent at some cost, of course, and after only a few weeks he was able to send me what he called an interim report. I opened it with shaking hands and felt a deep measure of relief when I read that he had established that Aliza and Bathsheba both left hospital together a month after the war ended. The report assured me that his investigations were continuing and that I could expect to hear from him again soon. In fact it was to be another eighteen months before he had anything more positive to tell me, leaving me in a state of ever growing anxiety in case, despite my best endeavours, Aliza had somehow fallen foul of the Russians after all.

Then in the autumn of 1947 I received a further report from him informing me that he had established that Aliza and Bathsheba had left Czechoslovakia, bound for Palestine and to the best of his knowledge were presently on a boat, which had left Trieste only a few days previously. I had to smile at the irony of this, remembering our journey back in '33, but was shocked by the size of the fee he wanted for pursuing his investigations further by following her to Palestine. I was anxious, too, that she had escaped one danger only to expose herself to another, given the volatile state of that country as the British Mandate entered its final months.

Again I hesitated, wondering what to do for the best. I was no longer as wealthy as I had been before the war and decided that it would be far more affordable to instruct a different agent who was actually based in Palestine. This proved to be a harder task than I had hoped, but finally in the last month of 1948, by which time the independent State of Israel had come into being, I received what I had been hoping for, namely a report giving me an address in Tel Aviv where I was informed she was now living.

Having established that Aliza was safe, I could have left it there. After all, I was not unhappy and, I'm sure, like many of my generation, sincerely grateful just to be able to enjoy as peaceful and untroubled an existence as possible, having survived two terrible conflicts relatively unscathed.

But all the same, Aliza had become part of my life, and a day seldom passed without my thinking of her. Clara, meanwhile, had made it clear that she had no wish to return to Berlin, which at the time was still very much a ruined city, with the French, American and British sectors having been placed under siege by the Russians. However, we still owned our house, which was now in the British sector, and I returned there occasionally, having rented out all but a small part of it, which I retained as a flat. In the spring of 1949, once the siege had ended, I therefore made up my mind that I had to write to her from there, explaining frankly that I had not been able to rest until I had satisfied myself that she was safe. I also expressed myself curious about how she was coping with her new life in a country she had once told me she did not wish to live in, while adding, too, that she was welcome to turn to me if she ever required any financial help. And then I waited with mounting expectation, hoping she would reply.

A month later she did so and I felt a glow of happiness when what I read expressed only pleasure at my having found her, politely declining my offer of financial help, and expressing a willingness to meet again should I ever be free to visit Israel. And so began many years of correspondence between us in which I would write to her whenever I came to Berlin and she would invariably reply a few weeks later. Her well-crafted letters were ever a joy to me but it was naturally a part of my life that I always kept from Clara.

Whether she ever suspected anything I honestly cannot say, but certainly corresponding with Aliza became more difficult from the mid 1950s onwards, once Clara decided that she was willing to return to Berlin occasionally, with the result that we would stay in the flat together whenever we did so.

Following Clara's death, I have enjoyed the pleasure of hearing Aliza's voice again at the end of the telephone, sounding as attractive as it ever did, and now at last we are about to meet once more. I have invited her to come here for lunch, and, glancing at my watch, I realise that it is almost time for her to arrive. I feel apprehensive, tense, almost like a young man again, and then as I look around… yes, it's her. Older, of course older, but still the Aliza I remember, still with that easy, graceful walk and possessing those dark, beautiful eyes so that

I feel close to tears. And then she smiles.

'Hello, Otto, it's wonderful to see you again. She looks at me tenderly, holding my gaze, enrapturing me just as she as always did with the sheer allure of her personality. Above all, I sense that though she must have been scarred by the suffering she has had to endure she has not allowed this to diminish her. She's still the same woman I have loved over many years and I am certain that her feelings for me remain as strong as they ever were. On impulse, I take hold of of her right hand and place a kiss on it just as I used to.

'My, Otto, you haven't changed. You're just as charming as ever.'

'And nor have you, my dear Aliza.'

'Flattery will get you everywhere, Otto.' And with that she places a kiss on my left cheek and I catch a whiff of the perfume she's wearing. Instantly, I recognise it from that occasion not long before the war when we met by chance in Berlin. Such a different world, now gone for ever. Yet, in my mind's eye it could have been just a moment ago.

'You know, Otto,' she tells me when we sit down together to have lunch, 'I've been thinking what a journey we've been on together. It's certainly been a friendship against the odds, hasn't it?'

I want to correct her and say *love affair* but I don't. 'Yes,' I reply, 'but we've always been such kindred spirits…'

She smiles at me and nods her head. 'I hope you've forgiven me for sending you away when we were in Prague?'

'It was for the best,' I say 'There's nothing to forgive. And I want to say that from the very first time I set eyes on you, I knew you were special. Not just beautiful, but forthright, brave, in fact the very antithesis of all the evil propaganda that the Nazi Party ever preached against the Jewish people. You helped open my eyes to that evil and for that I am extremely grateful. But now, after all these years, I want us to be much more than just friends; if you would like that?'

'Of course I would, Otto.' And with that she stretches out a hand across the table and places it upon mine.

I can't resist feeling for something in my the inside pocket of the jacket I'm wearing and taking it out. It's a small box. 'This is for you,' I say as I open it to reveal a diamond ring. 'I was wondering, my dearest Aliza, if you would do me the honour of becoming my wife?'

She looks understandably taken aback and I fear that I've gone too far too quickly but then she smiles. 'Oh Otto, that's so sweet of you, but you know, Israel is now very much my home.'

'I understand that, but I was hoping we could live together both here and in Germany. Of course, I'm still quite a wealthy man; we could travel… I'm sure we could work something out…'

'Yes, I expect we could…'

'So, will you say *yes*?'

' … I'm very set in my ways.'

'Oh, so am I, but I still love you very much.'

'And I you… So the answer's yes, my darling, I will.'

THE END

AUTHOR'S NOTE

It is a historical fact that in the 1930s the Nazi Party was willing, for a time, to support the Zionist movement. It had been encouraged to do so as a result of a visit made to Palestine by a Nazi aristocrat, who went on to write an acclaimed article in the Nazi Party newspaper *Der Angriff* and to become head of the Jewish Bureau before resigning, partly because of adverse criticism from Adolf Eichmann. When the aristocrat undertook this journey, he was accompanied, not just by his wife, but also by a Zionist and his wife, and they travelled on board the SS Martha Washington, otherwise known as *The Raging Moses*. Using fictional names, the opening chapters of this novel provide a completely imaginary account of how that journey came about, what it entailed, and as indicated above what its immediate consequences were.

The novel portrays in an entirely imaginary way some infamous characters from the Nazi era, particularly Joseph Goebbles and Adolf Eichmann. The latter served in the Jewish Bureau and became critical of the Zionists receiving any support, which would enable them to establish an independent Jewish State. Goebbels also first coined the idea of an Iron Curtain falling across Europe, rather than Churchill as is widely believed, whilst it's true as well that Himmler did order that prostitutes be brought into some concentration camps.

The defence of the Moltke Bridge and the unsuccessful

attempt to blow it up played a pivotal role in the battle for Berlin. Furthermore, some German troops did successfully break out of Berlin on the day it was surrendered to the Russians, although whether any individual driving a car at night through the shattered suburbs of the city would really have been able to succeed as well is quite another matter. It is also true that the concentration camp at Theresienstadt was administered by the Red Cross for a few days before the Russians arrived. Further, Prague did indeed only fall to the Russians after fighting between German troops and Czech partisans. For the sake of the drama, some licence has been taken with the minutiae of these events.

It was *A Nazi travels to Palestine* an article by Jacob Boas published in the History Today magazine in January 1980 and subsequently republished in 2001 that first drew the author to the historical baron. Further, in 2011, an Israeli filmmaker, Arnon Goldfinger, made an acclaimed documentary *The Flat* that throws further light on what really happened.

ABOUT THE AUTHOR

The author is a retired lawyer living near Canterbury, Kent. He is married with two sons and three grandchildren.

Other books by James Walker

Ellen's Gold

My Enemy My Love

I Think He Was George

Shamila

Ravishment

ACKNOWLEDGEMENTS

My sincere thanks to James Essinger and Charlotte Mouncey for all their help in the creation of this novel.